'Compelling' *Woman and Home*

'Through this lively, often funny, topical story of discovery
and reconciliation, ultimately of love, Libby Purves touch-
ingly and truthfully explores and extends the conventional
idea of family.' *Saga*

'Libby Purves writes with great humanity in this
engrossing novel that reveals there is more than one kind
of family.' *Closer magazine*

Also by Libby Purves

Fiction
Casting Off
A Long Walk in Wintertime
Home Leave
More Lives Than One
Regatta
Passing Go
A Free Woman
Mother Country
Continental Drift
Acting Up
Love Songs and Lies

Non-Fiction
Holy Smoke
Nature's Masterpiece
How Not to Be a Perfect Family
Working Times
How Not to Raise a Perfect Child
One Summer's Grace
The English and Their Horses (jointly with Paul Heiney)
Where Did You Leave the Admiral?
How Not to Be a Perfect Mother
Sailing Weekend Book (with Paul Heiney)
Britain at Play
Adventures Under Sail, H. W. Tilman (ed)
The Happy Unicorns (ed)

Children's books
Getting the Story
The Hurricane Tree

Libby Purves

Shadow Child

HODDER

First published in Great Britain in 2009 by Hodder & Stoughton
An Hachette UK company

First published in paperback in 2010

3

Copyright © Libby Purves 2009

The right of Libby Purves to be identified as the Author of the Work has
been asserted by her in accordance with the Copyright, Designs and
Patents Act 1988.

A CIP catalogue record for this title is available from the British Library

ISBN 978 0 340 83743 6

Typeset in Plantin Light by Palimpsest Book Production Limited,
Grangemouth, Stirlingshire

Printed and bound in the UK by
CPI Mackays, Chatham ME5 8TD

Hodder & Stoughton policy is to use papers that are natural, renewable and
recyclable products and made from wood grown in sustainable forests. The
logging and manufacturing processes are expected to conform to the
environmental regulations of the country of origin.

Hodder & Stoughton Ltd
338 Euston Road
London NW1 3BH

www.hodder.co.uk

Grateful acknowledgement is made for permission to
reprint from the following copyrighted work, 'Song of the
Old Mother' by William Butler Yeats, from *The Wind
Among The Reeds* © 1899 by William Butler Yeats.
Reprinted by kind permission of A.P. Watt Ltd on
behalf of Gràinne Yeats

I

Behind the stained-glass window I could see the grey shape of a tree, moving restlessly in the wind. Nine in the morning is early for a funeral: the autumn sun, I thought, must still be low above the ruffled North Sea. As the service wore on the light would come from higher above and that vivid shadow would vanish, leaving the bland, holy figures to cast their glints undisturbed on coffin and congregation.

For the moment, though, the branches tossed lively and untameable, surging with formless vitality behind the stuck, timeless saints. I fixed my eyes on them, forcing myself to accept the merciless ongoing life which mocks the ashy rites of death.

The vicar completed his dignified words of welcome – I saw his eye fall on me, alone in mid-pew, and caught a flicker of recognition and concern. I bowed my head to hide a help-less grimace. I hate pity. With a scrape and a rustle we rose to sing the first hymn, obedient, subdued voices requesting to be forgiven our foolish ways. And still beyond the glassy saints the shadow tree thrashed and danced, irrepressible. *Let sense be dumb, let flesh retire; Speak through the earthquake, wind and fire—*

No. Flesh does not retire, sense is never dumb. Life is merciless. The service flowed by; time stopped, as it often does for me these days, and when I blinked into awareness once more the sun was brighter, the colours fiercer. The tree was indeed diminished by the higher sun, but its few remaining branches flailed with wild life. *O still small voice of calm*, sang the congregation, but the tree in the window held me captive and calm eluded me. It was, as it happens, my second funeral in a week; a schoolfriend's father in distant Malmesbury on Tuesday, and now this Friday interment of a neighbour. Sid Featherben was well on into his eighties and had lived for years in a home. He had lost his awareness of most things ten years back, but in his day he was a renowned winner of flower and produce shows and a faithful churchwarden. I was here for the sake of his daughter, a school-gate acquaintance of years ago. Tom had raised an eyebrow when I said I would go to the funeral.

'Why? You hadn't seen Sid for years, Jill wouldn't expect you—'

'That's not the point. She'll be pleased to have a full church. People are. Remember—'

My husband flinched, and shook his head with a kind of weary anger. 'Well, go if you must.'

But he understood, however unwillingly. Tom does not react as I do. His griefs are different in quality: sometimes we are an ocean apart in feeling, and have to make effortful lunges to reach across the dark waters and acknowledge one another's sorrow. But he knows as well as I do the great social irony of mourning: we have discussed it, even ruefully laughed about it. The paradox is this: the first year of your own bereavement is the time of all times when people would gladly let you off going to other funerals. Yet it is also precisely the time when you realize how much it means to the main mourners if the pews are full and the singing lusty. Thus, at the moment in life when you are least emotionally fit to confront coffins, bearers, black coats, graves, crematoria, 'Rock of Ages' and vicars going on about ashes, you find yourself at more funerals than you ever normally would.

Mostly it is fine. Uplifting, even. Sometimes, in the most

unexpected cases, it is not fine at all and I have to hide my weeping from the properly and appropriately stricken mourners of a particular funeral. But still I go. I am in the Bereaved Club, a non-exclusive and ever-growing community.

At least this one was close to home, and fell on a windy, bright autumn morning with the brave sun rising from a milky sea. And I had liked chatting to old man Featherben when we first moved here years ago with our baby Samuel. He was one of the few proper locals in our commuterized village, and used to advise me about the garden with a bracing note of scorn in his voice. That was in the days when I had time and heart to garden, with my little boy beside me messing and prodding with his trowel in the heavy Norfolk clay. Sid was forever urging us to grow broad beans. We never dared tell him that we all hate broad beans in our family.

We all hate broad beans? I suppose, if I use the present tense, I should say – we *both*. For there are just the two of us now. No Samuel. He's gone. Not much of a family now, me and Tom: just a pair of middle-aged housemates, really.

Deep breath, watch the last branch dancing beyond the sainted glass. Say it again: my son is dead. I apologize for so harrowing you this early in my tale, and hope that my situation does not make you flee my company as if I were contagious. It has, indeed, done this with a few of my friends, and I do understand it. But take heart: the loss of a child is not in fact contagious, but merely random and comfortingly rare. And I promise that if you – like me – can squarely confront the fact that my only son died at just 21 years old and that I am still here, sentient and articulate, it will be the last full-dress misery that I will have to impose on you during the strange, true, and not entirely edifying story I am about to tell.

Tom and I lost Sam in the stupidest of accidents. It was the eve of his twenty-first birthday, and he was on a high stepladder in the village hall putting up balloons for his birthday party. Turning to laugh at something rude his cousin Harry said about the balloons, Sam missed his footing, fell and caught his head on the projecting bracket of the fire extinguisher. The damn thing had been installed days earlier as part of a health-and-safety overhaul to keep the hall open. I had helped to raise funds for it.

Everyone did the right things, but my boy never regained consciousness. On the morning of his birthday, at around the hour of his birth and his first cry, he died. Tom and I were by his side in the intensive care unit; there was no sign that he knew we were there, but it seems to me there is no way that such a surge of love and reassurance, admiration and warmth could not have reached him. The bland, technical little room was during those minutes almost holy with love. Sometimes I wish I was back there in that moment, terrible as it was, because of the shared and utterly united feeling that ran between the three of us, two alive and one departing. Family love is one of the most powerful elemental forces on earth, and at that moment, our last moment as a unit of three, we rode a great, curling triumphant wave of it, all together. Death may have thought that he had won, but I think otherwise.

Tom and I stayed for a while with our boy's cooling body, and I am glad. Not every parent in the world gets that chance, not in this wicked age when young men are daily thrown into the Tigris or blown to fragments into the desert filth. I remember looking down at Sam and thinking, numbly, how extraordinary a thing is a dead body. Whatever and whoever it represents, it is primarily just a fact. A big, solid fact, there in front of you. No pretence, no prettification, no ritual, no love can change it or delay its destiny. It is the most prosaically irreversible fact of all. Samuel had joined the vast majority of all human beings ever born: the illimitable, unknowable legion of the dead. I felt awe of him: my child had gone before, into some place of which I knew nothing.

It was a numb response, unrelated to the wild days and nights of shock and nightmare which followed, but it had its uses. His funeral was just as it should be, packed with friends of his generation who sang out for him. They came up to us with rough, awkward condolences in that same village hall, walking past that same fire extinguisher – drinking, indeed, the 21st-birthday beer. We were sensible, we were calm, we said things like: 'We were all lucky to have him.' We celebrated his life and lined the hall with pictures of him laughing and running and diving and playing tennis and graduating. We hugged and smiled and thanked our friends for coming so far at such short notice.

Especially we thanked the young, and did it with an extra pang, because that, too, felt like a farewell. We would not see much of them now. We would be the oldies in the end house; the bereaved wrinklies over fifty, poor old things huddling in the corner of life with only their tragedy and their curling photos and their greying friends for company. No noise, no mess, no life, no hope.

You may think me heartless to have considered our own social privation on a day when my son's coffin lay before us, but grief is full of small, odd pockets of unpoliceable feeling. There is irony, detachment, even flippancy. And the privation felt real. Sam was a social creature, and so am I, and it was not by choice that we had only the one child. So ever since he was small his friends had filled the house, some-times rather too obtrusively. In early years they romped and messed and demanded tea and broke things. In the teenage years they monopolized the video and slept in heaps like puppies on his bedroom floor. Later, in university vacations, our empty nest was refilled three times a year as old friends called by to catch up with him and he brought new ones home from Cambridge, generally preceded by a plaintive explanation – 'Denny's dad works in Dubai . . . Abeeku's from Ghana, he only goes home in the long vac . . . they don't mind sharing a room, in Ghana Beekie shares with his five brothers – and is it OK if Jackie dosses for a couple of weeks? She's had a bit of a row with her crap dad . . .'

I liked his kindness and sociability, but almost equally I just liked being surrounded by young life. Not all my friends feel this way, I know; Sarah, my closest supporter during that time, couldn't get it at all. She likes a tidy mid-life house, a bridge four, grown-up dinners and theatre trips and intelligent conversation. She finds the young adults messy and exhausting, with their giggles and big shoes left everywhere and their texting and weird social networks and addiction to wi-fi. Sarah would prefer small, biddable grandchildren, though heaven knows her equally academic daughter is thirty-two now and shows no sign of breeding.

Myself, I always enjoyed the young: I fed off their jokes and enthusiasms and savoured both their puppyish energy and their deep-sleeping langour. I liked their television programmes, too, and sometimes while Tom fled to his study I would sit in my chair, perhaps with a bit of sewing on my lap, as Sam and a couple of his mates lay around my feet on cushions watching *The Simpsons*. Or, if there were mostly boys there, it would be some incomprehensible sci-fi movie full of cod philosophy and stupidly jolting camerawork, and the sewing would progress rather faster. But still I stayed: I liked the sprawl of them, the long-limbed asymmetry, the invincible life.

My presence never seemed to inhibit Sam, either, at which my friends marvelled. 'Annie can't bear me round her friends, says I'm embarrassing . . .' 'Jake never brings them home except at one in the morning to clang around the kitchen heating up frozen pizzas. And when I say hello they just grunt.' No, I was lucky; I had young company and was grateful for it. Apart from anything else, it made me more tolerant of the semi-numerate young workers I deal with in my comfortable, bland, part-time job, supervising the accounts of three small firms on the industrial estate. Sometimes, indeed, I even considered going back to my old trade as a magazine journalist in order to mix with brighter youth. I am, after all, one of the dwindling band of trained sub-editors who can spell and remember the Beatles. But I am tired now, and fifty, and cripplingly sad; and anyway the magazines I once enjoyed have become shrill and harsh and obsessed with celebrity nobodies. I would only depress the staff by hating all that. Best to stay in my dull jobs on the industrial estate, stay quiet. Out of everyone's way.

Sam had no particular girlfriend, at least none was ever announced to us as important. I simply enjoyed the ebb and flow of his amoebic, ever-changing circle and asked no questions. So there they all were at the funeral, kind and sorrowful and shocked and shining with life, singing the hymns and signing the book. And afterwards we went home, Tom and I, and looked at one another in the tidy empty house and wept.

All this was back in the spring, seven months before the Featherben funeral, and we have walked through the minefield of loss with, I think, decent and dignified care. I waited a due time before going through his things, made decisions on respecting his privacy where letters and notes were concerned, sweeping them into a couple of shoe-boxes and taping them up. I cancelled his email and spent a foul half-hour online to a recorded message and banging rock music as I dealt with the morons on the 'Vodafone bereavement team'. I squared my shoulders to dispose of some clothes, for there is a limit to the number of tattered T-shirts and terrible surf-shorts that even a mother can cherish. A few went into sealed plastic boxes, being too iconic to part with. I had his laptop's hard disk wiped clear before giving it to a local teenager to take to university, and offered his sports kit to his cousin Harry.

I found that there are milestones in the never-ending journey of mourning. There is the first day that you can bear to watch television or read a newspaper without feeling a sense of betrayal at the frivolous, uncaring tone of the world. There is the scattering of the ashes; and there is the terrible moment when you first travel any distance from home and are surprised to realize, stupid with grief, that his absence is not only permanent but geographically universal. *He is not here either; he is dead everywhere!* I stood at a service station on the A14 in helpless tears one day, as if until that moment I had been kidding myself that he was only dead at home, in the village, in the house. Dead here, too . . . dead everywhere on the planet, everywhere in the universe. For the first time in twenty-one years I had no idea, no idea at all, where my child was.

Well, that was one milestone. Then there is the moment of going back to work, and the gradual degrees of renewed exposure to outsiders' scrutiny. What will people think, if you smile and laugh about some normal matter? Will they think you have no heart? Contrariwise, there is the strange and tiring duty of making other people feel comfortable with your loss and your new status as a tragic person. You have to mention your lost child in the first few minutes of any conversation, with a smile and a cheerful memory ('Sam always loved those Matrix films, I could never see the point'), so that people do not spend the next ten years tiptoeing round the subject, afraid to mention their own young, treating you like an invalid or an imbecile.

Small explosions in the minefield rock you: I hated the

date of his death – also, of course, of his birth – as it came round every month, and could not bear a calendar saying 16th. I would tear off two pages at once. To the bereaved there is something toxic about dates: at every milestone some small, mad, magical part of me was thinking 'OK, I have learnt the lessons of grief, I have been patient and kind and sensible, I have had to grow new strengths in order to bear it. I have done all that, I have passed the fairytale test and ordeal. Now can I have him back, please?'

But worst of all, and horribly private, was my dread of the nine-month mark. It was still two months off, on that day of old Sid Featherben's windy funeral. I woke on that morning, though, from a vivid dream of pregnancy and realized that what I was dreading was no less than pregnancy's negative: nine months for Sam to grow inside me, nine months for my motherhood to wither away again. The baby bones and teeth in whose interest I drank all that calcium-rich milk (I hate neat milk) were burned and ground to ash. The body I nurtured so carefully for two decades, fretting about vaccination and balanced diet and dentists' appointments, was no longer feeling any benefit from any of it, and never would.

I do not think Tom had these exact same feelings: I am not a father. His loss and mine are both different and the same, so we each had our own inner path to tread, and understood early on in the switchback of misery and acceptance that we should never drag one another down. So most of the sharing we did was of good things: sudden memories of our good, kind, gentle, happy-hearted boy, and of the eerily frequent messages we seemed to receive from him. Together we appreciated his crocuses which bloomed unexpectedly on days when we were saddest, the sunsets blazing over particular scenes he loved, the forgotten birthday cards in childish writing which suddenly appeared at the back of dresser drawers. We talked a little about the other child we lost – a miscarriage long ago when Samuel was three – and regretted together, soberly and without hysteria, the fact that we had never managed to conceive another. We both made a great performance of being thrilled about other people's grandchildren, and the great-nephew who was born to my niece and given Samuel as a middle name. Dear Carla wanted to call him Samuel right out, but Tom vetoed this, with more distress than he had ever openly showed. 'I won't have him *replaced*,' he kept saying, shaken out of his usual composure.

Anyway, we soldiered on. Diminished, lonely, but able after a while to read, go to the cinema, eat with friends and listen with real interest to the doings of their thriving families. I had feared that I would hate other people's healthy, lucky sons, but that never happened: none of them, after all, was a patch on Samuel. I didn't want their Donny or Dave or Matt or Paddy, not at any price; so I could sponsor the living boys' marathons or advise them on their first tax returns without any emotion beyond a faint, friendly interest. I suppose it was, in my mind at least, the sort of detached benevolence you might meet with from a very old nun making small-talk in the convent parlour. I became that starched old figure of humility: ageing, childless, benign, sad, sensible.

And that was how it was in the first months, which brought me to the hard pew at old Sid's funeral on that windy autumn morning. I did not know, as I sat there striving sensibly for acceptance, that the day was not only an ending but a beginning.

2

I got home to find Tom in a bad temper. He was doing his accounts, which generally has that effect, and often causes it in me, too. I am professionally adept at accounting because I retrained in my late twenties when I grew sick of working on women's magazines and wanted to move to the coast and start a baby. I have offered, several times, to look after this aspect of his professional life but some demon of pride prevents my husband from accepting help. For the first twenty years of his career, in any case, he had no accounts at all to do, being a salaried university lecturer – later a full professor. He had nothing more complicated than a monthly payslip to put in the drawer, and a self-assessment tax return to swear at once a year. Only when Sam was thirteen did everything change. Tom was persuaded to go into school and talk to the children about his area of research, at the time an unfashionable byway of biochemical botany concerned with the nutritional values of certain food crops. He did such a lively presentation that the head of science, whose hobby was local radio, asked him to talk about his experiments on a weekend programme.

The rest, to nobody's surprise more than Tom's, followed at breakneck speed. Suddenly in the nineties, after years of neglect, food science and farming became fashionable topics. Nutrition, organics, GM crops and 'superfoods' were suddenly hot news. Casting around for experts, a TV executive driving to his country cottage heard Tom being fascinating about parsnips, made a note on his cuff (nearly, he later told us, going into a ditch while doing so), and was on the phone to the department on Monday. *Faulkner on Food* was a six-part series which established the modest professor as the nation's nutrition guru; he is a handsome man, my husband, with the air of a slightly chaotic hawk, hair curling over his collar with badgery pepper-and-salt abandon. The camera loved him; he loved it right back, correctly regarding it as a slightly underpowered student with a shortish attention span.

His producers liked him, too, for his real knowledge, and were kept on their toes by his polite but just discernible contempt for the shallowness of their medium. Somehow, the alchemy worked. When his area of deepest expertise ran out, he moved on to allied subjects: *Faulkner's Farms* ran for three years, followed by the (wholly regrettable but irresistibly lucrative) *Faulkner's Families* in which he visited homes and discussed the nutritional patterns of people stupid enough to think that an airing on TV and a bit of free tofu were proper rewards for the loss of family privacy and the mockery of their neighbours. Sam used to invent new titles for him – *Faulkner's Fatties, Faulkner's Fromages,* or his favourite *Faulkner's Forks* – 'in which our expert explains the importance of tine-separation in the transportation of foodstuffs to the mouth'.

Faulkner's Families was too much for Tom, though. He could not bear the manipulation, the artful editing, which made him look like a bully and his subjects even dimmer and more incapable than they were. He felt during the months of filming as if he had – despite the high fees – been cunningly robbed of something, and became bad-tempered and unsociable. When it ended he moved back gratefully into the academic life which, technically, he had never really left. I thought he might return to the more serious kind of TV work he began with, but since

Sam's death he had done only two guest interviews, and it was noticeable in both that his old spark had not returned. We do not need the extra money because we moved to this pleasant house early in his television career, leaving the Cambridge flat where Sam was born, and we have more or less paid for it. When it seemed that the brief flare of media fame was over, neither of us much regretted it. However, in the same month that Sam died, Tom received notice of a tax inspection, something we have since learnt is common enough in the lives of media stars, however marginal.

Everything had, of course, been duly declared; we are tediously careful Middle Englanders. But the questions from the Revenue continued, stretching back first over four years, then over six, then seven. The months of our darkest mourning brought almost weekly demands for fresh evidence, bank statements and invoices. Sometimes I thought that the aggravation was helpful, distracting my husband at least from our joint misery. Mostly it felt like an additional curse and burden, a torment of Job, a fistful of salt in the wound.

Today, clearly, was one of the latter days. Tom threw down his pen on to his tidy little desk as I went into the room, trying not to flinch (I flinched for months when I smelt the lavenderish, woodsmoke scent of that room; we sat there with the undertaker – I cannot shake the memory off even though it has contained so many happier moments). He had clearly been waiting to let off steam.

'Bloody vultures! I've been through 2001 three times, and I can't see their problem. How *dare* they say this – look! – this . . .'

I put a hand on his shoulder and leaned over to glance at the letter. 'It is clear that there are culpable bankings,' he read. 'Culpable! Unresolved sums! They are *not* unresolved. They were probably payments left over from the second series the year before – there were repeats – it's in my book – I declared it all—!'

I looked sadly at his account book. It is honest, but messy.

'Sweetheart, they always get you in the end, specially if it's messy. You must have lost a couple of invoices – or is one of the deposits they mean perhaps the insurance payout from the time Sam dinged the car . . . ?'

'How dare they! I shall go to the European Court . . .'

'No, look, let me . . .'

He banged down the folder, closing it against me, his whole rage at the cruel universe focused on HM Revenue & Customs. But when he looked back up at me his eyes were bleak. I put my arms round his shoulders, and stood like that for a while until my back began to ache.

'It'll come good. At worst a few thousand. Don't worry. It isn't worth it.'

'It's not just that,' he said at last, shaking off my hug. 'This damned hippie woman got up my nose, too.'

'What hippie woman?' I moved away, easing my back, staring at the dead flowers on the windowsill and wondering vaguely whether there was a carton of soup left over for lunch. Tom is always happier after hot food, but I still found cooking a trial.

'Came to the door. Said she wanted to speak to Sam.'

Concern for lunch vanished. I stared at him. 'What?'

'I said she couldn't. I started to explain, and she cut me off.'

'What?' I seemed to have no other word at my disposal.

'Well, she got up my nose,' he said angrily, and folded his lips as if to close the subject.

'Did you tell her he's – that he died?'

'I was starting to, but it's hard to be quick – well, you know how it is. So she just cut across me when I hesitated, and just bloody rudely said I had no right, that there was no point my protecting him, that all men were stinking cowards.'

'What?'

'Then' – he was gathering steam, his voice taking on a reedy quality which I suspected was an echo of this interloper's own – 'she said that she had a right to speak to him and she knew this was his home address. Oh God, she went on, self-righteous bitch!'

'But you did tell her?'

'Why should I tell her anything? I lost it. I told her to sod off.' He looked at me, a little sheepish now. 'I won't be hectored on my own doorstep.'

'She might have been a friend, someone he was fond of . . .'

'She was forty if she was a day. And dog-rough. And rude. Not a friend.'

'What on earth can she have wanted?'

I turned the problem over in my mind, half-fascinated, half-repelled. For all my careful social structures of calm and matter-of-fact discourse about Sam, I was disturbed by the idea of a rough-spoken stranger taking an abusive line in connection with him, speaking his name with an insult attached.

Tears sprang to my eyes and I turned away from Tom, because of the rule that we don't drag one another down. If his anger was keeping him buoyant for the moment, good. When I had mastered my shock, and he was once more staring furiously at the Revenue letter, I tried one more question.

'What was her name?'

'She did say, actually. As she left. Said to tell him she'd called and wouldn't give up. Her name was as annoying as any of it. Djoolya.'

'Julia?'

'She spelt it out. D-j-oo-lya. Bloody affected, I thought.'

'Foreign? African, perhaps?'

'She was white as a maggot. Faded blonde. Scrawny.'

'What was the surname?'

'I've forgotten. To hell with her, rude cow.'

Tom clearly had little real curiosity about the visitor, writing her off as a passing lunatic. Perhaps this was because he was always less involved with Sam's friends than me; perhaps because he has been on television. Television people must get more experience of pestering lunatics than normal people do. But as I heated the soup and sawed off lumps of bread, I could not stop wondering about a Julia-Djoolya woman, dog-rough and fortyish, who felt so furiously that she had a right to see my vanished son, and yet who did not know he was dead. Not a friend, then. Not a friend of friends. A creditor, perhaps? A former tutor? Why?

I could not eat. While Tom drank his soup and talked about the tax inspector, I gazed absently past him at a tree thrashing in the wind beyond the leaded kitchen windowpane, and wondered. I hoped she would be back soon. I hoped I would be in, to see her for myself. Tom might chase her from the door but for me any tenuous link with my lost boy, even from a woman who called him names, could seem only a blessing. The greatest fear is that the dead will become mere legends, stained-glass figures of unreality. Even an insult, I realized, might feel like a flicker of life.

3

The woman did not come back in the following days, but the idea of her grew restlessly strong within me. I made basic mistakes at work and snapped at Tom more than usual. He was teaching again, and came home on his three lecturing weekdays grumpy and washed-out.

'Bloody students! It's all about their social life now, they don't come to university to learn, it's the last thing on their mind—' He would wander round the house complaining aloud, so that his voice rose and fell into indistinctness as he moved from room to room. 'Christ knows they ought to be spending most of the first year catching up, A-levels fit them for the square root of minus nothing as far as basic biology is concerned, and as for their maths—'

I tuned it out, as experienced wives must do. But one of these half-heard diatribes filtered into my mind and germinated as an idea. 'All about their social life', he had said. Sam's social life, surely, would hold some clue as to who this Djoolya woman was? I was pretty sure she was not local; I knew his home friends well, and most of them were connected to us by the net of local families and school. His university life was sixty miles from us, though, and, apart from the friends he brought home, there must have been wider circles – overlapping Venn diagrams – links to friends and acquaintances we never knew about. And, I told myself, if in some way he owed money or a favour to this hippie woman, it was our duty to repay it. For his honour.

This argument was one to cling to, obscuring the rather plainer fact that I just wanted another connection to his memory, another point of reference to make him real to me again. The daily terror is that his image will fade. So, even if I discovered something discreditable – some flawed behaviour or broken promise – it would be better than nothing. I knew it could not be very terrible: I knew Sam to be good. And if this ridiculously-named person could fill a narrative gap it would give me another morsel of my lost son to cherish.

So the idea began to grow. I would find her, and find out. I carried the resolve with me for several days without acting or making a plan. Tom continued to be moody and quiet and tiresomely obsessed with tax, and when I raised the subject at breakfast he refused even to join in my speculation. After a few more days it was Saturday, so I took the matter round to my friend Sarah's calm and tidy kitchen and related the whole incident to her. She sat there, fiddling with her reading glasses, frowning slightly, and then said:

'I think you'll find the answer might lie in the spelling.'

'Why?'

'Well, didn't Tom say she was some kind of hippie?'

'He says everyone's a hippie, unless they're either in a City suit, or cords and cardigans with egg down them and books stuffed in the pockets.'

Sarah is very clever. She was a senior editor on a top political weekly until last year, when she fell out with the owners and walked out ('Ah, the freedom of being fifty!' she said. 'Mortgage paid and no false pride!'). Now, when not gardening or reading, she is working on a history of centrist politics. She frowned, bit the earpiece of her glasses, looked up at me again and thumped the table with a flat hand for emphasis.

'Do you remember that girl Sam brought home, Jackie?

Little blonde one I thought was a girlfriend, but you said absolutely not, sleeping on the camp bed?'

'That was over a year ago – she stayed with us over Easter.' I frowned, trying to remember more: a flimsy pale creature, this Jackie, oddly silent for a Sam-friend, her personality drowned by a much noisier group camping out in the loft that week. She did not seem to be connected with any of them particularly, and looked at Sam, I thought, with an odd intensity. I had wondered whether she was in love with him, but since he demonstrated nothing but his usual puppyish friendliness towards her it seemed unlikely that he would have invited a lovelorn stalker to be so near him all weekend. He was sensitive that way, and kind.

And anyway, there was something in Jackie's manner which did not chime with being lovelorn. She did not flirt, merely seemed to look at him with heavy concentration, as if she were a portrait painter or a psychiatrist. I seemed to remember that when he was not in the room she was usually to be found stitching away with coloured wools at a big mud-coloured poncho garment. Funny little thing. Half-forgotten, now.

'Why would she be a connection?' I asked Sarah now. 'Because she was a bit of a hippie, too?' I thought of the poncho.

'Partly. But the spelling is the real clue. When we came over for Easter Sunday lunch, I tried to get her talking. I tried her on veganism, since she was eating the bean flan, but she didn't seem too enthusiastic about that; the only thing she got lit up about was feminism. Really snarky paranoid stuff-men feminism. Well, you know me. I can talk the talk, so I led her down that path, just to be polite. And then she said it.'

'She said . . . ?'

'She said that she had changed her name. Not the sound

of it, because she said that would be an abuse of her right to identity – she just changed the spelling. Like when the Greenham protesters called themselves wim-min, not wo-men. She did it as a protest against the patriarchal male-supremacist contempt' – Sarah grinned, quoting in a sing-song tone – ' "which insultingly makes Jacqueline into a mere diminutive of Jack". So I went on talking the talk, just to see how bonkers she would turn out to be.'

'So how was she going to spell it?'

The grin widened. 'D-j-a-k-k-i!'

I stared. 'You mean – this D-joolya nonsense – that they'd know each other?'

'Seems hard to believe there'd be two dingbats – sorry, Der-jingbats – with the same idea, both knowing Sam. Find Der-jackie and I bet you'll find Der-julia. Der-just like that! Der-jing!'

I was struck with admiration for Sarah's effortless brilliance, and only during the next few minutes' conversation did both of us realize that we didn't know where Jackie was, either. Except – and again, this nugget of information came from Sarah's remarkable penetration of the girl's surly defences – that she was not at Cambridge, but the London School of Economics, and had met Sam and his friends at an anti-war rally in his gap year. She had then kept up the acquaintance. I was crestfallen by the 'not at Cambridge' line, which seemed to put the lid on any hope of finding her through his contemporaries.

'But you should ask,' said Sarah firmly. 'Get to the bottom of this. I bet you anything that these D-women hang together.'

Sarah has been my lifebelt, these past months. We were casual friends in Sam's early schooldays, when she was a governor of the village school though her own daughter had left years earlier. We kept in touch lightly enough in Sam's teenage years, but only after the disaster did she become an all-important source of support: unembarrassed, unsentimental, astringently kind, matter-of-fact. I had never known her own history until then, either: her mother and brother both suicides, her father drinking himself into debt and early death during her teens, leaving her to live with an ailing great-aunt rather than be fostered.

Sarah won her place at the London School of Economics by sheer power of character and brains, and married her professor – a rumpled figure some twenty years her senior, who wrote speeches for Prime Minister Callaghan. They had one daughter, now in France, and lost another child to stillbirth. Somewhere in this life of tragedy and effort Sarah learnt how to offer what I needed – not comfort, exactly, not reassurance and certainly not fluffy or religious denial. What she gave was a kind of saving stiffness. When I was with her, it seemed obvious that nothing could be changed, that facts were facts, and that since I had no option but to stay alive and carry on, I might as well do so gracefully. She let me talk about Sam endlessly in the early days, but would not follow me down any of the wrong tracks – the path of guilt, the path of might-have-beens. She merely listened, waiting at the fork in the road, and when I moved back to a better path she showed gentle approval. Tom likes her, too. Once, when we had been grieving separately for a few bad days, I came back calmer from her house and found him also better, and reading Nietzsche.

'You make me ashamed,' I said, 'the way you sort yourself out by reading and thinking, and I just chat to friends.'

'Sarah,' he replied gently, 'is as good as a book any day.' It was one of the only times we ever discussed our different tactics for handling the situation, and the most apt definition of Sarah's support. Some of my friends apply nothing but feeling and empathy, and I love and need them too, though it is tiresome when they cry. But Sarah thinks. All the time. She can't help it.

On this occasion, though, I did not take Sarah's deductions home to Tom, nor tell him of my desire to track down his hippie interloper. Instead I sat quiet, looking into the fire all evening while he read, and tried to remember who else had been with us that Easter when the Jackie girl came. By bedtime I had visualized them all, and with a leap of my heart remembered that one of them was the Ghanaian boy, Abeeku. Who had told me at the funeral that he was short-listed for a job at an Africa Aid Policy think-tank, and was pretty confident.

So I Googled the think-tank that night, rang it up next day when Tom was out, found Abeeku still there, and asked about Jackie.

'Wah! I know,' said the distant voice, against a background of chatter and the occasional puzzling crash, as of chairs being dragged around on an uncarpeted floor. 'Jackie with a D. She was at the LSE, wasn't she? Actually, she worked here for a bit as an intern. Clever kid . . . I remembered her arguing about AIDS funding, at your Easter thing. There's someone here, Camilla, who might know where she went – hang on. Milla?' There was a crash, as if one of the chairs had tipped over, and some giggling.

'Yah,' said a cut-glass voice moments later. 'Camilla here, sorry, Beekie dropped the phone.' The sound of blithe young clumsiness sent a pang straight to my heart.

There was more scraping and a door slamming in the distance. I hung on, staring unseeingly at the calendar, the pictures in the hallway, the dried flowers on our calm wooden windowsill. I had a sudden sense of a journey beginning, a dangerous but necessary pilgrimage among strangers and monsters. My hand was shaking. But the brisk, unmonstrous Camilla-voice returned almost immediately.

'You wanted Jackie? She wasn't actually here long, it was a secondment thing. Learning charity politics on the ground, sort of thing.'

'But you know her?'

'A bit. She *was* working for Dan, with her scary girlfriend – sorry, that's not a person called Dan, it's Defeat Aids Now, which is a radical sort of charity.'

'Ah. And she might still be there?'

'I'm trying to think. We do a bit with DAN, but they're very anger-based, very leftie— What?' She turned away from the mouthpiece and a muttered conversation took place with some unnamed colleague. 'No, I remember now, she left DAN.'

I felt my trail going cold, and realized how much I minded.

'She went off with Julia Penderby – or was it the other way round? I mean, the girlfriend and Jules—'

Her voice muffled as she turned to the invisible informant. 'Was that Jackie girl some sort of item with the Dan woman? Julia?'

Julia. Julia Penderby. Der-Jool-ya . . . ?

After a moment the helpful Camilla returned. 'Got it straight now. Right. Jackie had a job with DAN – Defeat Aids Now. And we thought she was an item with the woman who ran it. But then she wasn't. And when she was with us for a bit she had this other girlfriend – she's, like, gay, obviously.'

'And?'

The Camilla voice was saying something to another person in the room, then came back into focus. 'And there was this huge bust-up. Because while Jackie was here doing her interning the girlfriend – Allie – actually went off with Julia Penderby. She's the one who runs DAN. And was an item with Jackie, before. So Jackie has a big flame-up and walks out. Of DAN, that is. Only the secondment to us was fixed by DAN, so she walks out of here too. Hang on, Molly here knows more.'

Another voice, less posh, came on the line. 'Sorry, I don't know much. I only really remember Jackie because I was doing the paperwork that month. We had to chase her up to do her expenses for going on a London Lighthouse trip with some African factfinders. And there was a mix-up with the National Insurance numbers, because she said her initial was D not J.'

'I know – yes, that's the right Jackie! She was changing her spelling!' I was exultant. I was right. There could not be two of them.

'Not by deed poll and law, she wasn't,' said Molly acerbically. 'We had an argument about that; you can't just keep calling yourself different things, it messes up the bookkeeping. It's just political, anyway, this lesbian thing where you put D on your name. You know?'

'Not really.'

'D for Dyke, reclaim the word. A bit like gay men carrying banners saying Faggots First, which I never got the point of. Cos faggot is rude, isn't it? Like dyke? I mean, we've got a gay guy here but he wouldn't go calling himself Fagandrew, would he?' Her tone changed suddenly. 'Hey, you're Sam Faulkner's mum, aren't you? I'm so sorry, he was really cool – I met him with Beekie . . .'

I had to head this off. Though it was nice to know that working at an Africa Aid Policy think-tank was a young and sociable affair, if no doubt woefully ill-paid. For a moment I envied them their lives.

'Jackie didn't leave a forwarding address, did she?'

'Haven't got it any more, I'm afraid.'

I thanked her, laid down the phone carefully, and looked down at the note I had scribbled on the back of an electricity bill. DAN, it said. And I had doodled a big D and a question mark. And a name: Julia Penderby. Who, given her status as former lover and boss and therefore perhaps mentor of the indignant Djakki, might be not Julia but Djoolya? I wondered, briefly, whether after the girlfriend-stealing incident Jackie had abandoned the extra D favoured by her old boss. I certainly would have.

That evening, Tom stayed out late; his computer was on, though, and I flipped through a search and found the Defeat Aids Now website, pausing on the 'About Us' page with the short staff list – only three – and thumbnail-sized photographs. *D. Penderby.* A thin, slightly hatchet-faced middle-aged blonde looked out at me, impassive, making it clear that the battle against AIDS was nothing to smile or be hopeful about. It was in a poor resolution, but around her neck was a hint of floppy, potentially hippyish, material. I dragged the picture on to the computer desktop and printed it, so I could ask Tom later whether this was his intruder, the woman who believed that our son owed her something. But then a moment later I remembered my husband's weary anger, and crumpled it up to put it in the depths of my dressing-gown pocket.

As I did so I felt something hard, a rectangle of pasteboard. Pulling it out I saw what it was. Sam's old gym card, picked up off his desk and thrust in there during God knows what tearful clear-up, back in the spring of our loss. I laid it down and put the dour blonde's grainy face next to him, as if to test what relationship there might possibly be between the blithe young man and this bitter-lipped woman twenty years his senior. I looked for a long time, and found nothing. But back on the website was an address and a phone number for DAN. I wrote down both, and stowed the paper away in the same dressing-gown pocket before Tom got home. It seemed to me for a moment that a warmth glowed from it, a kind of promise. I schooled myself, with weary skill, to ignore such delusional comfort. I have found, these past months, that it is important not to accept false relief lest the subsequent relapse prove too cruel to bear.

4

C arla – my brother's child – has always been my conso-
lation for having no daughter. Tom is fond of her too,
in a mildly exasperated way, though he wishes she was
brighter. In any case her arrival for Sunday lunch was enough
of an event to distract him from his bad mood and me from
the treacherously exciting pieces of paper in my dressing-
gown pocket. This visit was momentous, anyway. It was to
be the first time that my new great-nephew, Harry Samuel,
aged three months, would be brought into our house. I had
seen him in hospital and at their house but he was not, in
the first weeks, allowed to travel more than half an hour away
from the Norfolk and Norwich hospital where a small heart
defect was being monitored.

I like babies, always have. They know what they want,
demand it loudly, and offer a ravishing smile in return when
they get it. Tom is less keen on the very early stages of
human development, and enjoys children more when they
can talk and ask questions and look at worms in the garden.
When I heard Carla's car in the lane I went out to greet
them and carry in some of the baby's expensive and in-
ordinately complicated equipment, while my husband
padded purposefully towards the corkscrew and the wine
rack. Carla's husband Jeremy parked – crookedly as usual
– and began hauling frilled and rabbit-bedecked equipment
from the boot, amid flurried exchanges of 'Darling! The
changing mat—' and 'Darling, his hat! If we go in the garden

he'll have to have his *hat!*' Jeremy does some lucrative job in a merchant bank, offsetting emerging market risks or buying Bolivian paper futures or something. He has pale, smooth butter-coloured hair and pink cheeks and, it always seems to me, very little real sense indeed. In this he is the polar opposite of Carla, who has no intellectual qualifications to speak of and a horror of paperwork, but who in daily matters shows a great deal of instinctive sense. At school she was certainly not the sharpest knife in the box, and mortified my brother and his wife by leaving at sixteen and training as a beautician; I was, I hope, of some use to them all during that fraught time. My contribution lay in helping to persuade my brilliant brother and his intellectually snobbish wife that the most intelligent thing Carla could do was to use the talents she actually had, rather than try to fake some she had not.

In the end they cheered up when their younger daughter got into Oxford on a scholarship; and when pretty, well-groomed Carla snagged Jeremy and a big house, they became wholly reconciled. The marriage certainly seems to work. Jeremy plainly can't find his bum with both hands but runs his department as a rising star of the City with some sort of voodoo instinct for attracting money and immense personal bonuses; Carla can barely spell 'bank', but sends him out into each day's battle clean and tidy and properly fed, and so far seems to run a model nursery.

I helped them in and duly admired the cross, crumpled little face in the baby-seat, in return for which I was permitted by Carla to remove Harry Samuel's fleecy hat and further admire his butter-coloured hair.

'Hello then, great-nephew,' I said ceremonially, and called Tom over to admire. 'See? He's very alert, taking everything in.'

'I have no idea how you can judge that,' said my husband

a little repressively. 'They have no understanding of what-ever it is they take in. Can't have.'

'Yes, they have,' I said firmly. 'At three months they even understand jokes.'

'They can't,' said Tom with equal conviction. 'To under-stand a joke involves perception of incongruity, and a baby's experience is too brief to understand the concept of in-congruity.'

'Bollocks,' I said rudely, liberated from good manners by the exhilarating proximity of the young. To demonstrate my thesis I picked up a big red velvet cushion from the sofa, to balance it on my head. After a moment's solemn staring, baby Harry Samuel's face creased into a delighted smile and he gave a small unmistakeable crow of laughter.

'See? He knows cushions don't belong on people's heads. Perceived incongruity. QED.' Carla, transported with pleasure at her baby's brilliance, started playing peek-a-boo; Jeremy and Tom drifted purposefully over towards the drinks tray.

'You driving home, darling?' said the banker hopefully.

'OK, darling. But you're going in the back to amuse Harry.'

'Fine, sweetie.' He drank deeply, raising his glass to my husband. And there we were, a happy family gathering, the papers in my dressing-gown pocket almost forgotten.

Lunch proceeded cheerfully enough; Harry fell asleep after a brief breastfeed. He woke, though, just as we were drinking coffee, and proved to be one of those babies who wakes in a terrible temper. Sam was the same; it is, they say, connected to immature breathing patterns. Carla hurried to him, picked him up, shushed and tried to suckle him, but the child's hopeless fruitless rage only rose in a wail of pure despair. Jeremy shrugged apologetically but without distress, and Carla worked on, an efficient, preoccupied mother.

Things did not go so well with Tom or me, though; I do not think either of us was prepared for what happened to us in those minutes of wailing. The infant distress, the crumpled howl and baby tears seemed to pierce deep into me, opening a well of hopeless despair and searing through the barely formed scar-tissue in my heart. I saw – though I hope Carla did not – how vulnerable we were, how fragile our daily composure and how easily endangered. Where my great-nephew's laughter had lit up the room with disproportionate pleasure, his weeping brought an apocalyptic darkness equally beyond reason. In the sound of it Sam's death returned, Sam's coffin, the hollow unspeakable grief that was mine forever. Tears ran down my face. I carefully resisted the urge to brush them away, because I have, over these months, learnt the valuable lesson that tears are transparent: nobody sees them unless you rub and wipe.

Tom, on the other hand, jumped up and moved towards the kitchen, muttering an excuse. The child howled on, choking now on his distress; Jeremy grimaced and Carla soothed. Soon the sounds quietened, and the small face pressed against her soft cashmere bosom began to burrow and nuzzle. She pushed up her sweater and began to feed him again. Greedy, noisy gulps subsided into quietness. Tom came back, white-faced, his eagle profile blurred and puffy. I looked down at my hands and they were shaking.

It was time for the young family to go, in a flurry of bags and mats and blankets and safety straps. While Jeremy fumbled with the baby's impedimenta, Carla came back in and gave me a hug.

'We think of Sam, you know, a lot,' she began. 'You do know that?'

'Yes, sweetie. And thank you.' I was level again now, sensible, resigned. I hoped she had not seen the tears. 'It was lovely to see you, and Harry. Isn't he great?'

'Yes. But Auntie, the thing is – Jeremy and I did wonder . . .'

She hesitated, unusually, and I watched her pretty face crumple in concentration.

'You know how Jeremy's parents are both, like, dead?'

'Yes.'

'Well – Mum and Dad will obviously be Granny and Grandad, when he can talk, but we wondered if you and Tom might like him to call you – sort of – well, Nan or Gran or Grandpop, or something? Sort of less of a mouthful than Great-Auntie and Uncle . . .'

She must have seen something in my face which made her words tail off uncertainly. I took a deep breath, aware that Tom was standing behind me, and feeling – as if it were a solid thing – the wave of horrified revulsion coming from him.

'Oh, it's sweet of you – but I don't think that would be the best idea, I mean, would it? Him calling his grandad's sister Grandma? Be a bit odd . . . anyway, I'm sure he'll find his own name for us. Tarnetie or Gatie or something, for great-aunt . . . or just Marion and Tom . . . they do, you know.'

'Oh – OK. I just thought—'

'Lovely thought. But no, we . . . we're not grandparents—'

I had no more words. I hugged kind, silly Carla again and she tripped out to the car, to her tipsy husband and small, living son. Back in the house Tom leaned against the kitchen wall, his forehead on the cool tiles.

'You OK?'

'No,' he said. 'But I daresay I will be. No choice, really.' And that was the last we said about the lunch, or the baby, for some days.

5

On the morning after the lunch party both of us seemed to be back on an even keel. Ordinary life, it seemed, would press on. I was in the kitchen making Tom's morning tea when the phone rang; it was Eric, my Monday employer on the industrial estate. He owned a small firm making specialist packaging for medicines, and once a week I kept their books and did the wages for the half-dozen girls and boys who giggled through their working day there.

'Marion – thank goodness I got you.' He sounded flustered. 'Don't come in this morning – we've had a fire.'

I like Eric. You can hear his face in his voice, if you see what I mean: the nasal-clerical intonation immediately brings before you the threadbare comb-over, the benignly anxious wrinkles, the pale blue eyes behind the half-moon specs. He is one of the unsung heroes of the nation; his company will never grow vast and powerful but he provides jobs in this bleak coastal region where jobs are sorely needed, makes perfectly useful objects on a modest profit margin, and watches over his 'kids' with real affection. I did not like to think of Eric struggling with insurance assessors and suspicious police. It was a good little firm.

'Is everything OK?'

'Yes.' He exhaled, a long sigh down the phone. 'Fire wasn't big. Vandals, they think. Chucked something through the window, downstairs. I reckon I know why, and I could make a guess at who.'

'Ah.' I understood his reticence. Sukey Harmsden, sacked for pilfering petty cash the week before, was notorious for choosing boyfriends who specialized in brainless violence and extreme loyalty.

'I might raise it. But the police and the fire people are all over everything, so anyway we're not operating today. No point coming in. I've got the kids standing by to clean up, they won't lose wages. I'll take them to the pub at lunchtime, might get some ideas that would interest the police.'

Abruptly, and tardily, I remembered the nature of my own job.

'Hell, is the paperwork OK?'

'Yes, thank God. Well, thanks to you making us buy those cabinets.'

'Always worth it. In the computer age paper still matters, as my husband could tell you with a lot of swear words.' I had, during coffee breaks, confided in dear Eric about Tom's tax travails. He was one of the few people I felt I could decorously talk to about such matters. 'Shall I fit you in later in the week?'

'Be marvellous if you could. I don't want to get in a muddle.'

'OK. I'm free on Thursday.'

'Thanks.'

I poured the tea, reflecting how fond I had become of my little clutch of clients, and especially of Eric. The work I did for them was dull enough – certainly dull compared with my old, pre-family life as senior sub and staff writer for *Woman's Life* – but it had its satisfactions. Some of my friends wondered aloud why I didn't work for a charity or a community group, 'using my journalism skills, perhaps'. Others thought I must miss the glitzy world of magazine publishing. But I had that time, and remember it with amusement, and

I know it has gone and I don't really want it back. If I had sometimes entertained thoughts of returning to the planet Media, Tom's brush with national fame as Faulkner the Food-Guru reminded me how febrile and unsatisfying that world can be. Eric suited me just fine: there is a wholesome mercantile honesty about the human relationships in these small firms, an atmosphere of plodding, decent, productive labour. Besides, when Sam was growing up they were flexible and understanding, unlike the publishing giant back in London; and since he died I have drawn a surprising amount of comfort from my workplace. Tom, I felt, did not have this: neither the TV world nor his intermittent high-table life at the university seemed to feed his spirit in the way nice care-worn Eric and the others fed mine.

Still, a day off was welcome, and since Tom was off to a conference in Cambridge all day and planned to stay with a colleague after the dinner, I felt a sudden giddy sense of freedom. I could do anything I wanted, without guilt. There was no shopping, no housework worth bothering with, and in any case I was sick of the domestic interior.

I stood for a moment, Tom's mug in my left hand, considering. For a moment I contemplated a hike, a serious all-day walk down by the sea, but outside the kitchen window the Norfolk sky was Tupperware grey and a faint drizzle was beginning. Then my right hand slid into the dressing-gown pocket, and felt the slip of pasteboard and the crumpled cut-out photograph of Julia Penderby. D-jool-ya. I pulled out the photo and addressed it out loud. I do that far too often these days.

'What were you here for, you fierce woman? Why did you think my Sam owed you anything? What is it that you want?'

The picture stared up at me, impassive, unsmiling. I laid Sam's gym-card picture next to it and looked at them together: still no clue, no link. Yet she – I was sure in my bones it was she – had come to the house, berated my husband and slandered my son.

Moments later, I put the tea down gently on the bedside table and ruffled Tom's grey hair as it spread across the pillow.

'Sweetheart? I've got an unexpected day off. Thought I'd go to London, look for some duvet covers.'

He opened his eyes and tilted his head to squint at me against the grey square of the window.

'Really? Why not Cambridge? I could give you a lift – you could get the train back. Or Norwich.'

'Just fancy London. You know. Sick of Norwich shops. Trains from Cambridge take as long as London, with changes.'

'OK.' He closed his eyes again. 'Tea. Thanks.'

'I'll be off before you're up. Get the 9.15 Saver.'

'Mmmphm.'

It was strange to feel my spirits soar as I dressed hastily, in the bathroom so as not to alert him further. Normally I don't like London much. Years ago my life was there: I worked in a great buzzing tower near the Elephant and Castle, ran down the road in heels to swing perilously on to the platform of moving Routemaster buses, lived in a crumbling flat opposite Borough Market and cooked up the leftovers they sold cheap at the day's end. I was young and adventurous and bold then, an urban warrior. I spent the evenings happily crushed in wine bars and pubs, followed the Bonzo Dog band and other amusements, went to bed late and did my make-up in the lift at work. When Tom got the post at the University of East Anglia I was ready to move on from all this, and it made sense to have our children – well, one child, as it turned out – in a friendly middle-class commuter village with a good school.

I never realized that it would be a one-way move, not only

financially and logistically but psychologically as well. But the fact is that I have grown used to this provincial life and London only oppresses me, with its vast spread and its angry alien masses, its filth and roar and lack of calm. I avoid it, trying instead to lure old friends from their Islington or Hampstead houses to spend weekends in our backwater. Yet on that morning a sense came over me that this London trip was exactly what I needed. A journey would jolt me out of my sad routine; it would be a pilgrimage towards a mystery, a strange woman who – however tenuously – offered a link with my lost son. I even had, and instantly suppressed, one of those dangerous moments of magical thinking when you believe that if you can just solve this riddle and survive this ordeal, the dead one will be given back. Madness must be fought off, vigorously, by the bereaved.

I had no intention whatsoever of looking for duvet covers. We had enough to keep our pathetic little family of two in clean sheets all the way to the old people's home. My mission was to find Julia Penderby in her office. Or, at least (my courage was never strong) to look at it from the pavement. That was pilgrimage enough. Which, I suppose, is the measure of how little else there was in my life at the time.

I did some rapid printing of web pages before I left, and studied them on the train. I do not know East London well, and had to take it on trust that the particular inner suburb where DAN had its offices was a 'vibrant multiracial community with a lively gallery and Britart scene, and a rich history of immigration from the Jewish and Caribbean communities of the 50s and 60s to the modern-day Turkish, Bangladeshi, Vietnamese and Polish arrivals'. Vague memories of recent colour supplements told me that it was 'rapidly gentrifying' and a 'happening area, the newest hot urban village'. Be that as it may, it seemed to be accessible only by an overground train and a station of surpassing filthiness, where dried vomit from the night before was clearly visible down the walls and a couple of hunched young men in hoods exchanged something in foil at the far end of the platform.

I felt simultaneously disgusted and excluded: this was Britain, this was 'real' life in my country – it must be, it was the capital city and a rising, fashionable bit of it at that. Yet it had nothing to do with my life or the people I knew; Eric's young Norfolk employees (even sacked Sukey Harmsden) were another species: gentler and more naive, country kids for all their attempts at attitude and flirtations with drugs. I felt middle-aged and provincial in my chunky cardigan and wished I had dressed up; yet with a rush of something like shame I realized that if I had done so I would be unwilling to sit on these train seats in my best suit, or to pick up chewing-gum and worse on my good shoes.

As I hesitated at the station entrance, close to the wall to avoid being jostled, I stupidly wondered whether I would look less out-of-place if I bought an *Evening Standard*. Startlingly, an elderly Sikh stopped beside me with a large rottweiler on a lead.

'Can I help you? Are you lost?' he asked in a deep sweet voice, and my general revulsion at my surroundings turned to embarrassment at feeling it.

'Arigorn Street,' I muttered. 'It's an office, I need to find—'

'Is not far, madam. Down that way, go left after the shop with the red signs.' His smile was beautiful, and my shame increased. As he walked on, though, the dog turned its head and bared its teeth at me. I reminded myself that I had thought of today as a pilgrimage. Pilgrims suffer sloughs of despond and castles of despair. Squaring my cardiganed provincial shoulders I strode off in the direction he had indicated, past grimy kebab-cafés, phone shops with security grilles and a halal supermarket with angry red posters. Within a few minutes I was standing in front of a once-handsome Victorian brick building thick with grime, its sills and flourishes eaten away in places by the city's acid filth. An iron-sheathed door was fringed by four bells, the second from the top marked with a piece of card:

DAN International
Defeat Aids Now
reg.charity xxxxxxx

It took all my feeble nerve to ring the bell.

6

'Whozat?' said a woman's voice, abruptly. 'Chioma? Lost your key?'

'No. I've come to see Miz Penderby.'

'What for?' There was an aggressive abruptness in the tone which immediately convinced me that I had found Tom's ranting 'hippie woman'. I took a deep breath.

'I am Marion Faulkner. I believe you may have called on my husband, Tom.'

There was no reply, but the door buzzed sharply and I pushed it open. A gloomy hallway, lit by a single bleak neon strip, revealed a grubby but honourable old wooden staircase, redolent of Dickensian clerks. I began to climb it, breathless, stopping twice to fight down my nerves. Never confront an adversary until your breathing is calm. After three flights I found a dirty, frosted-glass doorway with another DAN sign. It had some kind of security device screwed on to it; there was a button, a keypad, and a slightly threatening 'Community Watch' poster with a black clenched fist superimposed on a giant eye. Once more I stepped inside on the buzz, and found myself in a surprisingly clean, cheaply modern little office.

Behind the reception desk a very young black girl with abundant hair-extensions sat behind an elderly Mac laptop, from which she barely glanced up at me.

'Julia's waiting for you,' she said, a touch accusingly.

'There were a lot of stairs.'

'Not *so* many,' said the child contemptuously. The urge to slap her made me suddenly feel better, bolder, an urban warrior again; and beyond that, a woman of the mother generation. I ignored her contempt and followed the wave of her hand towards another frosted door and the inner sanctum. I had found my Djoolya, at least: her name, with its superfluous consonants and perverse vowels, was tacked to the door. Pushing it open, I strode in and looked her in the eye.

Physically, Julia Penderby was much as Tom had evoked her: around forty, palely blonde with streaks of undisguised grey, her thin face deeply lined, her clothes vague gipsy draperies. All the same, there was something magnetic about her, a forceful and angry intelligence which gleamed from her huge, hard green eyes. I wondered again what her link with Sam had been. An older lover? It seemed unlikely, given the puppyish mob of his daily friends, and the fact that Abeeku's friends had pronounced her a lesbian homewrecker. But not impossible. Not given the look, the gipsy swirl, the intensity. I could see why she might be an adventurer in relationships, why Sam might have liked her and why his father certainly would not.

'I am Marion Faulkner.'

'You said so on the entryphone.'

'You came to see my husband.'

If she could fight in short sentences, so could I.

'I came,' said the woman, 'to have a word with Sam Faulkner.'

'Who is dead.'

Well, the shortest sentence won. There was a silence; for the first time she looked down as if abashed. She did not seem like a woman for whom such a feeling was familiar, and it took her a moment to raise her head again and look at me. Even then, I thought vengefully, her question was pathetic.

'What do you mean?'

'My son died last spring. An accident. That is why my husband didn't welcome your aggressive approach.'

I had not come to reprove her, but her sudden discomfiture brought out a little sadism in me. Death, after all, pays all debts and trumps all arguments. Sam did not deserve to be ranted at. Whatever duty she thought he had been derelict in, it was not his fault that he fell off the ladder and out of the known world. I kept my gaze on her, and kept it level.

After a moment's fiddling with a pen, she said ungraciously:

'Well, I'm sorry. So there's nothing to be done, then.'

'No.'

'Well, then.'

I was still standing, she was still seated at the desk. It felt as if the interview was over, and I did not want it to be. I sat down, uninvited, on the hard chair and placed my elbows on the desk. The great thing about bereavement is that you live with it daily. It becomes a familiar, like a dislikeable pet, until you are no longer afraid of it or embarrassed or even very interested by your own reactions. This gives you a bleak advantage over others, who are all these things in turn. A horrid power attaches to those touched by close tragedy. Very occasionally you can use it.

'I think I am entitled to know why you came and shouted at my husband. What did you want from Sam? Is it some duty we can fulfil, if it is due?'

'It doesn't matter,' she said, cool again. 'It was a matter of justice, on behalf of another person. Now that the justice can't be done, that person has a right to my discretion.'

For the first time I realized that she had a posh voice, very posh indeed: a Roedean or Benenden voice despite the gipsy clothes and the ratty building.

'I have rights too. I am Sam's mother, and I feel a duty

of my own, a duty to his reputation. His honour.' Clearly, her poshness was catching; I was growing Victorian in my language. 'I think you must tell me what it is he is meant to have done. And if it is something bad, I shall put it right. Myself.'

'I doubt that,' said Julia Penderby. 'Very much indeed. But, as I say, it is not my secret to confide, not in you or anyone else. Thank you for coming. It clears things up.' She stood up, as if to make me do the same.

'No it does not!' I stayed where I was, and looked up at her; her neck, I saw, looked older than my own. 'I have gone to a lot of trouble working out where to find you, and I am not going to be fobbed off now. What did Sam – do? Or not do? Tell me! I am not leaving until . . .'

She stopped me with an odd gesture, a petulant wave of her hand which made her abruptly less dignified.

'I will have to ask the other person concerned,' she said. 'If you care to leave a contact number I will ring you.'

'I want to know!'

'I know. But it's delicate. Have some respect for my feelings on the matter.'

'You came and shouted at my husband, and I won't be talked to about respect by someone who insulted my son's memory. Sam told me most things about his life, and I am beginning to suspect you are some kind of con-trickster.' That was a lucky shot; she bristled in authentic middle-class outrage. 'At least if you tell me something reasonable I'll know you're not.'

'I doubt he would have told you about this.' Her cool was returning fast.

'Why?'

'You are,' said the posh voice of Julia Penderby, 'probably too hidebound in your attitudes to be comfortable with it.'

I stood up and glared at her.

'Well, I know where to find you now. And believe me, I don't give up easily. I have my own ways of finding things out.'

I didn't, obviously. But I had scored some kind of random hit, and was surprised to see her thin hand tremble.

'I will be in touch. I give you my word. Whether or not I can tell you anything, I'll be in touch. But it is not my decision.'

I put out a hand and held it, defiantly, until she had to reach out and shake it. Her palm was damp, and I felt a perverse triumph at knowing that our meeting had afflicted her and not myself alone. Then I wrote my mobile number down on a piece of paper and thrust it at her.

'Don't ring the house. We're in the book, but don't ring. And don't bother my husband again, whatever you do. It's just me who needs to know.'

'OK.' She moved towards the door and opened it, and while it might have been a way to speed my parting, I thought I discerned something else in the gesture: a kind of grudging respect. She was a bully, and I had bullied her right back, and maybe she was not used to that.

'I will be in touch. And—' she hesitated. 'I do appreciate the way you came to find me. Men are pathetic. Your husband—'

'Don't you diss my husband. You burst in, shouting the odds . . . !'

'He shouted at me.'

The respect between us had evaporated and she was glaring like an angry cat. I half expected her thin blonde hair to rise like hackles. I was angry too, and halfway through the door I said:

'This other person – tell me – is it Jackie? Djakki with a D?'

She stiffened, then gave an odd little smile. 'I said, I'll call you.'

Only on the stairs did I remember the gist of the conversation with the girl Camilla. It wouldn't be Jackie. Jackie was history. An ex-employee and ex-lover, whose girlfriend Julia took over. Perhaps that was why she smirked.

The girlfriend. Who, then, was she? As I left the reception area the girl behind the desk was on the phone, saying, 'Allie? Julia said to tell you, five-thirty.' Allie? Was she the 'other person' who held the secret, or just another worker? The phantom figure of this Allie began to take strange, monstrous shapes as I walked back to the station in the fading London light, past the kebabs and the security grilles. It would be, I thought in my new mood of resolution, another clue to give to the private investigator, when I hired one.

I didn't have to. But it was not Julia Penderby who got in touch three days later. It was Sarah.

7

Sarah rang just before eight o'clock, when Tom was reading in his corner and I was watching *Coronation Street* on television with the sound turned right down so as not to disturb him. I took the phone into the hall for the same reason, and leaned on the wall, easing my stiff neck; I find I stiffen up very easily these days. Well, these last months mainly.

'You sound very up,' I said. Her tone was different from the calm, amused, donnish manner I was used to. 'Have you discovered some thrilling scandal about Shirley Williams or something?'

'No, it's not the book. Well, it came because of the book, oddly enough. I went to Cambridge last week to this debate, one of the student clubs. "Can Journalism Ever be Truly Radical?"'

'And can it?' I was still relaxed, fiddling with the flex, wondering what was happening on *Coronation Street*.

'Yes and no. But never mind that. I was just going into my spiel about Murdochization and the perils and possibilities of the profit motive, when guess who I saw in the second row?'

'Rupert Murdoch, taking notes?'

'No! Guess . . .' It was so unlike Sarah to be skittish that I frowned, twiddling the flex impatiently now, hunching and relaxing my stiff shoulders.

'Can't guess. You know I hate guessing games. Come on, who?'

'Jackie!'

I had tried to put the Julia Penderby interlude out of my mind for a few days, until she got in touch, so as not to torment myself with imaginings. It took me a moment to remember who Jackie was and why Sarah would know about her. Then . . .

'You mean – Der-Jackie? Djakki with a D?'

'Yes, but no D any more. Blushed when I mentioned it. Grown up, but still recognizable – smart jacket, hair tied back! A whole new Jackie with a J. Actually, she says she uses Jacquel*ine* more.' She dwelt on the 'ine' with a faintly satirical air.

'You *talked* to her?'

'Yep. She asked a really good question about the dem-ocracy of the blogosphere, and I gave a fulsome and flattering answer and straight after the session I dived down and grabbed her. Took her for a coffee.'

'Sarah! Did you talk about the business of Julia and Tom and all that?'

'No. Not a fool. But I did hire her as a research assistant over the Christmas vacation. She doesn't have family in this country, apparently. So . . . she's all yours. I got her!'

'I can't wait till Christmas!' I was squeaking now. The whole mystery, which I had tried to suppress, reared up again and overwhelmed me with need. The itch to know more about what linked Julia with Sam was overpowering, even as I told myself not to place any importance on it because it could never change anything that mattered. 'I can't wait, Sarah!'

'I know,' said Sarah calmly. 'So she's coming over tomorrow on the local train, to discuss the parameters of her work for me. And so I can see if I really want her in the house for three weeks or whether she'd better work by email. You're dropping in for coffee about eleven. I'm going to be called to the phone for a while. You can talk to her. If she knows anything.'

I breathed deeply. 'Sarah, you're an angel, but has this landed you with a useless researcher all Christmas?'

'No. Told you, it was a very good question, and she's grown up. You wouldn't know her. No ranting feminist stuff, no militant lesbian D on her name. Bright and keen. And I do actually need a researcher. *Hansard* wears me out.'

'Sarah . . .' I could not express what I felt. As ever, she understood.

'It's fine. It was just a bit of luck. It suits me and it might help you. Are you going to tell Tom?'

'Not yet. He was furious with the Julia woman. And I don't think he'd want to know that I was chasing after these people. It's not the kind of thing that helps him. He hates riddles, and mysteries, and stuff about who felt what about who and when.'

'Fine.'

I dreamed that night, strange, complex dreams in which my lost son was ever around the next corner, just out of sight, his voice and laugh muffled by something I could not see. Next morning I told myself severely that the link was tenuous, and that it was unlikely that Jackie knew anything at all of Julia's supposed secret and her relationship, if any, to Sam. It was, I said to myself as I brushed my hair with unwise vigour and shuddered at the strands I found tangled in the bristles, simply a nice thing to meet one of his old friends and houseguests. Civilized. It would give me another perspective on him, unthreatening, to be taken with my accustomed melancholy calm. But my heart raced with anticipation and a kind of dread. I walked so quickly up to the village that I was at Sarah's by half-past ten, jittering around annoyingly in her study while she frowned over some papers she wanted to post.

'Train doesn't get in till 10.45,' she said, a little crossly. 'She wouldn't be here yet.'

'Sorry.' I snapped the hinge of a stapler, accidentally opened it upside down and spilled staples all over the floor. So I was on my hands and knees picking up sharp little angles when the doorbell went, and in my haste to get up I stumbled forwards and impaled the ball of my thumb on two of them. When I went through to the sitting-room to join them I was sucking vigorously at the sore spot, flustered, my hair in disarray.

'Oh, Jackie – how lovely to see you – do you remember coming to us the Easter before last? With all those noisy friends of Sam's?' This was social reflex: always mention your lost one in a happy tone during your first sentence, so the other person knows it is a safe subject. Jackie came back calmly enough. Her voice was as I remembered it: slightly flat, with a permanent undernote of anxiety as if she had met with little approval in her life, and struggled too hard now to maintain control of it.

'Yes. I was so sorry when I heard. Too late for the funeral, I'm afraid. I was in America for a bit, early this year.'

Recovering, I looked at her properly. Sarah was right: the sullen, poncho-stitching adolescent had vanished, to be replaced by an apparently cool young woman, hair up in what was almost a French pleat, her jeans and trainers civilized by a clean white shirt, austere silver necklet and black jacket.

'Well, it's lovely to see you again. Sarah tells me she's struck lucky with a researcher, too.'

'I'm thrilled,' said the girl, though her voice did not sound capable of anything as visceral as thrill. It was less rough, less glottal-stopped than I remembered. Perhaps, like Julia, she was secretly posh underneath the radical chic. 'I'm doing a PhD at Lucy Cavendish, but I do have to earn as well and this is such a brilliant chance, because it all ties up with my own topics and I won't have to work in some bar all Christmas.'

We made small-talk for a few minutes. It seemed that Jackie had gone to the US to see her mother and new stepfather, and that the latter had offered, out of the blue, to fund her in a second degree if that was what she wanted.

'He's stonking rich. And he thinks it's a good thing for people to study political economy. I didn't want to accept, I hardly know the guy, but my mum said, hey, it was a chance to set everything right, because things haven't been good, you know? For years. In our family. And it *was* what I wanted, I always did, but everything was just impossible before.'

Sarah melted away towards the study, leaving us with our coffee-mugs. For a moment Jackie looked uneasily towards the door, anxious to be following and showing her interest in the work, but Sarah said: 'Leave me ten minutes, there's a love, I've got some stuff I need to get into the midday post and it needs a couple of calls. Sorry, Marion, you two will have to entertain each other.'

I picked up the thread. 'Things were impossible?' The girl blushed.

'Well . . . when my dad left and my mum went to America I got tangled up with some people. Political people, and a lover I had. And further degrees were considered a bit of a waste of time. And I got this job with a charity. I thought it was fantastic at first. But it all went pear-shaped.'

'It's not as much fun being young as people think,' I murmured, and she suddenly smiled, an attractive open smile I had never seen, and the anxiety faded from her voice for a moment.

'Yeah. That's about it.'

There was a silence. Then, gathering up my courage, I said:

'I'm glad to have run into you like this, anyway. I want to ask you about someone I met the other day.'

'Oh?' She was wary now, but not hostile.

'She runs a charity. DAN, Defeat AIDS Now. Julia Penderby.'

'Ah.' Jackie fell silent for a moment, then: 'You know, I thought this was a bit of a coincidence. Your friend Sarah, she's a crafty one.'

'You know what this is about?' I was thunderstruck, and she became shifty.

'I heard on the grapevine from another girl about Jules coming and shouting the odds at your house. I didn't remember that Dr Anderson knew you, though. Not when I heard she was at the uni. I forgot . . .'

'Just regarding Sarah,' I said firmly, 'she doesn't take on researchers to oblige her friends. She's been looking for a while, she's snowed under with this book. But OK, I admit it. It was a good coincidence for me. I want to know about Julia.'

Jackie got up, smoothing her jacket, and for a terrible moment I thought she was leaving. But she only paced towards the window and then turned, the light shining through the wisps of side hair.

'OK. You've been on my conscience,' she said levelly. 'Because I put my hands up, it was me that persuaded Sam to do it. I suppose I would have sought you out in the end, just to say sorry. After he died and all that.'

The clock ticked, oddly loud, or perhaps it was my heart. The words 'persuaded him to do *what*?' hung unsaid in the air; I did not trust my voice. It was Jackie who went on.

'And when Allie – Alexandra, my girlfriend – walked out and went off with my ex Julia, I prob'ly should have said something then. But I thought it might all go away, what with Julia's ideas – and then I went to America and everything changed, and I realized what a dickhead sort of life I'd been leading anyway. Maybe it was my step-father being so nice and normal with Mum. My dad, you see – uh, I s'pose he was the reason I went the way I did, went along with Jules's ideas about men. With Allie it was different. Only she'd gone.'

I was lost, but stayed quiet, hoping for the confusion to clear. She went on:

'And when I got back, it turned out Sam was – that he'd had the accident. So I didn't think about it hard enough to see that you and your husband had a sort of a right. Because that hadn't been the deal. I didn't know whether you even knew. But I reckon Sam would have told you, probably. He was really really nice about you always. I wished I'd had parents like that.'

I found my voice, and fought to keep it steady.

'Jackie, I have no idea what it was that Sam did, or what you had to do with it, or what the *deal* you talk about is. Or anything. Please . . .'

She stared at me. 'Holy shit, of course you haven't! God!'

Sarah came back in, sensed that the moment was not right, and made to retreat into the study. Jackie, however, put her hand out towards her, appealing.

'Please – Dr Anderson – I ought to be sorting out about work . . .'

'You can't leave me dangling!' I protested, and Sarah looked from one to the other, half understanding. That woman is very quick on the uptake.

'Tell you what,' she said. 'Let Jackie come and sort out her work stuff with me for twenty minutes, and everyone calm down, and then we'll have lunch. All of us. Jackie, will you promise to tell us what the hell this is all about, and why you've made Marion go white as a sheet? Over lunch?'

Her schoolmarm gaze made the younger woman blush
scarlet.

'Yes. Of course I will. I just panicked, it's like, embarrassing. But do you really *want* a researcher? It's not just all
a front? Because I'll tell you everything anyway . . .'

'I do. I have a lot of work to do. Come on. Marion, do
you want to faint right here or take a brisk walk round the
village before lunch and post these packets for me?'

When Sarah asks such questions, it is clear which answer
is required.

'Round the village.'

I suppose, looking back, that Sarah divined that Jackie
needed time to collect her thoughts before telling me the
story which follows. At the time I resented having to plod
and wonder alone on that November day in the grey village.
I even had to go to the village shop and buy an ice-lolly, the
kind I used to meet Sam with after school when he was five.
I sat on the bench opposite the little school and ate it, for
him, and wondered.

8

I got back to the house rather sooner than Sarah had ordered, and found both of them with their heads down, looking at an old *Hansard*. Sarah glanced up.

'Did you post those packets?'

I struck my head, felt in my bag and found the three thick envelopes still there. 'OK.' There was something unexpectedly comforting in being ordered around like a child, but then I have always taken comfort in Sarah's level-headed authority. I went back down the road, posted them with three heavy *thunks* and came meekly back. They had moved on to the kitchen, and I heard a little crow of laughter from Jackie; as I reached the doorway she stopped abruptly, and put her hand over her mouth.

'I'm really sorry,' she said. 'I don't mean to take all this lightly, it's just that Dr Anderson – it wasn't about you, it was about the Liberal Democrats.'

'Call me Sarah, please,' said my friend, whisking ham and potato salad out of the fridge. She handed me the plates and, still meek, I set the kitchen table. When we had settled down and taken our food, I reasserted myself and looked at Jackie.

'Right. You promised you'd tell me what this is all about. And don't worry, I won't freak out.' It was a hollow promise. I had no idea whether I would freak out or not. I kept seeing a clear inward vision of Sam in the hospital, after they took the tubes away, his face serene beneath the heavy bandage on his brow. I had a sudden mad vision of him opening his eyes, speaking, telling me his secret. I told myself I must not cry, but the sense of his nearness was almost unbearable.

Jackie took a deep breath and began. Sarah and I sat increasingly quietly, watching her, eating our food except when at certain moments our forks stopped in mid-air or landed sharply back on the plate.

'I first met Sam at a march,' she said. 'A gang of them had come up from Cambridge for a get-the-troops-out demo in London, winter before last. I was in the LSE student union group which was meeting up with them, so they had somewhere to sort out banners and stuff.' She glanced nervously at me, as if suddenly aware how little she knew of me. I might, for all she knew, be a convinced warmonger unaware of my son's feelings about the second Iraq war. I nodded helpfully, anxious for the story to unfold.

'Yep. We knew he went. Admired him for caring about it.' Her courage returning, Jackie went on:

'He was really great. Everyone was a bit nervy and aggressive that day, quarrelling about how to make an impact. Some people always want a ruck, you can imagine. But Sam just stayed calm, kept everyone on track, said we mustn't get stroppy with the police – he was fantastic to have around. Even the way he talked, slow and upbeat. He was – he was like a big, smiling sun, if that's not too stupid.'

I felt more tears behind my eyes, and a sudden affection for this girl. She saw the same quality I did. *A big smiling sun.*

'Anyway, we did the march and the two of us talked a lot. There's a lot of hanging around while the police put up barriers, you know? And afterwards we kept in touch, texting and all that, just jokey. And that's when I stayed at yours. I was a bit mixed up, I suppose. My dad was a disaster area, my mum had gone to America with her new bloke, and I thought I really hated men. Well, I did. And I'd never had boyfriends, because – because of my dad. I was safer with women. Sam was the first guy I'd really talked to. I was having this thing, quite a big scary thing, with Julia.'

'Julia with a D?' I said, more to fill the silence than anything else.

'Yes. She's a very powerful vibe, and not such a good one, I see that now. It felt like I'd got my mum and dad back, both of them in one person, you know? And she ran this AIDS charity, DAN. It's not like an ordinary medical charity, it's more sort of angry. Her thing is that it's men who spread AIDS with their randiness and promiscuity. And, and they have to be stopped, like, globally. I mean, do you know the figures? On how many partners men have in sub-Saharan Africa, and on this thing where they think a virgin child can cure HIV? It's, like, gross—'

Her eyes shone, her hand with the fork was starting to wag accusingly. It was Sarah's level gaze and an almost inaudible murmur of 'Sam?' which brought her back to the matter in hand. I sat quiet. Jackie, her campaigning zeal deflated, breathed deeply, as if dreading the next phase of her story.

'Anyway, this is kind of embarrassing, but I was in this affair with Julia Penderby. I never knew I was even gay, not before. But she really convinced me that it was my true self, and anyway it was the truest and most honest way for a woman to be. Free from the oppression of men. Phallocracy. She didn't even like me texting Sam, though he wasn't a boyfriend, obviously.'

The sun had come out; I watched a bright ray slanting across Sarah's kitchen table, the shadows of birds on the feeder outside throwing vivid shapes across the potato salad. I wanted to push harder, to make this annoying child get to the point.

'But Julia and I broke up . . . well, I sort of dumped her

but it was quite amicable, she's not the kind that freaks out. It only went on for about two months, but I went on working for her and doing training secondments with other charities she thought were good.' A deep breath. 'Then I met Allie. Alexandra.' I started momentarily at the name. 'And we got together. It wasn't specially smooth, we did fight, she's quite fiery. And that was when Sam said he'd help.'

'Help with what?'

'Help Allie to have a baby. She's a bit older, see, twenty-six, she works as a performance artist and a dancer and all that – it's not very stable, really. But she was just really set on having a baby. She doesn't have any family to speak to, I think that was part of it. So I asked Sam, because he was such a great guy and the only man I really was friendly with. She kept going on about sperm banks and the internet, and I was freaked, it might have been someone like my dad. Jesus, it might have *been* my dad. It was just too weird. So Sam was up in London and we went for a pizza and it was always such a relief just to talk to him, he was such a great guy—'

She paused, looking nervously at me. Sarah's slight frown kept me silent. 'Well, that was when I asked if he'd be our donor.'

My fork dropped on to the plate, with a clatter which frightened off the shadow-birds outside the window.

'You're saying that Sam donated his – his sperm, so your girlfriend could try to have a baby?' My voice was squeaky with outrage. Jackie rattled on, hasty and nervous.

'It wasn't something just casual, honestly. He thought about it a bit and we talked a bit, and he could see how we were placed. Allie was getting really impatient, she wanted to go to some awful clinic and be up-ended on some table – it felt like sort of rape. There were a lot of rows. And there was this new law that the baby could find its donor when it grew up, and I just kept imagining some stupid Tory-boy or something, a golf club type, and how awful that would be. And anyway I reckoned I needed to love this baby.' She paused, grimacing. 'Because deep down I reckon I wasn't ready to have one. Specially 'cos there was a risk it might be a boy. And I totally don't understand boys. I mean, Sam was different. The only one who was a proper friend, without any predatory shit. And I didn't want to lose Allie. So, I thought well, if he'd do it, I'd have more chance of loving it. I mean, if it was lovely like Sam.'

I opened my mouth but caught Sarah's eye again. She was shaking her head very slightly to stop me interrupting, as if she guessed there was more. Jackie ran on, hurrying now.

'So – Sam said yes. And the deal was, the deal *absolutely* was, that it would be anonymous, no stuff on the birth certificate, no child support claims or anything. We wouldn't tell the baby, we wouldn't tell anyone, certainly wouldn't tell you and Professor Faulkner. I got him to write a secret letter for Allie, in case there was ever some bone marrow thing or medical stuff like that and they *had* to know. Or if we were both killed. Sam said he needed to have rights. But otherwise it was never going to be out. I know you're supposed to let children have their roots these days and know about their DNA and everything, but . . .'

She was silent for so long that in the end I echoed:

'But?'

'OK. It was a horrible way to think. I don't think that way any more, I can see that babies do actually have a sort of right to know who their dad is. I was pretty messed up and immature, and Allie is – well, she's a bit like Julia. Not in the hating men thing, but she sort of carries you along with her. And she said she didn't want any complication.'

It was Sarah who asked the question I could not bear to frame.

'Did Sam go along with not being on the birth certificate?'

Jackie hesitated, and then spoke with more adult assurance than before.

'Yes. Technically. But I've thought about it a lot ever since, and my theory is, you know how laid-back he was, that he reckoned Allie and me would come round. I mean, he was my best friend in a weird way. So I think he probably expected that he'd sort of gradually, gently, work his way into being involved. At least so the kid knew. Lots of gay couples and donors sort of work things out like that. It's cool.'

'He said that?' Sarah was still in charge, giving sidelong glances at me. 'He said he'd be in touch if he was wanted?' I was quiet, my fork laid down to stop it clattering in my shaking hand. It was, for the moment, the mere fact of my son's kind, complaisant nature that made me tremble. Jackie frowned and answered carefully:

'He didn't say it quite like that. Well, I was in a state and Allie – like I say, she just wanted to get on with it, get pregnant, sort the rest out later. But not be a financial burden on him because he was younger than her, you know? So I brought the stuff from his flat in a cab—' She broke off, presumably motivated by delicacy towards a mother's feelings.

A conversation came back to me, an odd conversation with my son a few days before his 21st. It was about fathers, and Sam had asked whether I thought children always needed them. The conversation arose – or seemed to arise – out of a news bulletin about the dead soldiers in the Iraq and Afghanistan campaigns, and the plight of their children and widows. I can't remember what I said, but as a middling conventional family woman I dare say I replied that fathers were important, that a male influence was good for both boys and girls, all that stuff. I do remember that he said that perhaps the main thing was just to know who your dad was, in case you ever wanted to ask him things or know about his life. He said perhaps he needn't actually be there all the time, as long as he was sort of on tap. I assumed he was talking about soldiers again. I remember nothing else. I wish I had concentrated, but I was making a lasagne at the time.

Jackie was still speaking. 'Anyway, all I can say is that if I was still with Allie, and Sam had, you know, died . . . no way would we have come pestering you and Professor Faulkner. We wouldn't think of it. I hope not, anyway.'

This last observation had a ring of honesty, and I divined that she was thinking about the financially unstable Alexandra, who might have changed her mind.

'. . . And I do actually think,' continued Jackie, 'that it's disgusting what Julia did. I heard that she'd turned up, a friend told me, and I know how she is, I bet she really monstered at your husband. I don't see why she's doing it, unless it's just money. When I was with Allie she was really against him having to be chased about money. But maybe Julia made her change. Like she got me to put a D on my name. I mean, money isn't – but maybe it's, like, the principle. About men facing the consequences of their actions and lusts and all that – only it was only him being kind not, like, lust, so . . . but she might not see that . . .'

She was running out of control, wittering, her anxious eyes avoiding mine.

'. . . and I s'pose,' she concluded helplessly, 'that with the baby getting closer, they might change their mind about lots of stuff. People do get weird, I mean, don't they? It was one reason I was nervous about her having one. A baby.'

Sarah had quietly poured coffee for the three of us; my mug jerked in my hand as I heard my voice, rough and unfamiliar, saying:

'You mean – are you telling me – that this donor in-
semination, this turkey baster thing – that it *worked*?'

'You don't use a turkey baster any more, it's a special thing
you get online, a syringe without a needle . . .'

'I mean, are you telling me – Jackie, are you telling me
that this woman got pregnant?'

Jackie blinked, tired now.

'Yes. I thought maybe you knew. From Julia going to see
your husband.'

There was another silence. It was Sarah who said, 'How
long? When?'

'It must be quite soon.'

More silence. 'I suppose if I'm honest, that actually is why
Julia was after Sam. For child support.'

She looked at me, with visible pity. 'Mrs Faulkner – I just
wanted to explain – I mean, you aren't angry with Sam for
doing it, are you? I talked him into it, he was trying to help.
In the end he just laughed and said every baby was a blessing.
I remember that word, blessing, because it sounded so old-
fashioned. And OK, he said he'd help support it, and all,
and take it out and everything. If Allie and I ever changed
our minds. You're not angry?'

'Not with him,' I said. My voice was bleak, and the sun
had clouded over. 'Never with him.'

When Jackie had left, still apologizing, clutching her file
of papers, I sat in Sarah's kitchen and cried, longer and
harder than I ever thought possible. She did not try to
stop me.

9

I was lying, of course. I certainly was angry with Sam, and that is why I cried so hard. I suppose it was the first time since his death that I had felt such a normal maternal emotion, and the shock was considerable. When someone beloved has gone, your memory canonizes them. You remember only the shining goodness, the lovely qualities and moments. But those feelings can never be the whole reality of any human relationship, and without impatience and irritation and occasional resentment no love is wholly real. In that brief moment of fury, it was the sudden reality of Sam which hit me and the renewed shock of his permanent absence which made me cry.

Daft boy! How could he do such a thing, at twenty? How could he let his easy kindness betray him into such a casual, lethal contract with two flaky women in what was plainly an unstable union? How dare he – I am ashamed of feeling this, ashamed of my proprietorial instinct – how dare he lightly pass on to strangers the thing we gave him, his unique genetic material? How could he in such mad circumstances create progeny, Tom's and mine?

This child, if it were born, would be our first and only descendant. Our grandchild. And he was happy, was he, to let it be born to some stroppy lesbian witch who didn't approve of fathers and didn't want him or his family to know it?

I wept and snorted and gasped, there in Sarah's kitchen

as the sun went down that winter afternoon. I had never understood the expression 'to be beside oneself', but on that day I glimpsed the reality of it, as a part of me looked on in dismay at the crazy, uncontrolled grief and fury into which Jackie's tale plunged me.

Eventually Sarah spoke, gently, her hand on my shoulder.

'Marion. Settle down. This isn't doing any good.'

'Nothing ever can, now!' I heard myself, from a great distance, making this unconsidered announcement.

'You don't know that.'

She put the kettle on again, banging it down harder than necessary on the worktop and then turning back to me, pushing back her hair and frowning. She knew, better than anybody, that soft sympathy would destroy me all over again.

'Marion. Get a grip.'

So, after a while, I did. When I had blown my nose on large quantities of kitchen paper and accepted a cup of tea, she asked flatly but more kindly:

'Are you going to tell Tom?'

'No.' The answer was out before I could think. Again I heard myself, from a distance, making this sharp decision. Hauling the two parts of myself together, I found I still believed in it and more slowly said: 'How can I? He'll be furious.'

'Will he? I mean – look, Marion, I don't want to be callous about this, but thousands of young men donate sperm all the time. I used to go out with a medic years ago when I was a student and he did it, must have had about six kids, that's the ration. Never thought twice, just thought he was doing a favour for some couple he'd never met, and getting a few quid for it.'

'Yes, but that's different – and people don't think like that now. Do they?'

'Since DNA and stuff, you mean?'

'Yes, and – and racial roots, and everything, and—' I was

crying again. '—and it's not like a donor register and a proper clinic. He knew these people, or one of them anyway, and he was willing to have our grandchild grow up with lesbians – that awful hard-faced Julia—'

'It wasn't her then,' said Sarah thoughtfully. 'And it does sound as if he was really fond of Jackie, lots of texts and meet-ups – almost like a sister.'

'I wanted him to have a sister! Or a brother! It wasn't my fault we couldn't!' Hysteria, rising.

'I know – I didn't mean that.' She put a hand on my arm, tentatively. 'All I'm saying is that he may have felt it would all be OK. That the two women would come round and they'd all be friends. And at his age you don't really understand about children and how one feels about them. It's friends who are all-important when you're twenty.'

I was remembering how, as a little boy, he had constantly asked if he could have a baby sister. Not a brother to play with; his best friend had a little doll of a sister and he was enchanted by her. Carla was too old and scornful for him by then. Perhaps Jackie really was a sister-figure. Providing him with what I never did.

'Maybe,' I sniffed. 'But all the same, it's a hell of a way to have your first child, at that age.'

She shook her head. 'The other thing is, they're a new generation, they have to invent their own way of carrying on. I hear strange things all the time when I'm lecturing – they're completely at ease with the gay thing, for a start, much more than we were.'

'I am not homophobic! But . . .'

She ignored me. 'They're used to broken families, odd-shaped stepfamilies, gay adoption, surrogates, mixed up generations, IVF for old women, civil partnerships, all that. It's a new world.'

'So old values don't mean anything?' I was a little angry with Sarah now.

'Course they do. There's a whole set that never changes – kindness, and consideration, and unselfishness, and friendship. Maybe our generation's old values, the ones we got from our parents – maybe they sometimes left out plain old kindness. Sam was being kind.'

I was suddenly exhausted, and knew I would cry again any moment. I got up to leave, and Sarah did not try to stop me.

'Stay in touch,' she said. 'See you tomorrow?'

'Maybe.'

I did not want to see anybody. I went home, and mercifully Tom was out for a walk, leaving an angry scatter of accounts and scribbled additions on his desk; I left a note about supper, claimed a cold, and took myself to bed with a hot-water bottle to shiver into sleep.

Tom woke me with tea, toast, and the Sunday papers. I continued the pretence of a feverish cold and flicked through them, briefly enraged by a self-pitying article by some stupid bitch suffering from 'empty-nest syndrome' because her third child had gone off to university a hundred miles away. 'I go to her bedroom and weep,' she wrote. 'My family life seems to be over, discarded like the childhood teddybears gathering dust on the windowsill. To get through the next eight weeks without my beloved daughter seems, at this moment, unbearable. Nothing consoles me.'

'Cow!' I said, hurling the supplement to the floor. 'Godalmighty! Have these people nothing more to worry about than ordinary bloody life going on and their healthy kids growing up?'

Tom grinned, and picked it up. He seemed to be having one of his cheerful days. 'What were you reading?' He riffled through. 'This bit about the woman who wouldn't have radiotherapy?'

'No, what was that?' I tried to join in his bantering, and found to my surprise that I could, and that it made me feel better, because more normal.

'She's worried that it might damage her breast implants,' he said. 'Idiot woman. Natural selection, though – if she conks out she can't breed more idiots. Why do people write this stuff that shows them up?'

'Perhaps it's what Sunday newspapers are for,' I said thoughtfully. 'Setting before us examples of spoilt morons, to reassure us that we aren't screwing up our own lives nearly as much as they are. It's a kind of therapy. Like plunging into icy water because it's so nice when you get out.'

'Maybe.' He was wandering round in his dressing-gown and one sock, his badgery hair dishevelled, and I felt a sudden rush of pure love for him. My husband, the father of my child, the grandfather—

No. Not that. One must live in the moment. I took a deep, shudering breath, and watched as he flicked open the Money section and began berating the Revenue & Customs in a way that was almost soothingly familiar.

'Tossers! They go and lose 25 million people's personal details, including 350 families on witness protection, but if I can't find two bloody invoices from 2003 they're on me like ferrets – sanctimonious bastards with their Culpable Bankings and Offences Committed—'

I pushed back the bedclothes and got up, suddenly determined to face whatever the day brought with more courage than I had shown yesterday.

'Shall we go for a long walk?'

'OK.' I thought perhaps that I would tell him, on that walk. We would be honest with one another, face the situation together, make adult decisions.

As Tom got ready I dressed slowly and tried to rearrange

the revelations of the day before. The moment when sudden anger at poor Sam accentuated my grief still made me shake when I remembered it. But it released a flood of memory, lost in the months of canonizing sorrow. It was as if a Greek icon, flat-gilded and shining, suddenly heaved into three dimensions, losing lustre and gaining life. Through my mind ran a dozen moments of exasperation or real fury at my once-growing son: expensive school jackets forgotten in the school changing-room and never seen again, family DVDs and CDs left out of their cases and trodden on by big, careless feet, kitchen mess, bedroom chaos, staying out late at fourteen without remembering to ring.

But then I remembered other irritations, related more closely to what he had done for Jackie and her girlfriend. One teenage Christmas, soon after it was launched, Tom bought him an iPod: the original kind with the thumbwheel control. It was a more expensive present than we normally gave, over £200; but we were doing well on the TV fees and for fun Tom put it not beneath the tree with the 'big' presents, but into his stocking (we all have stockings. We are – were – that sort of family). Sam was thrilled, as we knew he would be; but he was never much of a listener on headphones, preferring to lie spreadeagled on his bed conducting an imaginary band, or dance around playing air-guitar with speakers blaring (another small irritation). Thus, two months later, we found that he had given the iPod to a friend at school. The mother of the other boy contacted us to check that this was all right, presumably worried it might involve bullying or drug deals. When I asked Sam he just grinned and said:

'Ma, Al just yearned for it, and his parents wouldn't ever give him one, they're skint.'

'But it was a present. From your dad. He really thought about it.'

'Yeah, and it was cool. And Dad was cool giving it to me, I appreciated it. But I really didn't use it much, after the first few times, and it had all my music on it, which Al likes. I've even got him into Dylan.'

This Alan was not a close friend, not a boy I saw often at home. But it would appear that my son, on seeing a need or desire which he could answer without much personal deprivation, had an instinct to fulfil it just to add to the general sum of human satisfaction. I sat on the bed again and leaned back on the pillow, tears pricking my eyes. Really, you have to honour that instinct. iPods, sperm . . . whatever he had he gave to make the world happier.

I went back into his early childhood: as a little boy on the common he would pick flowers and bring them to grown-ups, often total strangers. I asked him why, once, after he had thrust a couple of grubby daisies at a startled old man on a bench. 'He looked sad,' said the four-year-old Sam confidently.

Well, Jackie must have looked sad. A mixed-up kid with her troublesome father, still in awe of the chilly Julia and trying to hang on to a neurotic and flighty older girlfriend in the grip of broodiness. She must have looked sad, with her fear of having to feign affection for a strange man's progeny. So sunny, kindly Sam gave her what she wanted, in some sinister little bottle . . .

God! I could not let my thoughts roam down such improper pathways. And he did think about paternity, and whether he had the duty to give a child a father. I was sure of it, from that brief conversation in the kitchen. He would have wanted—

What? We cannot honestly second-guess the wishes of the dead, but we all do. Young as he was, carelessly living in the moment, I was sure he would have wanted to be some kind of father – at least an identifiable and findable figure, a known root. A root . . . a route for a curious child to tread towards its ancestry.

Did that matter to him? I tried to remember, riffling through sentimental maternal memories. As a child he had been typically curious about the 'olden days' and liked Tom's stories of the seafaring Faulkners he came from, admirals and captains all. My own family was less intriguing, being just dull old labourers-turned-clerks-turned-teachers, but I did have a great-grandmother who marched with the suffragettes. The interest Sam showed had been fleeting, and if I was honest it was mainly material for a ten-year-old's school project. But he wouldn't have wanted his biological child cut off from all that seagoing and suffrage. Would he?

I closed my eyes and tried to feel his wishes. I deceived myself. Sam's wishes were not driving me in this particular, inexorable direction. My own were. After the shock, the outrage, the cold horror of the mechanics of it all, I felt a treacherous groundswell of desire. Even of joy.

Tom began calling from downstairs for me to go for the promised walk. I laced up my heavy shoes, and went to join him.

10

We like to walk, my husband and I. We used to take intrepid walking holidays from inn to inn across European mountain ranges, ten or fifteen miles a day on wild terrain. Then, when Sam was a baby, I hefted him in a frame backpack and Tom carried everything else in his rucksack, and we walked the Pennine Way, staying at youth hostels with the baby corralled in a makeshift travel cot made of rucksacks. When he grew too heavy to hike yet too young to walk, Tom went alone a few times, pinning the excursion to research on wild food plants. From the age of six or seven Sam came with us on less ambitious journeys. He enjoyed running around the hostels in the evening, charming everybody and watching Venture Scouts on their Duke-of-Edinburgh-Award trips comparing blisters and cooking vast fry-ups. In his schooldays we took more conventional holidays, usually with other families so that Tom and I could do a few long days in the hills while the young played in the pool or the sea; when it came to the university years, in termtime we parents were alone together once more. So we did longer walks, reliving our courting days with journeys across the Picos de Europa and the Mediterranean Alps.

They have been some of our happiest times, these hikes, though Tom goes relentlessly faster than I like to. We stride out with walking poles, stay in ancient stone villages, shelter under olive trees in heatwaves or downpours with our packed lunches, and struggle to order drinks in remote bars while ancient, wrinkled sages stare at our walking boots and Boden anoraks in contemptuous disbelief. We talk as we walk: after Sam himself, these journeys have probably been the single most important cementing element in our marriage.

We have taken no holidays since the disaster, of course. But the day after Sam's funeral, when I still felt physically weak from shock, it was Tom who said 'Come on, we have to walk' and led a tearful two-hour trek out of the village and along the seashore in the wind and rain. I suppose it helped. You don't really know, at that stage, what helps. Or care much, either. But it tired us out and we slept.

After that, even these local walks tailed off. Tom grew preoccupied with the chaos of his tax affairs, and I grew lazy. There seems something pointless, now, about putting one foot in front of the other just for the sake of it. I know the countryside and coast around the village well enough and have no desire to see other lands, not any more. I would in many ways rather walk round in a town. The solitude of nature oppresses me with its shrugging indifference to pain; the erratic human footfall of the small cities is comforting. Not London. London is too *farouche* and unforgiving. Just Norwich, or Cambridge. But Tom's desire to walk seemed to me, for the moment, a hopeful thing. And it might provide a chance for me to tell him all, if I could raise the nerve.

But it was he who had something to tell me. We had gone in silence for ten minutes or so, moving fast, getting our second wind, when Tom said with an odd kind of artificial casualness:

'Have you ever thought that we ought to move?'

It was not an overture I was expecting.

'Why?'

'Well – because of Sam being gone. And we've been here a long time, and what's the point, really? There might be something else for us. It's a big world.'

'Where?'

'I dunno. Abroad. No point living in this bloody country any more, is there?'

I walked on, silent and startled. Tom grumbles a lot, as all of us tend to when we hit fifty. Like several of my friends' husbands (we laugh about it) he has been prone to start the day by throwing down newspapers and going 'Doh! Blair's Britain!' Or, more recently, 'Psha! Brown's Britain!' He is irritated by exaggerated political correctness, by health-and-safety nonsenses, by reality TV shows and pointless brown signs on the coast saying 'Beach' or 'Amenity area'. He is enraged by celebrity magazines, ministerial misdemeanours, drunken kids on Friday-night streets, and the increasing tendency of his students to cut and paste material off the internet and adopt an air of injured innocence when confronted. His tussle with the Revenue & Customs over his tax affairs was currently the front-running grievance against his country, and a strong one. But it had never occurred to me that he might want to emigrate.

'Well,' I said cautiously, 'it's our life, we have our friends here—'

'What *life?*' he asked. 'I've spent enough of my life teaching lazy spoilt kids, you've spent enough of yours adding up numbers in the cardboard factory. We've no family.'

He meant, I suppose, that both our sets of parents are dead, his father only the year before. Feebly I protested:

'There is family! You like seeing Carla and Jeremy and the baby . . .'

'How often? Out of the three hundred and sixty-five days we rot in this god-awful country, how many days?' He was on the edge of anger. 'They can visit if they want to see us. No need for us to bloody *live* in this dump.'

All this was so new, and frankly so frightening, that I drew on the skills of twenty-five years of wifehood and said nothing. We had moved from the beach to the clifftop, and I negotiated a ditch and stile with exaggerated concentration. I can feel the texture of the splintering rail even now as I think about it; every sense was heightened by alarm. When we had both reached the other side – Tom extending a courteous if tense hand to me as I stepped down – he said flatly:

'I know it's sudden. But I mean it, Marion. I don't want to stay here. Not the village, not the house, not the job. And the more I think about it, not the bloody country, either. I've worked and paid taxes for thirty years, I've done my bit. So have you. This country's not grateful, it's not considerate, it's barely civilized any more. The government just wants to bleed us dry and spend the money on Olympic stadiums and translating bloody road signs into Bengali. Once we've sold the house, we could live well in a lot of places where life isn't so expensive and oppressive. I can teach a bit, anywhere.'

He paused in his tirade, but kept on striding. I was short of breath and could barely keep up.

'There's no future in carrying on as we are. If Sam was here, obviously it might have been different. As it is, we've no future here and nothing to stay for.'

I took his hand, as much to slow him down as anything else, and we walked on in silence for a few moments. My own shock at yesterday's tale made me, I thought, wholly incompetent to deal with this new bombshell. Searching for a response, something to make him talk on while I collected myself, I said:

'Where, though? France or somewhere?' Several of our friends had bought French houses in the past decade and announced that they would retire there.

'No. Not the bloody European Union. It's all the same now. Under the iron heel. Useless fat chancers in Brussels making up mad laws and mad taxes.'

I recognized the tone now: it was definitely the all-too-familiar tax-inspection paranoia.

'Where, then?'

'I thought at first America, or Canada. As a scientist I can get a green card or a work permit, no trouble. I did the points calculator on the website for Canada. But then a better idea came up. New Zealand. There's a research institute in Auckland looking for biologists, long, short and part-time contracts. I emailed them. It looks hopeful.'

I was frightened now, and beginning to be angry: he had gone a long way down this track without me. But then, I had gone a fair distance down my own track with Julia and Jackie without telling him. And now, I saw quite clearly, I could not.

'You're saying you really want to sell the house and uproot us?'

'Yes. I do.'

A tightness gripped my heart, as a flood of absurd images tumbled and crashed: the view down the garden to Sam's old swing which I planned to refurbish for Harry Samuel's visits as the baby grew, the curtains, the wood smell of the hallway, the walk to Sarah's, the cupboard under the stairs where Sam made dens, the kitchen table, battered and scratched, which we three had sat round for years of family suppers. It was the table that made tears spring to my eyes; I pictured it standing lonely in an auction room when we had gone, leaving no trace of our broken, vanished family life. The gap we left would soon close; neighbours would say casually: 'Oh yes, we knew the end house when it was the Faulkners'; the new people have really opened it out with that conservatory . . .'

'There are no roots,' said my husband. 'No roots. Anything we want to keep we can carry in our heads. Can't we?'

'If there had been a grandchild—' I began, ignoring the warning bell still ringing in my head. 'If Sam—'

'Well, he didn't. He never had the chance.' Tom's face was shuttered, and he walked faster. 'He didn't have his life. We have. We ought to use it. Not mawk around doing nothing just because he's gone for good.'

The warning bell was louder, but I was so frightened now that I felt compelled to edge closer to telling him what I knew, to offer it up as the last bargaining counter before he blew our lives to pieces.

'If Sam *had* done – I mean, we don't know – it's a bit soon to leave the country—'

He looked at me, startled out of his own obsession for a moment.

'Are you trying to tell me something? Was there a girl-friend I don't know about?'

I could not tell him. Regaining control I lamely said:

'No, no . . . no girlfriend. But the thing is, people do say you shouldn't make any big decisions in the year after a bereavement. Maybe longer.'

Tom snorted, the phantom grandchild forgotten.

'Rubbish. Three months, maybe six. It's been longer than that. By the time the house gets sold it could be nearly a year. Then I could get sorted before the July semester, because the institute is attached to the University in Auckland.'

I flinched. Too much detail. 'Why didn't you tell me about this idea earlier? It's a bit sudden. It isn't fair just to . . .'

'Well, I'm sorry. But you have get through life the best you can, and I think we need to get clear out of England. Breathe some free air. I'm suffocating. This is self-preservation. It's hard enough to share a bloody planet with the incompetent hypocritical sharks in this regime, and I have no intention of sharing an island with them.'

'Perhaps just a holiday—'

'No. I want out. Something new. Definite. I need hard edges, I can't go on with this sogginess—'

'And me? Where do I fit in?'

'We'd go together. A new life, Marion! Can't you bloody see that? How much we need it?'

We do not, as a rule, call one another by our names when we are not in company. We use old pet names or absent-minded endearments – Badger, sweetheart, honeybun, dear-heart. This 'Marion' moment felt sinister and oppressive and I became angry again.

'It's something I would have to think about for a long time, *Thomas*. A long time. And emigrating is not necessarily the answer I'd find to our problems just now. I do have a life here.' Stupidly, I went on: 'And I do own half the house, let me remind you.'

The atmosphere had chilled and soured in seconds. It was physically colder, too: the sun had veiled itself in wintry clouds, and a sharp breath blew off the sea. We turned and began walking back. I pulled my hood up round my ears. After a few moments Tom said with a deadly quietness:

'Look around you! It's cold, it's flat, it's empty. We haven't got anything to stay for. At least, I haven't. And I'm going, Marion. I'd rather you came too, but don't doubt it for a minute: I am going. I'm not going to hang about like Miss Havisham, dwelling on the past. And I'm not going to fuck about in this appalling country any longer, with its crooked politicians and crap weather and idle students and conniving vultures in the tax office. You can do what you bloody want with your half of the bloody house.'

He accelerated, striding away from me. I did not speak again. Back at home I watched in silence, my accountant's soul appalled, as he gathered up the scribbled paperwork of untidy account-books and old bank statements from his desk and thrust them into the grate with a firelighter. In the blaze my husband's eyes flickered with a mad, fanatic light and I hardly knew him any more. He hauled and heaved and thumped around with suitcases for the rest of the day, still in silence, and did not come to bed. In the morning his car was gone.

11

'People do odd things in grief,' said Sarah. 'It's always seemed amazing to me that you and Tom stayed so level, so sensible after you lost Sam. You never broke down. Perhaps something had to erupt. Maybe it's healthy, his dashing off? Sometimes you have to do something physical, something a bit crazy, even?'

We were in my kitchen rather than hers; I had rung her in tears of fright and confusion at six in the morning when I saw the car gone and a lot of his clothes. Until then I had expected to find him asleep, as sometimes before, a cross but decently repentant hump under the spare bedroom duvet.

'How can it be healthy if you burn all your tax papers? The hearth is full of charred bits of adding-up and old invoices. It's frightening, it's like – suicide.'

Her voice was level, gentle. I was walking up and down the kitchen, fiddling with things, shivering.

'Suicides don't pack. And the documents are recoverable, surely? It might be just a fit of temper. You say he was excited about the idea of emigrating?'

'Maybe, and maybe I handled it badly. But – I don't know. Oh, his passport!' I left her, went to the desk in the living room and checked. 'Yes. It's gone.'

'So, probably not doing anything silly. I'm sure he'll ring.'

'He left his mobile. I found it in the bathroom, with the

screen broken as if he'd stamped on it. I can't even send a text.'

Sarah was silent then, turning her mug around in her hands, frowning.

'Marion, did you *tell* him? About the sperm donation thing? Was that what tipped him over?'

'No. I did say, just suppose Sam had had a child. But he brushed it off.'

'Probably thought it was a hypothesis, because you were panicking about New Zealand.'

'I was.'

Sarah yawned, not a bored yawn, more of a tension reliever. For the first time it occurred to me that these troubles of mine, and her role as my comforter and steadier over the past months, might have taken a toll on her too. She rubbed her head.

'Well, he can't go to New Zealand, can he? He said you'd have to sell the house.'

'I suppose that was if I was going too. He could perfectly well set off on his own to some bedsit, he's got savings. He never really spent the telly money. And it doesn't look as if he intends to pay the tax guys.'

'What do they want?'

'Last I heard they were asking for twenty-three thousand or so, including something called Penalties. It was terribly unfair, he didn't cheat at all, and it seems to have been the last straw. A sort of insult. I don't know whether they'll chase him.'

'Depends. They might not. Or he might rely on them not knowing where he was. Like that man who faked his death in a canoe and all the time he was in Panama.'

I found my legs weak, and sat down cold and shaking.

'Oh God, Sarah, this is unreal. I don't know whether he's left me, I don't know whether I've got a grandchild living with these crazy women in London – I don't know whether some bailiff's coming to the door. I want – I want . . .'

She was silent.

'I want *Sam!*'

More tears came, helpless tears. My friend watched me, murmured gently, touched my shoulder but withdrew her hand again in a kind of shyness.

'Would you like to see someone?' she asked after a while. 'You're not in any state to think properly, you know. Too many shocks, too close together.'

'See a shrink, you mean?'

'A counsellor. You never saw a bereavement counsellor, either of you, and some people say it's helpful.'

'No. Why would I?' I got up and walked round the kitchen again, restless for action, holding on to worktops to steady my shaking legs. 'I know what's wrong, I don't need some self-satisfied smug-arse going on about finding cognitive solutions or tracking it back to potty training. I'm not the one who's bloody mad! Everyone else is. Tom's gone off his head and there might be a weirdly conceived grandchild that I'll never see.'

Sarah sat quietly, watching me. 'One thing,' she said finally. 'Did Tom take his laptop?'

'What sort of question is that?'

'It's just that you know he left his mobile, but you could send an email, couldn't you? In case he checks his university address?'

'I could. Yes. Thanks.'

'You mainly want to know he's all right, really, don't you? Perhaps you should let him know that it's OK to take some time out from the – the situation. He might answer, and that would take the pressure off.'

I was silent. After a while, I heard myself saying calmly enough:

'I don't want to. I can't deal with him. I've pretended it's all right, but it hasn't been for ages. I can't be involved with whatever is going on in his head. It makes me feel . . .'

A pause. 'Feel what?'

'Endangered.' Again, I seemed to hear myself saying it from a long distance away. There was a band of tension round my head, and I sensed that it had been there for weeks, months even, but only now was it tightening like a cruel crown.

'Well,' said Sarah, and I could not read her expression. 'In that case, I'm going to email him. Then you'll know he's OK, and you can sort your own side of things out. Is that all right?'

I nodded. After a few careful, and again oddly expressionless, enquiries as to whether I would be all right, she left for home. I went back to bed and fell into tangled dreams; waking once or twice, I could not catch their meaning. I did not want to eat, but towards evening, awake and wandering round the house and garden without purpose, I heard the phone ring.

'Marion? Sarah. I've had an email back. He's safe. He's at a friend's flat in Cambridge. He said some things—'

'I don't want to know.' I really didn't. The band of tension round my head was too strong. I hung up without another word, took four paracetamol, stared at the bottle and said aloud:

'Oh, Sam. Four is too many. But not enough.' I went back to bed.

I should have been at work. Eric rang, and I croaked that I was ill and batted away his kind sympathy. After an empty time beneath the pale blue bedroom ceiling, it seemed that Sarah kept coming round; I never locked the front door. She would come up and sit on the bed, offering me tea and toast.

She became a nuisance. I wanted only to sleep, take pills

for my head, and sometimes read books I knew by heart, escaping into other lives. Most of them were children's books: E. Nesbit, Hodgson Burnett, *Just William*.

'Perhaps you're just having a reaction, and that's natural,' said Sarah. 'You've been so brave, for so long.'

I did not want to talk to her, and rolled away to look at the wall, sweaty amid my pile of books and tissues. After two days of this – it may have been more – I smelt rank in my rumpled bed. For a while I liked that: I was an animal in a hole, hibernating, sulking the winter away. I slept longer and longer, sometimes feigning unconsciousness when Sarah crept in and out with food, then later reaching out to gnaw it, cold, without even sitting up. The phone was off the hook now, and I hoped that Eric and my other employers would just give up and find someone else.

It was not purposeless, that time. I came to feel that I had a job to do, and that the job was to be accomplished in dreams. They went on, ever more vivid and memorable. In each of them Sam was a baby, brand new with solemn, wondering eyes. Sometimes he changed into nightmare shapes and I woke gasping. Sometimes he grew, through remembered childhood stages yet preternaturally fast, and became the last Sam I remembered: the sunny young man. Those were times when I woke to bleakness, knowing him lost, and dived deliberately back into the dream. Temazepam helped. They were left by the doctor after Sam died, and I found them in my bedside drawer like a forgotten blessing. Maybe I took too many.

In the last, long sleep of this visionary time – though I did not think I was asleep, I saw the messy bedroom and dirty plates around me all too clearly – Sam spoke to me, clearly and in his own familiar voice.

'Mum. My son's going to need you. Get up.'

I heard myself answering. 'Where? Darling, where?'

'Get up, Mum. I need you.' The voice had changed again, back to his insistent three-year-old pipe. He used to wake me up at five or six to make cardboard models for him, or help with some Lego. Tom was always a little surprised that I didn't seem to mind, but I actually liked those early-morning sessions constructing games and stories at the kitchen table, him with juice and me with black coffee. Mothers with several children would tell me that this was clearly because he was an only child, and spoilt. They just batted theirs away, or told them to watch cartoons on television. I liked to get up for my secret early mornings with my Sam.

'Mum. Get up.'

My legs were weak, but the tight band of headache had gone and I felt a strange, irresponsible lightness. The phrase *Unbearable lightness of being* kept running through my head, and I tried to remember what that was about. Something to do with the terror of eternity, and that if we are immortal souls which never die, the weight of unbearable responsibility lies on every move we make. Nietzsche, was it? Sarah would know, it was the sort of thing which you heard discussed at her dinner-table. Was Sam feeling the eternal heaviness of responsibility even now? Wanting to protect the child he made?

'Was that why you got me up?' I asked him, aloud. 'I'm up now, sweetheart. I'll go and find him.'

I put on my dressing-gown, for the heating seemed to be off and the room felt dank outside the shelter of my duvet. Feeling in the pocket I pulled out the gym-card picture of my son and the printout of Julia Penderby's gaunt face. I laid them carefully on the bed while I took a shower, washing away the rankness of nightmare, and pulled on trousers and sweater and flat walking shoes. I ate a piece of toast and cold, old scrambled egg which seemed to be beside the bed, and said aloud: 'Food for a journey.' There was something satisfying about the words and I said them again. Downstairs the kitchen was tidy, with stacks of post neat on the table and a note from Sarah.

'Hope you're better. Give me a ring. Tom fine. Will be round about three.'

The clock said half-past two. I looked out: it was light, despite the winter greyness, so it must be half-past two in the afternoon. Sarah would be here soon. At the thought a wave of cunning swept over me. She mustn't know. She would stop me. I gathered up my purse and a cloth shopping-bag into which I threw a spare pair of pants and a T-shirt and the tired remains of the fruit bowl, three clementines and two apples. Soon the house was switched off, locked and empty, and I was on my way to the station. There was a five-to-three train which would do nicely. On the way I thought I glimpsed Sarah's red raincoat through a hedge on the corner, and jumped into a front garden for cover; but it was only some stranger, who swung past without glancing at my crouched form behind the fence. I caught the train with a minute to spare, and bought a single to London.

12

It was half-past five before I got to Dalston, a journey of which I remember nothing until a lucid moment when I walked through the grimy station and saw a clock. That was the moment when it occurred to me with a sudden sickness – or a flash of sudden sanity – that the office of DAN might already be closed. I shook my head to dislodge the thought: it could not be so. I was doing what Sam's voice had told me to do, and he would make sure it worked out. I could always wait till morning. I walked on, past the kebab shop whose smell woke in me a faint memory of hunger and normality. That made me hesitate again, though not for long. Then I turned down the side road to the dirty brick building I remembered. Something was different: the ironbound door hung open to the street, pieces of litter blowing inside on the sharp wind: a polystyrene cup broken into a white claw, a page of newspaper in some exotic script.

All the better. She would have no warning of my coming, this time, and no defences. I climbed the three flights and found that the landing door too stood carelessly open, its Community Watch eye-and-fist poster staring uselessly at the unguarded office and computer. There was no sign of the surly receptionist, but a light was shining through the inner frosted glass door, which stood just ajar. Against that light a vivid shape moved, a tossing flapping shape which – turning to reveal a lifted arm – resolved itself into human form, oddly distorted. The voices from the inner office needed no resolution. Both were raised in angry argument.

'—And I say it's bloody racist, and sexist, and it'll make you a laughing stock,' said the first, an unfamiliar woman's voice with a faint but vigorous South London twang. The other, deeper and sharper and now unquestionably posh, was Julia Penderby's.

'You're *so Daily Mail* sometimes, Allie,' it said. 'I tell you, the Portweigh Trust is interested in funding it—'

'Only if they're as mad as you are. Wouldn't work, anyway. Some women *want* men. Live with it, Jule, we're not all witches from the sixties!'

'If women want to take the risk of intercourse with men . . . !'

'If you want to help African women, then help African men as well!'

'Look where that's got us! Ten, twenty million children with AIDS—'

I made out these words, which meant nothing at the time: only the name 'Allie' struck through my aching head, telling me that Sam had done right to send me here at this moment because this was where the woman was. And therefore – my heart hammered – the child. I pushed open the door without knocking and stepped in.

Julia Penderby was at the desk, in a dark-blue woollen garment with some sort of Indian pattern on it. She looked different today: her thin, grey-blonde hair awry, her cheeks flushed, pupils wide and dark in the hard green eyes. The other woman had stepped aside in surprise when I pushed the door open, and I had to turn to see her. When I did, it hit me like a blow.

I see now that it was the most superficial of resemblances. No actual feature made her a true twin of my son Sam. Yet there was the dark-gold tumble of hair waving across her forehead, untidy as his when he was too far from a haircut; there was the square jaw, the pale skin, the blue eyes and long lashes. Even the set of her mouth – always a touch satirical, always ready to laugh – gave an instant and breathtaking sense of *déjà vu*. Yet Alexandra or Allie was not at all mannish. Rather, she was one of the most beautiful women I had ever seen. She carried her vast late pregnancy with impossible grace. She too wore smocky Indian clothes, but on her they looked imperial, not gipsyish. I stared at her, and swayed, holding the door frame for support. She looked back at me, her face calm, one eyebrow raised in interrogation.

'What the hell are you doing here?' asked Julia sharply. She was more flustered than I had imagined she ever could be. 'How did you get in?'

'The doors were both unlocked,' I said, the second question being by far the easiest to answer.

Julia turned on her girlfriend, even angrier.

'Allie, did you leave the bloody street door open?'

'Prob'ly.' The other woman still seemed not at all discomposed by my arrival, indeed faintly amused. She glanced at her fingernails, which I saw were immaculately kept and polished, like a model's. 'Need some bloody air in this place, more ways than one.'

'Oh, for Christ's sake – go and shut it, you know the kids get in downstairs and piss all over the place.'

'I'm not climbing up and down your bloody stairs in this state,' said Alexandra, baldly. 'Do it yourself.'

Julia hesitated, and through my turmoil I even felt briefly sorry for her, torn between her responsible desire to shut the door, the reasonableness of not letting a heavily pregnant woman go and do it, and her reluctance to leave me as a cat among her pigeons.

'Oh, I'll bloody go!' and to me, sharply: 'You wait here, if you must. I was going to text you, but since you're so fucking impatient—! Allie – don't talk to her till I get back.'

'Charming,' said the pregnant woman as her friend banged off down the stairs. 'How are you supposed to amuse yourself without me to talk to? Tell you what, read the latest lunacy from Man-hater Central.' There was a pile of cheaply printed flyers on the desk, and she shoved one at me and plonked herself down in her friend's office chair. I stared at it and began reading, though at the time little sank in. Beneath the DAN logo of *Defeat Aids Now* the text ran on:

> In Sub-Saharan Africa all strategies against HIV/AIDS have failed. Twelve million children are orphaned, and two million a year die.
>
> Why have they failed? Because of men's sexual self-ishness. A true and vigorous feminist perspective on AIDS is long overdue, and championed by DAN. Globalization, patriarchy and first-world phallocentric oppression of celibate and lesbian womyn form the crucible where the historic predation of the man-rapist flourishes.

I glanced up at Alexandra, and saw that she was smirking, on the edge of laughter, watching my expression.

'You got to the man-rapist?' she said mockingly. 'Julia, on the other hand, is a head-rapist. Batters her way in there.'

I looked down again at the leaflet.

> Womyn's only hope is where secure refuges and secure work environments are freely provided and barred to all men, including male aid workers. DAN's first refuge is planned to open in Mozambique as soon as the medical centre is complete. But we must go further. It is womyn's right to have children, and where men are irresponsible

we should not be made dependent on their diseased selfishness.

For Africa, the next stage is to fund and staff facilities for IVF and donor fertilization from screened males. Maternal antenatal and postnatal care is a priority, as is gender-screening, which is an absolute necessity to keep the male population from dangerous increase in the continent's future . . .

I laid it back down on the desk, next to her. She was perched on the edge of the chair, arching and easing her back, breasts thrust towards me under the Indian smock.

'That's what I have to put up with, day in, day out, all in the name of lerrrve,' she said. 'Grim, huh? You might wonder what poor bloody African men ever did to her, seems unlikely that they'd dare.'

I was at a loss to enter this mad debate. She went on, unbothered by my silence:

'Anyway, what did you want with St Julia of the Castrating-Knife? You looking for a job?'

I shook my head.

'Because I'd say you were a bit too old and a bit too white for her. She likes to employ teenage morons with hair extensions and attitude problems, who are too thick to know there's a minimum wage.'

'I'm here,' I said, and my voice sounded faint even to me, 'because I am—' I could not take my eyes off her triumphantly swelling belly, straining like a boat's spinnaker beneath the Indian cloth. The room swayed a little and went white. I don't know whether I finished the sentence, because the next thing I was aware of was that Julia was back and her voice was saying 'Oh, shit!' There was a pain somewhere and blood in my hair and I was looking at polystyrene ceiling tiles.

I shut my eyes again against the glare of the desk light.

'You fainted. You hit your head on the desk,' said a cross, authoritative voice. 'Nobody touched you. You do not have a case for assault. You came into this office without permission . . .'

'Oh, shut up, Jules,' said another voice, contemptuous. 'She's out of it. Give her a break. Anyone can faint.'

'Out of it? Drugs?' said Julia sharply. I opened my eyes again and croaked 'Certainly not' and the pregnant woman, still sitting by the desk, said in her lazy, amused tone, 'You tell her!' Then she added, 'Jules, we'd better take her to the flat and sort out that cut.'

I was helped to my feet, dazed. The two of them supported me, one stiff and resentful, the other more gentle, and led me up another short flight of stairs where a door opened into a surprisingly light, airy space. It was a loft for servants, I suppose, in the Victorian heyday of the house. Later – Allie was to tell me in our long hours of conversation – as the area went downhill it became a sweatshop, whose huge skylights enabled Edwardian seamstresses to work late into summer evenings without gaslight. Now there was a wooden table in a kitchen corner, with four rickety bentwood chairs around it, two modern tubular easy-chairs with no arms, and a couple of floor cushions. Two doors, roughly painted red, led to unseen spaces. My knees buckled and Julia lowered me on to a cushion on the floor, her partner neatly kicking a second cushion under my head.

'Better down there. Less far to fall. Jules, she ought to have a cup of tea or something.' The pregnant woman lowered herself on to one of the chairs beside me and put the back of her hand on my clammy forehead with what seemed to be genuine concern. Through the fog of confusion the maternal gesture warmed me.

'We don't have milk,' said Julia repressively. Addressing

me where I lay on the floor she continued: 'We don't do dairy. We're vegan. On environmental grounds.'

'Oh, for Christ's sake, give her some green tea', said Allie. 'Poor woman only comes up for an interview or whatever, passes out cold. Doesn't need you going on about cows farting methane and drowning fucking polar-bears. Hey, you OK?'

I felt far from OK: sick, a spinning head, a curious faintness. My outflung hand was shaking, knuckles drumming on the floor. Allie leaned forward in her low chair with difficulty, and put her warm hand on my neck to feel the racing pulse. Julia spoke again, in a low aside:

'She didn't come for an interview. I know who she is. She came to see me a while ago. I was going to talk to you about it, when you weren't in such a princessy mood. She's Sam Faulkner's mother.'

The chair creaked on its steel tubes as Alexandra jerked in shock. But she kept her hand on me. She, too, spoke in a low voice.

'Sam Faulk— Jackie's friend Sam?'

'Yes. I went to find him, after you and I had that talk about child support.'

'Jesus!' The hand vanished; lying with closed eyes I found myself listening hard. The voices rose. 'You never told me you were doing any such fucking stupid thing!'

'You have a completely unreasonable attitude to male responsibility—'

'I told you, Jacks and I absolutely agreed *not*! Not to chase him, he was only being kind! And you went to see the poor bastard?'

I opened my eyes: Alexandra was standing now, her hand raised as if to hit the other woman.

'I told you I would,' said Julia flatly.

'Months ago! And I told you not to, and I *assumed*,' she

said sarcastically, 'that you would do as I asked, given that it's my bloody baby – you cow!'

She seemed to think better of her physical aggression, and sat on the chair again, easing her shoulders. 'I suppose I should have expected it. You and your money fixations. Christ!' She leaned back and glanced at me. 'So this is his mum? You dragged her into it?'

'She came to see me. I told you. I only saw the father. He was highly unhelpful and rude. As usual, the women pick up the pieces. This woman came and told me that Samuel Faulkner died earlier this year.'

'The donor? Poor old Sam? He's dead?'

I was watching them now, fascinated; they had almost forgotten me lying on the floor. Alexandra was breathing fast, her hand on her swollen belly, genuinely shaken, her lazy composure vanished. It was me, now, who was worried for her, and I raised myself on my elbow with a feeble instinct to protect her.

'Oh, poor sod. And poor Jacks! She really loved that guy, more than she loved me, I sometimes thought. What the hell did you say to the family?'

'I told you. The father was obstructive and rude, and patriarchally arrogant. He didn't even tell me the donor was dead. Then this woman – the wife – came to the office. She didn't know about the baby. I told her I couldn't break your confidence. I was considering when to discuss with you the matter of whether she should be told.'

'Oh, thanks a bunch! You didn't mind barracking some poor dead guy's father for child support, and then you didn't even tell his mother what it was about, and you told me fuck-all about any of it. Oh, shit, Jules! You are such a cow sometimes!'

'And you are an irresponsible little bitch,' said Julia, not apparently at all surprised or upset by the vituperation. 'You insisted that this baby you cooked up with Jackie shouldn't be any kind of responsibility of the man—! I was just sorting things out, making sure he paid up at least a bit. Men cannot be allowed—'

My anxiety about Alexandra ebbed, as I saw her fold her arms and narrow her beautiful eyes. She was, I decided, enough of a vixen to see off most aggression. I closed my eyes on the conflict, and tried to breathe evenly. The shouting went on for a few minutes, then there was an odd silence, with breathing and sobbing, and I opened my eyes. Julia was kneeling at Alexandra's feet, head buried in her swollen middle, and the younger woman was ruffling the thin pale hair, almost absently, in a gesture of casual forgiveness. It was she who turned towards me and said, to the weeping woman at her feet:

'Mrs Faulkner's still here, by the way, Jules. When you've finished the drama-queen act, I'd better do that bandage.'

Julia rose, glaring eyes in a tearstained face and vanished through one of the red doors in the corner. Alexandra went through the other door and ran taps and opened and shut cupboards, returning efficiently a few moments later with warm water, a sponge and a bandage. I flinched a little at her touch, and she said, with that faintly sarcastic but benign smile that reminded me so much of my son: 'It's OK. I was a student nurse for a year, till they threw me out.'

'What for?'

'Satanism,' she said amiably, dabbing at my head. 'But never on duty. Shut up, sweetie, don't move while I look at this cut.'

13

It was not the bandage nor the green tea which revived me enough to get off the floor, but Alexandra's nurselike decision that I needed food. After I had lain for a while, watching the dirty orange of the city glow through the skylights, she brought me a Marmite sandwich and a bowl of thin spinach soup, and I hauled myself up, pulled on the few clothes I had discarded, and sat at the wooden table to eat it while she ate the same and watched me with detached interest. Twenty minutes, maybe half an hour had passed and still Julia was nowhere to be seen; when I glanced at the door in the corner my new acquaintance said:

'She'll be online, working. She works up here as well, hammering the laptop in the bloody bedroom, would you believe. Three in the morning if she suddenly thinks of something. I suppose it's good practice for being woken up by the baby. Plus, she doesn't eat after four in the afternoon and she doesn't like dealing with ill people at any hour, so she'll be hiding. Don't you fret. It all makes a nice change. Think of yourself as the floor show.'

I drank my soup, took a bite of the sandwich and felt better.

'You're being kind to me. Thank you. There's a lot I want to talk about.'

She grimaced. 'Mmm. Maybe. Maybe not. Have another sandwich. When did you last eat?'

'No idea. I've had a bit of a shock. Several shocks.'

'You surprise me.' Her ironic tone made me smile in spite of myself. 'Presumably the main shock was about the baby?'

'Yes. But I dunno—' I was surprised how much I wanted to confide in this odd young woman. 'My husband's sort of vanished rather suddenly, too. We live in south Norfolk and he's suddenly said he's going to New Zealand, and I don't know where he is. Except my friend Sarah says he's in Cambridge, only he took his passport so he might be really going away.'

'Ah! Jules will be pleased.'

'Why?'

'Because all men are bastards, and she needs to keep on collecting proof in case one turns out to be nice. That would be a *real* disaster. Whole life's work wasted. Mrs Pankhurst's ghost wailing in dismay.'

'Why are you with Julia?' I marvelled at my own light-headed courage, questioning this woman in her strange world of lofts and crazy ideological pamphlets and shouting-matches and tearful reconciliations and deliberately manless pregnancies. 'Jackie seemed such a sweet girl—'

She laughed. 'Ah. You met Jackie. That explains you turning up. No, I love Jacks, I really do. But we were hopeless together. Jules and I fight all the time, but we fit. You know—' there was a girlish confidence in her tone now. 'Thing is, with Jackie, she was crazy about your Sam. Even though she was with me. And hush ma mouf, don't let Julia hear this, but there are some girls who just need a man to lean on. Sorry, I forgot, don't cry—'

'It's just that you look a bit like him,' I said, wiping my eyes with the piece of kitchen towel thrust at me. 'And I miss him so.'

'I only met him two or three times. Didn't think he looked like me, though.' She stood up and crossed to stare into a small mirror on the back of the door. 'But if he did, hey, that explains Jackie.'

I was still dizzily brave, light-headedly determined. 'Why didn't you want Sam to have anything to do with the baby?'

'We-ll,' said Alexandra, wriggling her shoulders like a child caught out in a lie. 'I actually didn't mind. I didn't want him on the birth certificate, or being made to pay anything, that was so unfair. He was only doing us a favour. And the government's so down on us benefits people – you remember that case? The fireman?'

I frowned. 'What?'

'Some poor fireman donated sperm to a lesbian couple out of the kindness of his heart and the benignity of his bollocks. And they split up, and the Child Support Agency made him take a DNA test and pay for it. Gross, huh? You'd think Jules would have a campaign against stuff like that. But no. It's always men's fault, whatever. Anyway, I'm always on and off the social, and if he was on the birth certificate they'd chase the poor sod, just when he was paying off his student loan. So I told her to keep him out of it.'

'But Julia?'

'Well. When we got together I was two months gone. *Fait accompli.* She wasn't that keen on the kid, but very keen on making Sam pay his bit. I wasn't. We threw a lot of crockery during top-level discussions on the subject. But we didn't know Sam died. That would have changed the picture, even for bloody Julia. I'm really sorry. You shouldn't have been dragged in.'

'I should,' I said, feeling faint again now and hearing my voice shake. 'I want to know this child. He's going to be my grandson.'

'Granddaughter,' corrected Alexandra, patting her bump. 'We did a test.'

'A scan? CVS?'

'Nope. Julia says medicine is an invasive patriarchal conspiracy to keep women down. She even wanted me to have a bloody home birth up here with some Moroccan doula woman in a fucking kaftan and feathers or something, but I put my foot down.' She yawned, showing pretty kitten teeth. 'We know the sex because a friend of ours does divining, copper rings and stuff. Shona is never wrong. She's from Orkney, her auntie was a witch. It's definitely a girl.' She paused, a little shifty now. 'Just as well.'

I looked at her in dawning horror.

'You mean – if it had been a boy – that leaflet, gender-screening—'

'It was probably too late anyway,' said Alexandra hastily. 'For terminating a boy, I mean. And I don't know that I'd have gone along with it. Even if she'd wanted me to. I don't have to do what Julia says, *I'm* not stuck in a loony refuge in sub-Saharan Africa being refused food unless I toe the line.'

'But she wouldn't really . . . ?' My voice was high, sounding hysterical and silly even to me.

'Oh look,' said the pregnant woman uneasily, visibly groping for her old composure. 'In India they're always terminating girl babies to get boys, so it would only be evening things out, doing it Julia's way.'

'That's appalling!'

'Mmph.' She picked up the plates, with too much clattering. 'Look, I'm sorry, but talking to you is weird for me. I don't hang out with many respectable grown-up types these days. I don't want to shock you. But people have terminations for lots of reasons. Fact.'

'I'm not shocked,' I lied. 'But I want to know this child. He – she – is the only future—' To my shame, I was choking again, the band of pain tightening round my head as I began to cry. 'Sam's baby – and now Tom's gone—'

I looked up at Alexandra, hoping to see the crooked smile, hear the friendly tone in her voice again. But she only looked bleak and said a little harshly:

'I don't know about that. You've seen how it is. We fight, me and Jules, but we're good together. And with our daughter we'll be a three-way family. We've got plans.'

'And you're happy for your child to grow up hating men?' I was angry again, and it strengthened me.

'I don't hate men.'

'Julia clearly does. Your daughter will pick that up.'

'Look,' she said patiently. 'We're not monsters. Gay women are mostly really liberal, the ones I know. Very tribal, they like having men around, kids, grannies, all that stuff. But Julia's different. She's pure 1970s. We balance out, I argue with her, and I won't talk crazy to the kid. But we have to keep the peace.'

'What does that mean for me, then?' Great bitterness was rising, choking me.

'Honey, I do see your point. But Jules comes first, and I don't see her buying the idea of grandparents. She was going on and on the other day –' her voice hardened into an uncanny mimicry of Julia's clipped sour tone – '"*Have you any idea how many layers of toxic patriarchal assumption lie in the word grand-father?*" And that was just because I said I liked an audiotape of *Heidi* when I was a kid.'

'I'm a woman,' I said weakly. '*I'm* not a patriarch.'

'No,' said Alexandra quite kindly. 'But you're not our type, are you?'

As if on cue, Julia reappeared like the Demon King from the other room, her eyes and nose still red.

'Do you want a cab?' she asked abruptly. 'It's dark out there now.'

I hesitated, but Alexandra, who had been watching me not without compassion as her previous speech sunk in, said with

one of those flashes of unanswerable authority which seemed
to affect even Julia:

'For God's sake, Jule. It's dark, it's raining, it's getting late
and she lives on some bloody seashore. She's half crazy with
shock, and all the minicab drivers are stoned by now.'

'She can't *stay* . . .' But Julia was wavering, under her girlfriend's gaze.

'She can. She can sleep right here, with the spare duvet.
Get sorted out in the morning. I'm knackered anyway, and
I've had my soup. Let's all bloody well go to bed.' And to
me: 'The bathroom's over there. I'll chuck you a duvet. You're
not fit to walk down the street till you've had a rest, and I'll
take the bandage off in the morning.'

I lay for a long time under the skylight, letting my mind
go blank. I hoped for more dreams, with Sam directing me
how to carry on, but none came.

In the morning footsteps circled round me, doors opened
and shut. I heard murmured conversation and strained to
catch the words; my sense of cunning was returning now,
and I hoped that Julia Penderby would go away and leave
me with my unborn grandchild and the odd but not unlike-
able woman who looked a little like Sam. If we talked again,
perhaps I could make her understand that the coming
daughter might benefit from having grandparents. Or, at
least, a grandmother.

Hope was answered; while I continued to feign sleep I
heard Julia's clear, high voice saying:

'I've got to go to this meeting with the Portweigh Trust.
What are you going to do, when you've got her out of the
way?'

'Library, probably,' said Allie. 'I'll get a sandwich. I don't
have to answer the phones downstairs, do I?'

'No. Chioma's coming up at nine. But anyway I want you
home by five.'

'Oh, for God's sake! I'm only pregnant, I'm not ten years old. Get to your meeting. They won't give you the money for the bloody IVF nonsense, you know.'

'We'll see about that.' The door opened and closed, not softly. When the footsteps had retreated on the echoing wooden stairs, I sat up and said:

'Hi. Thanks for letting me sleep here, that was kind.'

'No problem. Toast? I've got some real butter, haha!'

'Not vegan?'

'Nope. Real butter, immorally pillaged from mummy cows by phallocratic capitalist farmers, and sneaked into the back of the fridge by me. Julia never cleans out the fridge. She's a bit of a man that way. Hey, should I tell her that and start World War III?'

I could not help laughing at her playful treachery. After the first mouthful, as she still looked relaxed, I asked:

'Do you take the mickey out of all her ideas?'

'Not all,' she said, her mouth full. Then, swallowing, 'I am a feminist, honest. I do performance art when I'm not up the duff. I'm pretending to work on a book about women poets. I've got my union card all right.'

'But you're not like Julia.'

'Ah, shit. She just goes a bit far, that's all. There's a thing with her dad, and her first girlfriend was bi, and died of AIDS that she got off a bloke.'

A cold fear gripped me, a thought of my grandchild.

'She's not—'

'No. Course not. But Jules will calm down in the end, and DAN has done some good work. And I love her, obviously.'

'But if she doesn't really want this child you're having . . .'

'She'll get used to having a mini-me around. I want my baby girl, Jules wants me – look, I don't have to explain all this to you, do I?' A light edge of irritation entered her voice, and I backed off. It was growing harder and harder for me to take my eyes off her magnificent belly, and stop thinking of the curled infant within. Sam's child.

'No. I'm sorry. I was just curious. I'm not myself, anyway. Ignore me.'

'What you said yesterday,' she said more kindly, 'it was all a bit of a surprise talking to you. I've been thinking. It does seem a bit hard, what with you not having your boy any more.'

'You mean you might let me – let me in a bit? When the little girl is born?'

'Umm. I dunno. But I didn't want to be mean. It's not personal.'

'I wouldn't interfere.'

'Yeah, but—' suddenly this assured young woman seemed like a teenager, uncertain and awkward round a strange adult. 'There's Jules. And it's sort of difficult—'

'I'm not your type. You said so.'

'Oh God – that's not what I mean . . .' She was embarrassed now.

'Why do people have to *have* types?' I seemed to draw confidence from her discomfort. 'Why is it that cool radical-feminist lesbians in East London can't be friendly with a person just because she lives in Norfolk? You probably think I play golf, don't you?'

'My dad moved to Essex,' said Allie crossly. 'And he prob'ly plays golf by now. I speak to him, about once a year anyway. He tells the neighbours I haven't found the right man yet. My stepmother collects pictures of Princess Michael. They'd never, ever, ever have come to one of my shows. I'm not being unfriendly, I just know that there are some people that don't mix that well.'

'And you think I'm one of the sort that can't mix with you?'

'In a nutshell.' She got up to put more toast in the machine, and slammed the handle down hard. With a spurt of anger I asked:

'Then why the hell didn't you get pregnant by someone whose world you *could* bear to mix with? You must know lots of men, even if Julia doesn't want to.'

'Jackie,' she said, between gritted teeth, 'said she could only love a child if she knew it came from some guy she trusted. Look, I really don't want to talk about this. You should go.'

I was silent. For someone as tough and stroppy as I had seen this woman act with Julia, she had been oddly compliant and conversational so far. Perhaps, at some level, she did want to know me. And her moods swung erratically enough; in a moment she was looking at me with a faint smile and said more softly:

'But anyway, the thing is, Sam was cool.'

'So he *was* your type?'

'Yeah, all right.'

'How can my son' (I fought the tears valiantly) 'be your type, and me not at all? Not even enough to be in touch with the child?'

'Dunno,' she said again. 'It's seeing you with Julia, p'r'aps. Oil and water. Look, before you go I'd better sort out that head.' Her tone swung back to the centre; not unfriendly but utterly matter-of-fact, convincing me that this was the last word.

Breakfast was over; Allie moved towards the bathroom and began running the taps. I put my hand to my bandage, realizing that once she had taken it off and examined the damage I really would have no reason to stay one minute longer in this odd, important attic. A cold, dark weight in my heart told me that I might never see this interior again, never see this woman, never meet her child. My genes, Tom's genes, the last and only remnant of Sam, would whirl away into an unknown life. This pair would move and I would not know where; the child would grow and smile and play, unseen. Knowing this was another death to me, and as in too many unexpected moments of the past months it brought back the first shock and the familiar shaking. The world went pale and I thought I would faint once more, and hated myself for the weakness. I should fight, not flop. I pulled myself upright, battling the whiteness and the stony grief, hoping to show at least some dignity in my departure. I would step on to the scaffold with head held high.

But it was Allie who cried out, dropping the basin and sponge in the bathroom doorway, clutching her stomach, her mouth a circle of shock.

14

Childbirth can be quick or slow, calm or crazy. When Sam was born I went into hospital with pains ten minutes apart and lay around for some hours moaning intermittently, sucking on the Entonox cylinder and having strangers probe my privates. Finally I was transported by trolley to a labour room and duly, as Victorian chronicles would put it, brought to bed of a fine boy. The whole process, from stumbling down the stairs at home to holding a wrapped infant, took nine hours and progressed according to every textbook I had carefully read. Other women's stories bored me slightly, seeming exaggerated or melodramatic: waters breaking in Sainsbury's, days of agony, forceps, precipitate labour without warning and emergency delivery in the back seat of the car in the doctor's driveway.

I had little interest in all this drama; childbirth was, to my ignorant understanding, a thing you should conduct in as dignified and predictable a way as possible. Carla's chirpy account of the birth of Harry Samuel sounded so like mine that it confirmed this view. So I was as unprepared as Alexandra herself for what happened in the next half-hour.

Her cry roused me from my moment of fainting, fatalist stupor. It was a primeval yell, unignorable, and sent a shot of adrenaline through my body so that every muscle tensed. She yelled again: I moved towards her where she stood clutching the door frame and saw that her waters had broken, faint colours mingling with the water from the dropped

basin. Then she was leaning on the door frame, knees buck-
ling, falling, crying out again; it could not be a minute since
the last cry. Putting my arms around her for support I felt
her belly rock-hard, an alien thing, pulsing sharply. When
it eased again I helped her to the floor and the cushions I
had slept on.

'Jesus!' she shouted. 'Godalmighty!'

'I'll call 999.' I groped for my phone, but another wave of
pain and terror overtook her and I could not free my arm
from her clutching, bruising hand. I saw why men in in-
numerable societies have considered labouring women as
objects of voodoo dread, and gratefully allowed themselves
to be excluded from the hut where the grim old women rule.
I saw why doctors, from the age of chloroform and stirrups
to the age of the epidural, have wanted to calm this tumult
by any means available. Allie's labour was frightening, primi-
tive in its intensity.

'Hospital,' she said in one brief moment of rest. 'Number's
inna kitchen drawer. Oh – aaaah!' I found a piece of paper
in the drawer and was about to dial the midwives' emergency number when a scream from the floor called me back.

'Don't fucking *leave* me, bitch!' she said. 'Hold – help –
hold – turn—' I saw that she was trying to roll on to all fours,
and helped her, and for a few moments all was quieter. I
rubbed her back and said:

'I'll ring the midwife. Give me a moment. Remind me, the
address? Aragorn Street – what number?'

Amid more screaming I achieved an answer, one of us
knocking over one of the bentwood chairs in the process, and
when I had made the call I went back to Allie. She now wanted
to squat, with me supporting her. I feared the baby would
come before I could find towels, or anything clean; helpless,
I clutched her under the arms and hoped for succour. None
came. Minutes ticked by, the pains and the terrible hardness

of her stomach seemed to become constant, with no intervals; I could feel her weakening, her tears running down over my hands as I numbly supported her helpless weight. At last I laid her down on her back, moaning more softly, and nerved myself to reach down and pull off her pants. The top of a head was visible now. Already. A head. The word *crowning* returned to me from some dimly remembered prenatal manual. It looked wide enough, ten centimetres? What the hell was a centimetre, how did one measure, when – 'Aaaah!' she howled again, her face contorted, glazed with sweat and tears.

'I think you have to push,' I said uncertainly, and was drowned by another howl, too near my ear, not of pain but of rage. 'I-fucking-KNOW!' she snarled.

And then it happened; the head, a monstrous unrecognizable thing it seemed between her slender thighs. The head was in the room with us; I put my hand to support it, instinctively. One more howl and a torrent of obscenities saw the rest of the child, and a red snaking umbilicus, squirm on to the cushions. Looking wildly around I saw my discarded jacket, reached with my free hand and wrapped it round the small body. Allie fell back, groaning.

'It's born! It's OK – are you OK?'

'Afterbirththing,' she said indistinctly. 'Has to come out, yeuch, it was in the book.'

'Oh yes.' The baby had made no sound, and I panicked and put a finger in its mouth in case it was blocked. A tiny cough, some dribbled filth, and then a thin faint cry rose like a bubble of life and there were three of us in the suddenly silent room, under the skylights and the scudding London clouds.

'Nothing's clean, nothing's sterile, where's the ambulance?' I was babbling. 'Even this jacket—' I was afraid my very anorak would kill the baby. Allie croaked 'Gimme' and winced at another pain; I could see now that the afterbirth was here, and wondered about cutting the cord. 'Gimme.' I put the baby, still faintly whickering, on to her chest and she tore at her clothes and laid it on a warm, sweaty breast. Magically, calm returned to the room; two women, messy cushions, an upturned kitchen chair, a newborn miracle.

We stayed almost motionless for a few minutes, all three of us exhausted. Then I got up and looked round, wondering how to begin straightening this chaos.

'You ought to get to hospital. Make sure everything's all right.'

'Yeah. S'pose. She looks all right, though, doesn't she?' She was staring down at the baby's crumpled face and sharp little eyes. 'Taking everything in.'

'I think we're meant to cut the cord. Tie a knot in it or something.'

'Shit. I'm not doing that.'

'Better wait for the midwife or ambulance guys or whoever.'

As the shock subsided, the significance of what had happened came to me and I said hesitantly:

'Might I hold her?'

'OK.'

I knelt down at her side, feeling the middle-aged creak in my knees, and took the bundle carefully, trailing its cord. Some memory of films about childbirth returned, and a story of my mother's about a cousin born with six fingers; and I thought I had better check beneath the wrapping. When I did, I saw something unexpected in the waxy red confusion of its tiny curled-up form. I wrapped it up again.

'Allie,' I said after a minute of cradling. 'Allie—'

She was lying flat now, breathing heavily.

'Mm?'

'It's a boy.'

She had no time to answer before the buzzer rang, impatiently and repeatedly, from the entryphone in the corner. I put my grandson back in her arms; her hand came up to support the child, automatically, but her eyes were wide with shock.

'They're here.' Moments later, two brisk, kind paramedics were gathering up the baby in clean, soft wrappings, cutting the cord expertly, and assisting Allie to her feet.

'Can't get a chair up here too easily,' said the Asian one, who seemed to be the boss. 'Can you walk down with me, love?'

'Reckon,' said Allie, shakily. And to me: 'You'll come? Could you bring the keys? They're in the drawer where the number was.'

I followed them down to the ambulance, uncontrollable tears running down my face, and wept in shock all the way to the hospital. The kindly paramedic strapped in the back seat next to me said, 'You did well, love,' and gently reached across to feel the tattered remains of my own bandage. 'You're going to have to get that head to A&E and tidied up.'

Allie said nothing, only stared at the van's ceiling, her face unreadable.

15

The young Asian doctor, weary-eyed, came out from the side ward where Allie lay to find me loitering helplessly in the corridor.

'Ah,' he said, glancing at his notes. 'There you are. Mizz' (he buzzed the z sound, cautiously) 'Penderby? D. Penderby, I have you here as birth partner—'

It took less than a heartbeat for me to decide not to set him right.

'How is she? And the baby?'

'OK. No great worries. It was a first labour, I gather?'

'Yes.'

He frowned and looked down at the papers again.

'It's unusual to have such an accelerated precipitate labour with a first child. She'll have to be very careful over any future births. Very careful indeed. And we'll need to keep her in for a day or two, keep an eye. I gather the placenta was delivered?'

'Think so. It was all a bit chaotic.'

'Terrifying.' His professional veneer cracked a little and he suddenly looked much younger. 'To be honest, I've never attended a full-on precipitate case. Less than two hours, she thought?'

'A lot less. A sort of tornado.'

'Well, she's come through it but there's been a lot of strain. We have to watch for side-effects. The baby's fine. AOK.'

'Is it – is he with her?'

'Not right now. She's tired and we wanted to run a couple of quick tests on him. Midwife will try and get baby feeding as soon as possible. She'll want to see you, of course. Nurse?'

The nurse, officiously junior, bustled up as he vanished along the corridor, opened the glass door and said brightly:

'Your *friend* to see you, dear.'

Allie was lying flat, her hair spread on the pillow, her beautiful face white as the hospital sheets. Seeing her brought a shocked, lurching physical memory of the terrible violent hardness of her belly, the struggle, the blood. I felt moment-arily sick, and fought the feeling down.

'Well,' she said faintly. 'What about that, then?'

'You did brilliantly,' I said automatically. 'The baby's fine.'

'God. The baby. Yes.'

'He's beautiful,' I said, again without much thought; it is what you say to new mothers. My head was swimming, unready for the swirling battle of thoughts and feelings. Allie, too, looked as if she were in shock.

'The bloody baby,' she said again. 'Too tired to think about all that.' She closed her eyes. 'You have to help me. Please.'

'You'll feel better when you've slept.'

'Stuff from home. Keys – you got the keys?'

'Yes. What do you need?'

She wanted a nightshirt, a book, a hairbrush, make-up, jeans and a T-shirt.

'And you'll have to tell Julia.'

'I could leave a note. Or you could phone her mobile?'

'No. You. You have to help me. You know why.'

I felt pity for this beautiful weakened creature, golden and wary as a cornered stag.

'But she'll be pleased, surely? You should tell her—'

'I told you, no. Too tired.' She shut her eyes again, with an air of finality.

'Go. Please. You.'

I took her list, muttered some vapid reassurance, and went back out into the main ward corridor. The same young nurse was there, walking from the desk towards me with an air of proud helpfulness.

'I can take you down to see Baby in SCBU now, if you like.' She pronounced it Skiboo, and I was suddenly taken back to the day Sam was born, back in the time when one automatically spent three or four days in hospital and learnt its ways. A woman with a premature baby had talked constantly about Skiboo, the Special Care Baby Unit. I had not heard the expression since. I blinked stupidly, transported and suddenly emotional. The nurse was leading me onward, talking over her shoulder, her rubber shoes squeaking on the lino.

'They're keeping an eye, but he's a big strong lad and he's not even in the incubator! You can hold him if you like! Sorry, but it's quicker if we take the stairs, is that all right, dear? The lifts are supposed to be for clinical need, of course Baby was taken down by lift!'

Even in my confusion I was amused and a little touched to realize that she was being exceptionally solicitous, polit- ically correct in the rare and spooky presence of a supposed lesbian life-partner. An old one, at that. I followed meekly down the echoing flight of steps and through a rubber- fringed swing door into the purposeful quiet of the unit. She cleaned her hands with gel from a wall bracket and motioned me to do the same, then led me along the row of hunched neonates, barely human in their Perspex tanks. A single open cot stood slightly apart. It was labelled BABY MORRIS/ PENDERBY and in it lay the child, apparently asleep. She reached down without hesitation and placed him squarely in my arms in his white hospital blanket.

Those who have felt it do not need to be told; to others

it is probably inexpressible. But the boy opened his eyes as I took him, and looked up into my face with that calm, wondering solemnity of the newborn. And they were Sam's eyes from years ago. I cannot say more. I held the child for a few moments, silent, and felt myself begin to shake. The vigilant little nurse saw some change in me and gently took him back.

'He'll want to feed now he's awake. Mummy is breast-feeding, isn't she? I'll take him up if Sister says. Aren't you a lovely boy, then? Miss Penderby, are you coming back to see Miss Morris?'

I did not want to see the child at another woman's breast. Not yet.

'I've got to fetch her things from home. I'll be back as soon as I can.' In the lift and along the ground-floor corridor I found myself weeping, but hospital walls and hospital staffs are used to that.

It took me some time to find my way back to the DAN office building and the loft, and even after regaining reasonable mastery of myself I felt shy of using the key. I rang the office bell and was buzzed in without question, and once I reached the third floor I hesitated. A figure beyond the frosted glass stood up and moved towards me to open the door. It was a black girl; not the surly receptionist but a stouter, smiling version.

'You lookin' for Julia?' she asked. 'Only she rang in, she's still in her meeting. I'm jus' Chioma. Can I help?'

'No – it's just that I've got the keys—' I jangled them. 'For her friend, for Allie. She asked me to fetch some things. She's in the hospital.'

'Oh my Lord! She OK? Is it that baby already?' Chioma, whose face I liked on first sight, struck a not unpleasing dramatic attitude, hand on heart, mouth agape, eyes wide.

'Yes. She's OK. Just wants some clothes and things.'

'You best go up. Julia might be 'way till afternoon, she says. I'd best tell her, yeah?'

'Yeah. She'll know which hospital, won't she?' In my preoccupation I had forgotten its name myself, remembering only the road. I climbed up to the loft and looked in dismay at the terrible slaughterhouse mess created by the baby's abrupt arrival. I did what I could, mopped and wiped and stacked the ruined cushions in the far corner and put the bentwood chair upright. The room looked better and I paused for a moment, unwillingly appreciating for the first time a certain peaceful grace in its proportions. Not a bad place to live, up here under the rafters; an eyrie of calm in this teeming corner of the capital.

Going into the bedroom felt invasive and uneasy, but I soon found the few garments Allie had named, and her washbag, and the novel carelessly thrown on the floor by the bed. I added a paperback baby-manual I noticed in the corner of the main room, unobtrusively tucked at the end of a shelf full of radical, feminist and AIDS-related volumes. She might want to read it, if they kept her in.

Looking at it, I remembered the manuals I had read when Sam was new: Penelope Leach, Hugh Jolly, good old Spock. As I flicked through, this one seemed OK: I noticed that it had a whole chapter on 'Same-sex families', but what was within it made good enough sense. It laid great stress on the desirability of having extended family and friends of both genders in the child's life, and a deep pang went through me at the thought of a boy – my boy – growing up not with a friendly father like Tom or Jeremy, but with the innately hostile Julia. He would have to learn to spell it Djoolya, too. Would he get bullied at school? No, probably not. These two would find some painfully right-on primary school, full of children with two daddies or two mummies.

I put the book with the rest in my canvas holdall, on top of the small change of clothes I had grabbed yesterday – a hundred years ago – in the silent house in Norfolk. The thought of home briefly made me wonder about Tom, but he too was impossibly distant, a figure from another life, tiny through the wrong end of the telescope. For the moment, my duty and desire alike lay here in East London, undeniable.

16

The partition walls were thin and an angry woman's voice is piercing; I heard Julia some distance down the hospital corridor. Chioma must have rung her and sent her straight here. I quailed, wondering whether my brief imposture was the cause of her audible outrage. Silently I practised excuses . . . 'It was all a bit of a muddle, did they really think I was you, I am sorry—' But when I got to the door of the side ward, standing ajar, I saw that it was Allie she was berating.

'Why didn't you ring me? For God's sake – you could have died, with nobody there—'

'*She* was there. The mother. Christ, I don't know her name even—'

'Marion Faulkner. The busybody! Did she interfere? I'll . . .'

'No! She helped!' A choking sob. 'I couldn't help it, it just came, if she hadn't been there I could've died, I thought I was going to—'

'Beloved—' Julia's voice quietened, became almost pleading. 'I know, I know, I'm only freaking out because I might have lost you – don't cry – don't—' There were inarticulate murmurs and I retreated a step from the doorway. I was touched in spite of myself. Poor, shocked Alexandra deserved some love right now, and clearly she had it. Even if it was stormier and more combative than any kind of love I would have welcomed myself.

After a decent moment I knocked – there were for once no nurses anywhere in sight on the long wide corridor – and cautiously stepped in, holding the bag with Allie's things on top in front of me, as a kind of safe-conduct talisman against Julia's wrath. She whirled round and glared at me.

'You!' she said. 'Couldn't keep away!'

'She's brought my stuff,' said Allie with a defiant sniff. Her nose was red with weeping. 'For God's sake, Jules! She delivered the damn baby! I told you!'

'Well, leave it here,' snapped Julia, glaring at me and reaching for the handle. 'I'll sort it out. She is going to be in for days, they say.' She glowered as if I was responsible for the situation. Which, I thought light-headedly, I almost was. I had given birth to Sam, Sam had become the donor, Sam's child had arrived too fast . . . he always was an impulsive boy . . .

Sam's child, the child with Sam's eyes. The child over whom I had no rights, no influence, nothing but overpowering, sudden love born in that moment in the Skiboo. I decided to ignore Julia's snatch for my bag – it was, after all, mine – and fought against tears as with deliberate slowness I unpacked Allie's things to put them, item by item, on the bedside cabinet as if laying my last hopes on an altar. I felt both of them watching me, and kept my head down over the bag. Something else was nagging, though, apart from my grief; I felt there was an absence in this sickroom colloquy. As I pulled the last item of Allie's out – a pair of rolled-up black denim jeans – I realized what it was. As did the new mother herself. I straightened up in time to see her stony face as she said to Julia in a flat, accusing tone:

'You haven't asked me anything about the baby.'

'I was worried about *you*,' said Julia, again with that unexpected tenderness. 'Obviously. So OK, how is she?'

Nobody spoke until Julia, impatiently, asked again.

'How *is* the baby?'

Allie gave her lover an oddly nasty smile.

'Male,' she said. 'So get over it. I have a son.'

Julia's silence hung in the room. I found myself taking a step back. At last she said:

'Don't fuck with me, Allie. This is no time for your mind games. Shona did the test, it's a girl, we've known that for ages. Stop shitting me.'

'Tough tit,' said her lover with something that was almost pleasure. I was getting used to the veering variability of tone between these two; there was no affection in the way she snapped 'It's a boy. B-o-y. Geddit?'

Julia turned to me. 'Is this you?' she asked fiercely. 'Have you got anything to do with this stupidity?'

I gaped. 'It isn't stupidity,' insisted Alexandra. 'I am not joking. Shona got it wrong. Stupid witch. I've had a boy. And the more I think about it, the more it's fine by me. It'd better be fine by you. And I'd be obliged—' Suddenly her brittle aggression crumbled and she began to cry. 'I'd be obliged if you wouldn't refer to my *son* as shit.'

I thought Julia was going to walk out. She was deathly pale, and shaken as I had never seen her. But the tenderness in her returned with its usual lightning speed and she took Allie's hand and murmured, close to tears, 'Our daughter . . .'

Allie kept on crying. 'I know, I know—!'

'Our Tamasin – everything we planned . . .'

'I know! When the nurse brought it in I couldn't feed, there wasn't milk, I was too upset, I knew you'd hate me. But then when she took him away I knew, I knew – it's such a mess – don't hate me . . .'

'I don't hate *you*!'

More sobbing. They had forgotten me. And, with a spurt of hot anger, it seemed to me that they had also forgotten the infant on the floor below, the boy with Sam's eyes and golden wisps of hair. By now the nurses might have given him formula feed, deprived him of the colostrum, the first mother's milk with its precious immunities. For all these deluded, hysterical women cared, the child could get every damned ailment going: he might gasp for breath with a tiny stuffed-up nose, croak with croup, be racked with baby coughs.

Anger gave me courage.

'Alexandra, you really should try to feed the baby. At least for a few days. The early milk is vital, it gives him your immunities.'

Julia turned on me, venomous. 'You have no idea what we've been through. You're probably glad that we're going to have to raise a boy – a lord of the universe – oh, you'd like that! You probably think it's funny!'

'I don't think Alexandra minds him being a boy,' I said, still brave. 'It's only because of you she's upset. And you'll get over it. Boys are not evil.'

'In this patriarchal culture—' began Julia, but Allie caused a diversion by pressing the call bell, struggling out of bed, wincing, and stumbling towards the door, sobbing.

'She's right. I made him, I owe him the bloody milk at least. Nurse!'

I took her arm, afraid she would fall. The nurse came hurrying in her squeaky shoes – a different, older one now.

'What's this? Mummy, back into bed! Bed rest!'

'I wanna feed my ba-a-by!' She was wailing.

Behind us I heard Julia start to remonstrate, whether with the nurse or with her lover I could not tell.

'And I want *her* to go away!' cried Allie.

I thought she meant me, but she was clutching my arm.

'No, Julia! I want Julia to go away!' Her hair was down over her face, one swollen red eye showing. Pointing a trembling finger at her lover she looked like some amateur dramatic society's idea of Mrs Rochester.

The nurse, clearly accustomed to such outbursts of post-natal emotion, turned a quelling eye on Julia.

'Perhaps it would be best. Mummy's a bit tired and overwrought just now. Visiting starts tomorrow at ten.' She turned to me with the same incipient message but Allie clutched me.

'No. I want Mrs – thingy – Marion – to stay. I don't want to be all alone . . .' She began weeping again, and I led her back to the bed and asked the nurse:

'Can you bring her baby? She tried to feed, earlier, but she'd like to try again.'

'I'll see,' said the nurse, still narrow-eyed, assessing the strange situation of three women at odds. 'You stay there, keep Mummy calm. You –' to Julia – 'I think you should do what your friend asks and go, for the moment. Things always look different after a nice sleep.' The moderation of her words was belied by a steely edge in her voice; even Julia was subdued. She only managed to hiss at me as she left:

'You. Don't interfere with things you don't understand.' Given that I was the only person present actually to have raised a baby, I allowed myself a momentary sneer at her back. The nurse opened the door wide and Julia swished out, an angry cat with hackles raised.

Allie lay back on the pillows, cupping her breasts in her hands. 'They hurt!' she said. 'My tits hurt! They're hard!'

'Milk's coming in,' said the nurse briskly. 'Good sign. I'll fetch Baby. I told nurse not to feed him just yet, so he'll be good and ready for you.'

Despite my bravado sneer, Julia's last words had more effect than she knew. I felt inhibited from talking to Allie in the ten minutes it took for the baby to be brought to her, and she seemed to feel the same. We were, after all, comparative strangers and I had just witnessed a major drama in her personal life. British reticence reared up again in both of us. Once, though, she took a hand off her breast and reached out for mine, holding it for a wordless moment. The nurse came back, pushing the transparent cot whose white-wrapped bundle uttered a thin, high wail.

'You're in luck! Baby just woke up and they were about to give him formula! Nice and hungry now, he'll feed beautifully! Who's a lovely boy?' The response was a louder, angrier wail. She gave him to Allie, and with a firm practised hand which made the mother jump, squeezed the left breast into a position where the child could reach the nipple. Eyes tight shut, head shaking with urgency, the baby fastened its wide mouth on and Allie winced in surprise.

'Bloody hell! It's like a suction pump!'

'See? Good baby, he knows *just* what to do!' said the nurse, and to me: 'Call if there's a problem.'

She strode out, to bestow her bracing welcome on some other neonate.

'How the hell,' asked Allie, shocked out of her weepy decline, 'does he know what to do?'

I laughed at her, and the tension in the little room ebbed and vanished. I wondered how I had ever felt reluctant to see this baby feed.

'They just know! I was amazed, too. But you're lucky, he's obviously getting what he needs very quickly. My Sam was a bit slow. Longer labour, perhaps.'

A dribble of pale, greenish milk was, indeed, running from the corner of the gulping baby's mouth. Allie looked down.

'Yeuch! Doesn't look like milk—'

'It gets creamier later. This stuff is gold dust, though – colostrum – first milk – even poor little dairy calves are allowed to have that.'

'I'm a cow!' said Allie. 'I'm a bloody milker! Moooo! Who'd have thought it?'

The baby sucked on; she had almost recovered her normal spirits, and when the nurse came back and put the baby on the other breast for a moment, to ease it before taking him away, Allie shook her head in amazement.

'I need him – he needs me – how cool is that? I never thought a baby would actually be helpful, not for years!'

'More efficient than a breast pump,' I agreed, and the nurse smiled.

'Lovely. Now. Mrs Morris. I think you need a sleep.'

'It's not Mrs,' said Allie. 'Miss. Or Miz.'

'I call my mummies Mrs,' said the nurse firmly. 'It's how I was trained.'

'I suppose it's a sign of respect,' I said vaguely. My own head was spinning again now, with a pleasing tiredness. 'Everyone equal, sort of thing. Or like that old country-house thing of always calling the cook "Mrs" even if she'd never married. It's a sort of honorific.'

'Julia would knife you for that,' said Allie, settling back. 'When do I get to do that feeding thing again?'

'Few hours,' said the nurse. 'He needs a rest too, don't you, beautiful? You sleep when the baby sleeps. That's the rule. You can have him with you tomorrow, but for tonight we'll bring him up from Skiboo. Keep an eye. Don't you worry about a thing.' She bore him off. I gathered up my bag, not knowing at all where I would go next.

'Allie,' I said tentatively. 'Are you and Julia all right?'

As I said it, I realized with surprise that I wanted them to be. I wanted the child to have two people, younger, stronger people, to protect him. Half an hour earlier when I thought him rejected, the thought had crossed my mind that I should run down the stairs, snatch him and take him to safety to be my second Sam. The feeding scene restored my sanity. I looked down at my hands, not yet elderly but not young either; the skin was wrinkling, a miniature brown ocean beneath the wind of time. I am too old for a baby, I told myself, I am fifty and it wouldn't be fair. The thought sent a pang through me, but I recognized its truth and it did more to sober me up than anything in the past days. A baby needs someone younger. Someone like this shining, laughing Allie. And Allie needed someone of her own, a back-up, a supporter.

I wished she would need me too, but sadly accepted that this was not so.

'Will you two be all right?' I asked again. Her silence bothered me.

'If she can accept him,' she said at last. 'And I think she can. I think so. She's a much . . . bigger . . . person than you might think from all this annoying crap about hating men.'

'You sent her away,' I said.

'Oh yeah. We have rows, you know? Slapping screaming rows – it's how we are. She'll be back.'

I did not like the sound of the rows, slapping screaming rows. But Allie's eyes were closing. Impulsively I said:

'Can I come and see you tomorrow?'

'Yep.' It was faint but distinct. 'You do that. Thanks.'

She was asleep. I walked out of the hospital for the second time that day, not weeping this time.

17

Outside the hospital I paused, stunned by the roaring traffic on the main road and the realization that I had no idea where to go. I had left the keys of the loft on Allie's bedside table, and in any case Dalston was the last place I wanted to be and certainly the last place where I would be welcome. I looked at my watch; it had stopped as it often did, so I pulled out my mobile phone and switched that on for the first time in days. 7.45.

Too late to go home, and in any case I needed to be back at the hospital in the morning. The little screen blinked as I stared at it, showing missed calls and an envelope symbol. I flicked to the text messages.

U OK? CALL. TOM FINE STILL IN UK. SARAH
and

ME AND J AND HARRY SEND LUV DO CALL XXXX CARLA

I flicked back to Sarah's message and after a moment's hesitation, leaning on the edge of that hospital door in the traffic, texted back.

AM FINE TAKING FEW DAYS BREATHER M

That should settle her. I found with only slight dismay that I was thinking of Sarah as an enemy, a danger to be outflanked. I did not think that rational, sensible, kindly woman would approve of what I was doing. Whatever that was. She would be afraid for me.

I knew also in my bones that Tom would not approve.

In any case I did not want advice from anyone. There was a path before me, only faintly delineated as yet, and I needed times of quiet and solitude to negotiate it step by fearful step. For too many months there had been no path at all, only a scrubby wilderness offering neither shelter nor direction. Tom and I had dwelt in this arid place, stoically pretending, and now he had found an outward track I would not follow. But his desertion set me free to find the beginnings of a better path, or a mirage of it at least; it brooked no interference. Kind friends, kind Carla, would only drag me back into the wilderness. Of course they would. The wilderness looked all right to them, from where they stood.

It was not an easy or flowery track that lay ahead. Julia loomed as a (screaming, slapping!) peril, not to me but to the peacefulness of the child. For him my feelings were strange, pure, intense. In the days of shock after Jackie's revelation I had feared that I might be graspingly maternal about this baby, long to possess him, do something crazy to achieve that. An hour ago I had been really afraid that I would snatch him in spite of myself and go on the run like some madwoman in the papers. But oddly, it was not so. The temptation was only momentary, and the love that sprang in me when I saw the baby's calm blue eyes contained little possessiveness, only an overwhelming desire to protect him. If he, the new and nameless one, was safe and nurtured I would sleep easy. I would weep that I could not hold him, but such ordinary sorrows can be borne. I was not like that idiot in the Sunday supplement who whined when her child went to university.

But if I did not know that he was in a safe and happy home, even at the ends of the earth, I would have not a moment's peace, ever. I understood now that while I did not need to possess him I would always need to know. And Allie would, I thought, have grace enough to tell me. She had reached for my hand in her moment of trial.

So I must stay close. I set off along the roaring city road looking for somewhere to sleep. After a while I came upon a budget chain hotel, checked in, threw off my shoes and jacket and lay down, dazed and unexpectedly happy, on a clean, bland bed. Faint pangs of hunger were overwhelmed by weariness and I was asleep in minutes, only waking in the small hours to pull the covers over me. Once, between dream and waking, I thought I heard a baby's thin cry somewhere far away, and heard it stilled by kind voices. Sam's child was safe for tonight. That I knew.

I had left my phone on without meaning to, and when it rang I groped around in panic, thinking it was still night. But the curtains of the hotel room were thick and effective to give rest to jet-lagged travellers, and when I looked at the lighted figures on the phone's screen I realized it was after nine o'clock.

SARAH, said the message, still flashing. I pushed 'Accept' and croaked, 'What?'

'Are you OK? Seriously? Where are you?' asked the peremptory voice. 'Tom's been worried.'

'Tom!' Indignation pierced my drowsy confusion. 'He walked out on me! To New Zealand! What effing right—!'

'He's not in New Zealand. He's in Cambridge. He's fine. He's worried about you, we all are. Carla rang, says she can't get you on the home line or the mobile. I don't even know how she got my number.'

'I am fine. I am busy. Everyone can leave me alone.'

'Marion, you sound odd. What is happening?'

'Nothing. Just – I'm fine. I'm with friends. I needed a break.'

I got rid of her with relief, and spelt out a cheerful text message to Carla to head her off. Then I switched the phone off with a sense of finality. These clutching fingers from the other life must be prised off. They would pull me back to the old and arid ways of grief, depleting the new energy that filled me. I swung my legs off the bed and stood up, realizing that I had lost a certain stiffness of the muscles – familiar for months, and put down to inevitable ageing. It was gone. Stretching felt good; walking across to the bathroom my steps were light, and the hot shower was a benison. I stuffed my grubby shirt into the bag and pulled out the clean one, admiring my reflection in the mirror with unwonted pleasure. I looked pale enough, middle-aged and staid, but my hair sprang strongly from my brow with little grey in it and my eyes were clear.

I smiled at the woman in the mirror: she had come through fire and had dignity. She was a grandmother. An ancestress. Her line went on, stretching immeasurably into the future of the race, woven in to the tapestry of time for good or ill. For this I had another woman to thank: the beautiful, bruised Alexandra. Strange her life might be, troublesome her lover; but she was the mother of my boy's boy and therefore my kin for ever.

I ate a sawdust-tasting muffin in a coffee shop and got to the hospital just before ten. At the entrance to the maternity ward I thought to ask the young nurse – yet another one – whether 'Mrs' Morris had a visitor.

'No, she's had her breakfast and Baby's with her. Are you Mrs Penderby?' She glanced at a list on the desk, presumably of approved fathers and birth-partners, and gave me a suspicious glance.

'No. I'm a friend, I brought her in yesterday. Actually, I delivered the baby.'

'Ooh! I heard about that! The paramedics were full of it. Floor cushions, they said. Well, you'd better come and see the pair of them.' I felt stupidly pleased to have got this officious child's respect. We squeaked along the lino to the sideward and found Allie leaning back, still pale but with her golden hair washed and shining, loose on the pillow. A transparent cot lay alongside like a dinghy by a great yacht, and I could see the white covers moving gently with the baby's breathing, and a tiny hand thrown up near his face.

'Marianne. No, Marion. Here we are, then,' she said vaguely. 'Sorry. Don't know what's happening to my brain.'

'Marion it is. He looks peaceful. Has he been feeding?'

'Only half the bloody night, he has. I ate two breakfasts. The girls had one left over and they were so impressed by how fast I ate the first one that they let me nab it. Need all I can get. This boy is a greedy pig. Aren't you, Piggy?' She addressed the remark to the cot, whose occupant snuffled briefly as if in reply. 'Sucking pig.'

I was glad to find her in good spirits, and reluctant to break them by mentioning the matter of Julia's exit last night. I asked after her own recovery, and gave her a couple of magazines I had picked up on the way – not without hesitation, since I had no idea of her tastes and a healthy fear of getting on the wrong side of Julia's politics. Allie crowed with delight, though, throwing aside the *New Statesman* and the newspaper to seize the glossy weight of *Vogue*.

'Oh wow! Haven't seen one for months!' She began flipping through the pages. 'I used to sneak down to the library and read it when I was meant to be looking up women's writing. This'll have to go under the mattress when Jule gets here.'

'Is she coming? Should I get out of the way?'

She raised her eyes from the magazine and grimaced at me, but with an air of friendly conspiracy.

'She'll drop by later, I should think. She had another meeting with her bloody Trust thing about Africa, and they always seem to be in the morning because the woman who runs it is an MP. I wouldn't expect her for a while.'

'I don't want to intrude,' I said rather primly, though I wanted more than anything to stay here in this quiet little white cubicle, with this woman and baby.

'Not a problem,' she said, returning to *Vogue*. 'Brat'll be awake soon and feeding away, and nurse Ratchet out there says I haven't got the hang of the burping bit yet. They sick all down you, did you know? Oh, of course you did. You had one. Sorry.'

'Alexandra,' I said, gathering all my courage and wits together. 'We've met in rather odd circumstances—'

'You keeled over, and then I did,' said Allie, still flicking pages. 'I put a bandage on you and you delivered my baby. Yes, a bit odd, I s'pose. Like being in the war together, really. How is your head, anyway? I'd almost forgotten.'

I went on determinedly. 'Fine. What's even odder is that you don't know me, you've no reason to like me or trust me, but I am this baby's grandmother. And I know I don't have any rights at all, Julia made that perfectly clear—'

'Julia can be a cow sometimes,' said Allie, herself still placid as a milker. 'But she's not a bad person, you know.'

'I can believe that if you say so. But she's not happy that he's a boy, is she?'

'Oh, that. No. Humm. Daresay she'll get over it. Time she did, frankly. She can't carry on as if everything with gonads is an AIDS machine or else her demon dad. Did you know who he was?'

'No?'

'His Honour Justice Macallan Strang Penderby, that's who. Remember?'

The name was immediately familiar; the scandal had dominated days and weeks of headlines some five years back. I searched my memory for details.

'The one who attacked his wife with a mallet . . . oh, I know, something to do with her finding some photos?'

'The very same. And the wife had cancer, and the photos were pretty ripe.'

'What happened?'

'The establishment won, as usual. Wife wouldn't testify, girl wouldn't testify, turned out she'd had her sixteenth birthday and they couldn't prove the photos pre-dated it. Scot free. Resigned for health reasons.'

'And Julia? She wouldn't have been living at home, would she?'

'She ran away when she was, like, sixteen or something.' Allie's eyes rolled skywards and she shook her head. 'Join the dots.'

'You mean her father—'

She shook her head again, this time a fierce negative. 'Look, Marion. It's her business. It's her life. If she thinks men are crap and cause all the trouble in the world, she's entitled to her view like any flat-earther. She'd kill me if she knew I talked about it. Christ knows why I just did. I keep on telling you things, it's freaky.'

'I think,' I said slowly, my eyes on the baby rather than the speaker herself, 'you were trying to convince me that it wasn't spite or lack of goodness, and that therefore Julia will be an OK parent for this baby.'

'Yup. Probably.' She yawned and hauled at the front of her nightshirt.

'Pig there better wake up soon. My tits are like cannon-balls.' She had, I had noticed before, a remarkable ability to switch off during a conversation, change the subject and lower the temperature. Perhaps it came in useful if you lived with angry Julia Penderby. I could see that I was losing her attention and said desperately:

'Never mind anything about Julia. It's not my business. All I wanted to say is that if you need any other support, anything at all, practical or financial or – anything, I'm here.

I care about this baby.' I hesitated, then ploughed on, feeling
a hot blush rise. 'And actually, I care about you.'

Her attention switched back to me with a wide, beautiful
smile.

'Gaw, that is so sweet!'

'I don't mean to be obtrusive—' A snuffle from the baby
alerted and distracted us both, to my relief. Her smile had
reassured me. In moments the snuffle had become a wail,
not a full-blown 'Nwah!' but that newborn mew which for
a mother pierces every other sound, while it passes almost
unheeded by outsiders. Allie jumped, and said:

'Oh God, pass him to me, my back still hurts. You have
to get him plugged on the tit before the key changes – once
he starts really howling it takes ages.'

'I remember it well – you're a quick learner, I must say.
Whoops – here—!'

The baby latched on to her swollen breast with fierce
avidity, and the two of us watched his concentration with a
kind of awe. After a few moments Allie looked up at me.

'I will remember. What you said. How would I find you?'

I wrote my mobile number on an old receipt from the side
pocket of my bag, then hesitated, and wrote down the home
number as well. I would have to go home, at least for some
clothes and for somewhere to sleep without paying hotel bills.
The idea was not attractive; the thought of the house and
garden wearied me, like the thought of going back to a
schoolroom calculation you have got wrong before, an
exercise-book covered in scribbles and tearstains.

'Try the mobile first. Then the home number. The mobile
doesn't work too well when I'm in the house. It's a bit bleak
and rural.'

'Did your – did Sam grow up there? Was he a country
boy?' Her voice was soft, vague: she was relaxing into the
feed now, feeling the warm flow of oxytocin, the natural high

of the feeding mother. I had forgotten the sensation but her face brought it all back: eyelids drooping, Mona Lisa smile. I answered in a voice as soft as hers.

'Yes. He was a real village boy. Loved London, though. And loved the city when he was at Cambridge.'

'I grew up in the city mostly,' said Allie. 'My dad moved to Essex later.'

'Is he still there?'

'Yep. With the wicked stepmother.'

'Any brothers and sisters?'

She was silent, then, 'Sort of.' Suddenly, I knew that I must urgently withdraw. A warning voice told me that Allie was revealing more than she would wish to, and that if in a more brittle mood she came to regret it, she would close herself off to me entirely. I stood up.

'I'd better go. You've got the numbers?'

'Do you have to?' She sounded like a child now. 'Jules won't be here for ages . . .'

Raised voices in the corridor indicated that she was wrong. I grabbed my bag and looked wildly around for another exit; there was none, so I slipped through the door and turned in the wrong direction, away from the entrance so that my back was to the new arrival. There were swing doors at the far end of the ward corridor; rather than walk too obviously towards them I turned my face to a noticeboard on a screen which partially hid me. Through Allie's door a moment later I heard a familiar, cutting voice:

'Who was that just came out?'

'Oh, social services or something. I have to register the birth. Bureaucracy. Told her to come back another time.'

She could lie smoothly, this girl. I smiled; featuring in a lie between her and her partner brought me and Allie closer. Which brought me closer to the child. I stifled this thought, because it was wrong to want any wedge driven between the two who would share a home with the baby. The mention of registration, though, made me realize with a shock that I did not know his name. Allie had not mentioned one. I had not asked. I suppose this was because, to me, his name was Samuel.

18

I went home. Sometimes it is the only thing to do. After the fear, exaltation and bewilderment of the past two days you might think I would head for peaceful Norfolk with relief, at least to recharge my batteries, as the cliché has it. In fact, I shuddered on the train north, dreading the empty house, the faded flowers, the rank and sweaty bed where I could barely remember spending the days of shock. And there would be Sarah, all concerned; and her researcher Jackie, formerly known as Djakki, who was altogether too close to my new unfolding world. She might – I shook with alarm – even have heard on some grapevine about the birth of Allie's baby. And, therefore, of my part in it.

As for Tom, I could not even begin to think about that problem. Christmas was only weeks away, and I had no idea what would happen: I felt sick at the thought of the first Christmas without Sam, and at the certainty of every other Christmas being without him until the crack of doom. Carla and Jeremy would invite us, that I knew. Even a week ago I would have liked the idea of spending the dangerous day with them and their baby. Not now.

No, home was not attractive. But it was, for the moment, the only logical destination. I changed on to the branch line and sat, forehead on the cold window, looking out at the flat, darkening landscape and the tossing trees. It was an east wind, freshening, and when I got out on to the blustery platform I could smell the sea. Sam loved that smell and wrote childhood poems about it.

> *The seawead smell*
> *Is like a spell*
> *The magik sea*
> *Is calling me . . .*

My eyes pricked with tears and the wind whipped them as I turned to face it, so that the salt droplets were driven back towards my ears. I ran a sleeve over my face – a hospital smell clung to it still – and trudged down the dim lane towards home. I had to pass Sarah's house: all the lights were on and for a moment the memory of calm evenings and confidential afternoons under that roof made me waver and think I might knock on the door and return to that world. But I heard from deep within me once more that odd, crafty voice that told me Sarah was a danger and an impediment. I hurried on. In parenthesis now, and sanely, I should say that I speak of it as a 'voice', but it was no such thing. Rather a feeling, a warning, an inhibitory power from a part that I was never before aware of possessing.

In the house, though, it was impossible not to think a little kindly of Sarah. The kitchen was clean, with a note saying 'Lasagne in freezer, salad in fridge'; the dead flowers were gone from the living room, and upstairs the bed was made with fresh sheets. There were no dishes or mugs lying around, and the old bedding was folded, rough but clean, on top of the tumble dryer. The untidy heap of clothes which tends to lie around on the bedroom armchair was untouched, and the post lay in heaps on the kitchen table. I appreciated the delicacy which stopped Sarah – for she alone had a key – from intrusive sorting of letters or invasive tidying.

'Sorry,' I said aloud, meaning it for her. 'You're a good friend.' I riffled through the letters, but none of them tempted me to reach for the paper-knife. There were two for Tom from the Revenue, and I hesitated before angrily throwing them back on the heap. Suddenly, the prospect of the home-made lasagne in the freezer became over-whelmingly attractive, and I pulled it out and put it in the microwave. When did I last eat properly? The night before, in the loft room, there had been soup and Marmite sand-wiches with Allie. Two days I had been away, two and a half. What days!

I should have known that the light in my window would be seen and reported. I had not been home an hour, had barely finished my greedy and much-needed supper, when the phone rang.

'Marion! You're back!' said Sarah's voice. 'Everything OK?'

'Yes. Fine. Thanks for the lasagne. How did you know?'

'Mrs Pollick saw the light on. She was wondering about you doing the flowers on the 23rd. She rang me, I suppose out of tact, poor old thing.'

'Can't.' I hated the church flower duty, even more during the past year. It was an especially uninspiring task in the winter months when one was supposed to do creative things with holly and ivy and dried lavender. I had never had the resolution to have myself struck off the rota. I rarely went to church on Sunday now, anyway. 'Just can't. Not this week.'

'I'll tell her. Don't worry. Main thing is you're back. I was worried. That flu you had—'

'Wasn't flu.' In spite of myself I could not sustain these artificialities with my best friend. 'You know that. I was having a wobbler.' The childish word hung on the air, and it was a moment before Sarah said:

'Well, glad you're better. Can I drop in tomorrow?'

I hesitated. 'I'll come to you.'

'OK. Coffee?'

Memories of the last time I sat in Sarah's kitchen came back, with an echo of the cold, numb shock.

'Will your researcher be there? Jackie?'

'Well – I could fix it so she's not,' Sarah sounded doubtful; we were into the Christmas vacation now, and I supposed Jackie was a fixture. 'She's living in right now, it's more convenient for nine o'clock starts and she's a fiend for work. But I can shut her in the study, she won't care. Or send her out on a hike . . .'

'It's fine. No, I'll come over. Say hello to her.' It occurred to me – or to that crafty, anxious voice from deep below my surface – that I could have a word with Jackie. I could suborn her, prevent her passing on any gossip she picked up on what I presumed was an efficient Sapphic grapevine. As if she had read my mind, though, Sarah suddenly said:

'Incidentally – you might be faintly interested to know that there's a beau on the horizon.'

'Oh? Another girl?'

'Bloke. Visiting lecturer at Lucy Cavendish, over forty, very correct. Former Young Conservative. She's all aglow.'

'Oh. Hum. Well, see you about eleven.'

The effort to sound normal had me clenching my free hand into a fist so tight the nails scored my palm. Rage surprised me, releasing all the screaming demons. So she was no longer gay, this Jackie? Turned back to the main-stream, had she, after persuading my poor son to pass on his genes by syringe to her ex-girlfriend, dooming his child to be brought up by the volatile, the misanthropic, the 'screaming, slapping' Julia Penderby? Meanwhile she, Jackie, prepared to sail on regardless into a life with some safe fortyish academic? So they could have children called

Tycho and Zack who played the bloody violin and spoke Greek for fun? And that was fair on everyone, was it?

My rage abated slowly. I had, after all, seen the living child, seen him feed with glee and regard the world with newborn wonder through Sam's great grey-blue eyes. Perhaps after all it was always better to be born – into any ménage – than not to be born at all. I could not be sorry that he existed. Only tormented by his future, a hostage to fortune and to flaky and volatile mothering.

And here I must tell you something shaming and terrible, but nonetheless true and probably more common than any bereaved parent will admit. A month or so after Sam died it occurred to me that a duty had fallen away from me and Tom for the first time in two decades: the duty to worry about our son's welfare and future. The day he was born the duty had begun, and the weight and wonder of it took my breath away: suddenly there was someone more important than either of us, whose feelings and welfare would come before ours for ever. The day he died – though in that moment we could never have thought it – that duty died, too. No point wondering whether he had seen a dentist lately, or remembered to wear his bike helmet. The stars had gone out, the sun was dim, the wilderness stretched around us; but a tiny, shameful consoling voice said that well, at least now there was nothing left to worry about. No point.

And now the worry was back. I threw the lasagne's tinfoil tray into the rubbish, not caring about the recycling bin, rinsed my fork, and gripped by a need for green stuff, stood by the fridge door and ate some of the salad leaves. Then I took myself to my familiar bed with Radio 4 and a peppermint tea. I wondered whether Allie had blagged a second supper, as well as an extra breakfast; I wondered what she and Julia had said to one another, and whether the baby's downy perfection had softened the older woman's heart. Tears flowed again, dampening the pillow, as I told myself that I had no right or ability to find out. As I fell asleep, though, I saw Allie's smile again, felt that brief grasp of her hand, and was a little comforted.

19

It was Jackie who opened the door when I knocked on Sarah's back door, clearly feeling well at home. She looked even more conventionally tidy and groomed than before, her hair twisted up in a knot with pretty tendrils round her narrow face and a new air of self-assurance. Born, no doubt, of the sudden declaration of love by her damn lecturer.

'Do go through, Sarah's in the kitchen – excuse me, I'm in the middle of some papers—'

At least, I thought sourly, the changeable child was now less likely to be plugged into any kind of gay-political London grapevine which would bring her news of the baby. She had moved on from that world into a cosier one; was probably being taught golf and monetarism by now. Fickle and mutable, the young!

I stopped myself, remembering some enthusiasms of Sam's which had not lasted – his extreme-Green phase, his flirtation with Marx at sixteen. I must not become a harrumphing old harridan. The thought of Tom flickered across my mind at this point, just as I was entering the kitchen, and I pushed it resolutely away. Tom was one problem too many.

'You look *well*,' said Sarah admiringly, as she fiddled with coffee filters. 'Have you been having some long walks?' She and I had always shared an almost superstitious faith in the curative power of walking.

'Not really.' I thought about Dalston, and the floor of the

loft, and the bland Travelodge night, and the howling road past the hospital. 'But I feel OK.'

'Tom's OK, too,' said Sarah. Her laptop was open on the table, and I thought she glanced at it and then too quickly looked away. She filled my mug and with a slightly distracted air, said:

'Look, two minutes. I have to set Jackie on a particular trail and I hadn't finished explaining it. Is that OK? The newspapers are here—' She pushed a *Times* and a *Guardian* towards me. 'Five minutes max.' She eased the lid of the little computer shut and then I was alone at the scrubbed table, looking out at the birds on the feeder outside the window.

Something nagged at me, though: I could not remember ever before seeing her bother to close her laptop when she had work on in the kitchen. Ever since the blessing of wireless internet dawned, it had become a commonplace for Sarah to desert her well-equipped study when her thoughts were racing. She would throw together meals or tidy up with the machine in the room with her. I had seen her pause halfway through whipping up cream to answer an email or pin down an idea.

But she had never closed the lid just because I was in the room. Until now. I looked at the grey laptop for a moment, ignoring the newspapers, and then pulled it towards me and opened it. Her Mail program was open on the screen, and I recognized all too well the second name from the bottom of the Inbox. Tom.

I clicked; a long trail of messages, back to front as usual, opened before me. In the study beyond the hall I could just hear Sarah's voice explaining something; her closeness panicked me and I rapidly clicked 'Forward' and spun the whole of the message chain through the ether to my own email address. She might not notice the little bent arrow which indicated this; I restored the machine to its previous state, closed the lid and pushed it away, engrossing myself in some *Guardian* headline just in time for her return.

The rest of our *kaffeeklatsch* passed normally enough; Sarah told me about work and Jackie's usefulness, I fibbed about my time away, inventing a friend far from London. She asked whether I had heard from Tom and I told her that I hadn't, but was quite calm about it, since he clearly needed time to think about his various problems, which were too much for me to take on. After a while she said tentatively:

'What Jackie told you, last time you were here – I can see it must have been an awful shock. But Sam meant it for the best, I'm sure. He was a kind boy.'

I agreed, heart thumping, trying to avoid her eye.

'Anyway, it doesn't look as if that woman Julia is going to be any more trouble. Jackie was saying that she's very fair-minded, she wouldn't expect to involve Sam's parents in a thing like this.'

'Mm.'

'And obviously, you wouldn't . . .'

'Mm.'

I could not wait to get home, to my stolen email; I refused the offer of lunch and walked back through the biting wind to my own hearth and elderly computer. It blinked into life and claimed to have 23 emails waiting, but I was interested in only one. I read the correspondence between my husband and my friend from the bottom up, chronologically, and only later reversed it until it lay in the correct and damning order. Another's take on one's own history is always, I suppose, painful to endure. I cannot bear to read through it again these days, but for the sake of completeness, here it is.

from: sandrson2100@hotmail.com
to: foodfaulk01@aol.com
subject: Where?

Tom, I have just seen Marion and she has no idea where you are. Are you OK? Is there anything at all that Edward or I can do? I could tell her you're safe, at least. Sarah

from: foodfaulk01@aol.com
to: sandrson2100@hotmail.com
subject: re: Where?

I am safe. Tell her. Thanks. I'm at a friend's, nobody she really knows. In Cambridge. It's not a woman, nothing like that. But I need a breather from it all. T

from: sandrson2100@hotmail.com
to: foodfaulk01@aol.com
subject: re: Where?

I've told her you're safe, which I think helped. But she's not well, Tom. She's staying in bed a lot and I can't get her to eat properly. It's not like her, she doesn't want to talk and makes no sense when she tries. Are you sure you shouldn't be here?

from: foodfaulk01@aol.com
to: sandrson2100@hotmail.com
subject: re: Where?

I think I make it worse. We haven't been able to talk for a long time, and the sleep thing was finishing me off. She talks and cries and shouts for Sam in her sleep,

Sarah, night after night. She doesn't know, she won't
believe it when I say so, says she sleeps absolutely fine
it must be me dreaming. But it's got worse, not better,
as the weeks went by. I once actually woke her and
asked, at two in the morning, whether she thought we –
I said we, to soften it – needed to see a counsellor. But
she was all calm and rational and said she didn't need
some trick-cyclist telling her what was wrong, she knew
what was wrong, Sam was dead and grief was natural.
She said it was me who perhaps should take
Temazepam. Then more sleep and more shouting.

But next morning she was normal, chatting to Carla
and Jeremy about the baby. I haven't slept properly for
a long time, and lately a lot of things got on top of me.
Don't think I'm not ashamed of running away, because I
am. But I can't see a way through it. Not while we're in
the house, in the village, with everything the same
except the one thing, Sam.

from: sandrson2100@hotmail.com
to: foodfaulk01@aol.com
subject: re: Where?

Thanks for explaining. Yes, I see all that. I don't think
Marion's been really open about what she feels, even
with me. She's been impeccably sensible, but I've been
worried that something might erupt. And perhaps the
night terrors are a sort of safety valve. It must have been
hard not to be able to share her grief more openly, for
whatever reason, and she'd probably have done better to
see someone. A psychiatrist once said to me that the
English professional classes are the most difficult to deal
with because they just won't acknowledge the depth of
their pain, they deny it with self-control and cover it with

bright good behaviour. Then they suddenly implode and do something crazy. He said there was a lot to be said for a Mediterranean or African behaviour, howling and throwing yourself on coffins. But the way we were all brought up, I suppose, we can't do that. I was the same when I lost the baby.

from: foodfaulk01@aol.com
to: sandrson2100@hotmail.com
subject: re: Where?

It's an interesting theory your shrink friend has, but I don't know about it. I've always believed in not wearing your heart on your sleeve, like those terrible people who moaned and wailed about Diana in the street. If you're not a Mediterranean howling type it just feels self-indulgent, at a time when you should be putting yourself last, because the tragedy is someone else's. It was Sam, after all, who was cheated of his life. For us to carry on as if we were the damaged ones would just seem disgusting, wouldn't it?

But it was Marion's nights that were doing for me. I feel more normal now than I ever have since it happened. I talk to my friend here all the time. I even cry. I begin to see a way forward.

The thing is, I never cried with her. Marion and I made a pact in the first week that we wouldn't bring each other down. Grief seems to go up and down like a rollercoaster, it isn't a smooth slope. Sometimes you do actually feel quite normal. So we thought that if we took care not to show each other when we were down, we'd avoid doing a weatherhouse-family thing, one in and one out, and therefore getting to a state with us both staying permanently upset. It made sense at the time.

But then the night thing started. And OK, some odd reflexes of my own which I'd rather not talk about.

I'm a biologist. I never thought about stuff like this before.

from: sandrson2100@hotmail.com
to: foodfaulk01@aol.com
subject: re: Where?

I don't suppose any of us do, until it happens. When I lost my baby – the stillbirth – all those years ago, I felt as if someone had taken away one of the walls and a huge new landscape opened up, a really terrifying Bosch landscape with black rocks and deep ravines and demons. And even though there had been the old tragedies in my family, it was hard to realize that the big dark blankness had been there all the time, behind the cosy walls we live in. It's as if we live in a stage set, with three walls, and never look out into the void beyond the footlights where the dark universe is laughing at our antics.

from: foodfaulk01@aol.com
to: sandrson2100@hotmail.com
subject: re: Where?

Yes. Cosy lab walls for me, I suppose. And TV studio walls. So when the edges fall away into blackness you turn your back and look for new walls to hammer on, you pick any pointless fight you can, as long as you're facing away from the ravine. I've been hammering at the Inland Revenue for months as if they were the problem. God knows why – they only want about £20k and I do have it. But the day I left home I decided completely, in

a sort of crazy fit, that the only thing to do was to leave the country, walk out with the clothes I stand up in, go as far as possible. New Zealand, was the idea. Just to say sod everything, sod the taxman, sod the system and its heartless nitpicking incompetent meanness.
Apparently they don't bother following you for sums like that.

But I've almost forgotten that idea after two nights staying on Malcolm's futon. I even sleep, though the damn thing is hard as nails.

from: sandrson2100@hotmail.com
to: foodfaulk01@aol.com
subject: re: Where?

So are you perhaps ready now to tell Marion where you are?

from: foodfaulk01@aol.com
to: sandrson2100@hotmail.com
subject: re: Where?

Please don't ask that.

from: sandrson2100@hotmail.com
to: foodfaulk01@aol.com
subject: re: Where?

Why? She's your wife.

from: foodfaulk01@aol.com
to: sandrson2100@hotmail.com
subject: re: Where?

I can't. That's all. I wish you hadn't said that. Even the word 'wife' sort of upsets me, as if 'husband' was a job description I'm never going to be up to, not any more. I can't sleep again now, I keep hearing her crying and muttering like she did night after night. And I dream about Sam and he's angry with me, like when he was thirteen and Marion and I had a bit of a fight over some stupid thing and he walked in on the shouting. I think I'm going mad. I've let him down, and her, and everyone.

from: sandrson2100@hotmail.com
to: foodfaulk01@aol.com
subject: re: Where?

Tom, I'm sorry. Please don't cut off. I got it wrong.

from: sandrson2100@hotmail.com
to: foodfaulk01@aol.com
subject: re: Where?

Tom, seriously, I'm sorry. Please don't cut off. Really. I won't ask you about Marion again. She seems to have left the house, I'm going to text her but if she's gone to visit a friend as well then that's all to the good. She might have gone to that schoolfriend in Ely she sometimes talks about. Don't worry. I'll keep an eye. It's not your sole job to make everything all right. It takes a village, and all that . . .

from: sandrson2100@hotmail.com
to: foodfaulk01@aol.com
subject: re: Where?

Tom, I'm really worried now. Mail me that you're safe.

from: foodfaulk01@aol.com
to: sandrson2100@hotmail.com
subject: re: Where?

I'm OK. Had a bit of a thing, sort of short-term breakdown thing. Might even have been cathartic, curing. Malcolm says I have to see a therapist. I don't think he wants me here in this state. But don't think I'm not caring about Marion, because I am. I know I'm a louse and a useless husband. It's just I can't face her. She's so sensible and I feel such a fool. And now I'm not a father any more, I don't know that I've got any talent for being just a husband. Useless.

from: sandrson2100@hotmail.com
to: foodfaulk01@aol.com
subject: re: Where?

You're not useless, dear Tom. You're just stressed and shocked and need to look after yourself first. There are times when that happens to all of us. Not something to be guilty about. But are you OK? Is your friend OK with you staying there? Can Edward or I be of any, any help? You are the absolute priority, for both of us, please know that. Should I come to Cambridge?

from: foodfaulk01@aol.com
to: sandrson2100@hotmail.com
subject: re: Where?

You're an angel. Perhaps it would have been better if I'd talked to you and other people sooner. But as I

say, I'm a biologist. And a bloke. And talking to
Marion wasn't something I could do. In case I made it
worse for her. Hell and damnation, what a muddle it
all is.

from: sandrson2100@hotmail.com
to: foodfaulk01@aol.com
subject: re: Where?

You'll be OK. Hang on in there. Seeing the therapist
mightn't be such a bad idea. They don't take over or
interfere, you know. They just help you work it out for
yourself. In some ways you may have been hit even
harder than Marion over Sam. People underestimate
what fathers feel. And women are very strong.

from: foodfaulk01@aol.com
to: sandrson2100@hotmail.com
subject: re: Where?

I think you're right. It has hit me harder, if that's
possible. I will see the therapist. Malcolm's booked it
anyway, he seems very adamant. He's amazingly bossy,
for a philosopher. Sarah, I can't say how grateful I am
for all this. I sit here all day on my own mainly, I'm not
lecturing at all or going out. I'm writing some stuff down.
That seems to help.

from: sandrson2100@hotmail.com
to: foodfaulk01@aol.com
subject: re: Where?

You're getting there. Hang on. I admire you for it.

I stopped reading, and pushed the keyboard away from me with mingled horror and outrage. Tougher for him, was it? A job to be tackled, was I? Oh, and he was Sarah's top priority, even though she knew the shock I'd had about the pregnancy? Oh, poor diddums Tom!

Perhaps it is the peculiar quality of email which made it so painful: without the slightest impropriety there was nonetheless a wifely, pillow-talk intimacy in their tone which made me shake with jealousy, shock and rage. How dare Sarah, how dare Tom? I was sure I did not shout and weep in my sleep. He must be making that up. For sympathy. To justify his own babyish cowardice in pretending to abscond to New Zealand without paying his twenty thousand back-tax, which was his own bloody fault for not keeping proper accounts. Never once in his endless complaints and cursing of the Revenue did he admit to me that it was an amount that he had got in the savings account. Admittedly I rarely asked, because he gets so angry about his financial affairs. But all the same it rankled.

And Sarah! Treating him so understandingly with her motherly calm – or was it motherly? Did something lie between them that I had never seen? I dismissed the idea, but not without briefly, shamefully, relishing it first.

The exchange was not quite over; I had frozen the screen on her sycophantic 'I admire you for it', but there were a few more messages. Scrolling up, breathing heavily, I read on. There was a gap of a day, a longer gap than any of the others, then a new tone. I saw to my amazement that they must have met the day before yesterday. Perhaps the lights in Sarah's house as I walked past in the dusk shone not only on her and her researcher-guest, but on my husband too.

from: foodfaulk01@aol.com
to: sandrson2100@hotmail.com
subject: re: Where?

I've been in some sort of shock since our meeting last night. I'm sorry if I left abruptly, I needed to think. But I'm glad you came clean, and that I got a glimpse of Jacqueline. I'm not sure I'd have been able to believe the whole farrago if I hadn't met her. What a mess.

I can't believe Marion was so stupid as to want to get herself caught up with these people. I can hardly believe she went to find the madwoman, and if what you suspect is true about her carrying on down that track, she really has to disengage. I hope to God she really is in Ely, and hasn't gone looking for them. There is no way that we can have any relationship with these crazy dykes and their manufactured child – excuse my bluntness, but I am in no mood for political correctness. Remember, I've met one of them, she was a sort of nightmare gipsy thing who came and ranted at me on the doorstep. Are they trying to get money off Marion, do you think? The whole thing is outrageous.

from: sandrson2100@hotmail.com
to: foodfaulk01@aol.com
subject: re: Where?

Perhaps you and Marion need to talk about this, quietly somewhere. Shall I try and fix it? She's back. I just walked down the lane to check, and saw her light come on.

from: foodfaulk01@aol.com
to: sandrson2100@hotmail.com
subject: re: Where?

Yes. Perhaps that would be best. Thanks. Though I shall have trouble controlling myself if it turns out she really is chasing after this rainbow. Maybe you should be there when we first get back together.

The messages ended. Yeah, right, I thought. Sarah the fixer, Sarah the all-wise, the Henry Kissinger of our emotional Palestine. And Tom, the bigoted despiser of 'crazy dykes' and 'manufactured children', Tom who had never seen his son's son feeding, newborn, at golden Allie's breast. I 'had to disengage', did I? We'd see about that.

20

I walked by the sea for a long time that afternoon. It was one of those shining winter days with a touch of frost on the pebbles and a vast blue sky; a day to lift the heart. My anger and humiliation faded a little. Tom was clearly in grievous mental trouble, and he had loved Sam, and Sam was the son we made together. And our family life had been good, or as good as most. It was hard to remember how we three had been before our boy died, but on the whole yes: good. Too small a family, I saw now, but all the same a good one.

I was still surprisingly raw and offended about the 'crazy dykes' line, thinking protectively of Alexandra. I knew my husband to be of the old school, dismissing gay men as a bit cissy and lesbians as virulent man-haters, objects of far greater suspicion. Even his brief television career did not seem to have cured this, though heaven knows that in that media life he must have worked with a rainbow diversity of sexual inclinations; and in our social life the issue had not sufficiently often arisen for it to be a problem. On the other hand, a small, honest remnant of me had to admit that if you wanted to point at a violently misanthropic and aggressive lesbian, Julia Penderby was probably the closest you could get outside a cartoon strip.

As for Sarah, I became a little calmer about her part in all this. But only a little. It is a curiosity of female friendship that when it goes deep and close and confidential it risks tipping over into resentful hatred when things go wrong. Perhaps we give too much of ourselves, too rashly, in conversations with other women, and only too late do we realize we can never reclaim our lost reserve.

Maybe I always knew this, and that is why I felt warning twinges in my sudden intimacy with Allie, and pulled back. In the case of Sarah her kindly equanimity and my bereavement may have made me give too much and take too little, making me the weaker party and afflicting me with the resentment which the weak always secretly feel for the strong. For nearly nine months I had wept on her, talked erratically and compulsively at length about every shift of sorrow, guilt and bewilderment. I had accepted her care and distracted her from her own hearth and husband and perhaps her own troubles. I never knew her in her early marriage, when she lost the baby, so Sarah had never needed to lean on me. I had never been the strong one. Lately I had needed her, and as a result it seemed that I now hated her.

Yes: hated. Patronizing cow, with her theories about my middle-class reticence and hidden grief! Soft fool, to believe Tom's nonsense about night terrors! I was sure I did not cry out in the night. I was fine. I was resigned, I was dignified. I am an adult and I accept bereavement. I am a grown woman of the older generation and I know that, as the young so elegantly put it, shit happens.

Doubts, delusions, denials swirled around me that day on the beach as the soft waves rippled on the cold pebbles. One thing remained constant: I would not be bullied or persuaded by this smug pair of emailers into ignoring or forgetting the child – the nameless boy – who lay in Allie Morris's arms in the clattering London hospital.

I was bound to the child, the boy who would not go home to a calm house and a friendly Norfolk village but to an uncertain life with two combative women in a Dalston loft.

I had seen his eyes and they were Sam's eyes. Even though I longed for the touch and smell and feel of the baby, ached for him, I had learnt in a merciful instant that by some miracle I loved him enough to want another woman – younger, stronger – to hold him to her heartbeat. If Tom could not see that glory and that sacrifice, if he thought it was a squalid 'manufactured child', then to hell with him. And to hell with Sarah. Though Sarah, I had to admit, had noticeably failed to join in his condemnation of my quest. On the screen, anyway. Then I remembered her tentative 'You wouldn't . . .' as I was leaving this morning, and hardened my heart again.

When I got home the phone was flashing a message. I put the kettle on and then went back to listen to it, and without surprise heard Sarah inviting me over to supper the next day. She added, her gently modulated Radio-4ish tones unchanging, that she was hoping Tom would be there and that we'd have time to talk alone.

I wondered why she admitted this degree of intimacy and ownership of my husband's movements. So far, after all, she had told me only that she knew him to be safe. Then I realized that with her tidy scholar's eye she would have noticed the little curly arrow next to Tom's last email, indicating that it had been forwarded. She would have seen in her Sent box who had got it. So she knew that I knew. In other circumstances I might have felt pity for her embarrassment. As it was, I ignored her message. If my husband of a quarter of a century wanted to see me, I said aloud to the drooping pot-plant by the phone, the lousy fucking coward could bloody well come round and face me in our own house. Without his Nanny Sarah's skirts to hide behind.

I had just enough self-awareness, as I slammed down a mug and viciously clattered with instant coffee and hot water, to realize that I was starting to sound a bit like Julia Penderby.

* * *

He came over next day, of course. After sorting out the house, ringing Eric with a promise to come back on Monday, and putting Carla off visiting for a while ('I've a streaming cold'), I had walked more miles along the beach, this time in grey drizzle, and come back to light a fire in the sitting-room and consider beans on toast and a mindless hour with the television. The kitchen was a mess – I am not much of a housewife when Tom is away, and tend to tidy up for his return – and when the key turned in the back door I felt a familiar but treacherous lurch of guilt on realizing that he would walk into chaos. Then my inner Julia Penderby reasserted herself, and I was positively glad of the chance to annoy him.

When he appeared in the sitting-room doorway there was a strange, refocusing moment: in my pique and embarrassment about the emails I had built Tom into a caricature, but the man before me was the old familiar husband with his hawk profile, badger-striped hair over his collar and a slight donnish stoop. It was impossible to connect this familiar Tom immediately with the angry broken-down creature of the emails, and I just blinked stupidly and said:

'Hello. You back, then?'

'I got asked to supper at Sarah's. She thought you might be coming. We could walk over together.'

'Well, I'm not coming. Why didn't you tell me where you were? All those days?'

'I didn't know where you were, either.'

'You didn't ask. I had my mobile.'

'Mine got broken.'

We were glaring now. Then Tom sat down, suddenly, on the sofa and said:

'I've been a bit of a dickhead, haven't I?'

It was impossible not to soften towards him.

'Perhaps you just needed a bit of space. Reaction.'

'Perhaps we both did.'

'No, I'm fine—' I was combative again, without completely knowing why. 'Nothing wrong with me. I had a touch of flu and then I went to see some friends. Sarah told me you were OK.'

'Marion,' he said in a new, rather irritatingly gentle tone. 'I'm seeing a therapist. Who specializes in bereavement. It might be an idea if you did, too. We're not coping.'

'You may not be. I am.'

He sat for a moment, looking at his hands as if he had rarely seen them before. When he raised his head again his tone was different, artificially bright.

'You're the judge of that. Of course. But I think I'll go back to Cambridge for a couple of weeks, see this therapy chap. I'm on sick leave but it's the vacation next week anyway.' And then, in another tone again: 'So are you coming to Sarah's for supper?'

'No. Not up to it. You go.'

He looked at me uneasily, but I held him with a level gaze and his eyes dropped first. 'OK.' As he left, I reflected that we had done well. We had not had a row, I had not revealed my fury about the emails, he had not tried to coerce me into anything. We were adults: balanced and sensible, middle-class and self-controlled. No screaming and slapping. Something to be proud of, that.

21

He came back one more time, after his supper presumably; I was in bed. I heard the key and latch rattle, the front door open and shut, footsteps in the hall, lights clicking on. A voice called up the stairs in a half-whisper: 'Marion? You awake?' and I did not reply.

The footsteps came softly up the stairs, the bedroom door opened and a weight creaked on to the far side of the bed. There was a faint glimmer of light in the room now, from the downstairs windows – I never shut the curtains, not since Sam died, it feels like bad luck. As if he might be out there on some wild night, tapping on the window like Cathy's ghost calling to Heathcliff. In the faint light Tom loomed, a dim silhouette. I reluctantly pushed myself up on one elbow as he spoke.

'Sorry. Did I wake you?'

'You have now.'

'I just wanted to say that Sarah's pretty worried, she thinks she's upset you. She's a good woman.'

'Mmph.'

'It's your business, she's always been more your friend than mine.'

'True. Until you became email pals.'

'Marion, she's been helpful. A lifeline. What did you expect? Do you think that nobody can talk about this problem without you policing every word?'

'Enjoy your little pen-friend,' I said spitefully. 'I'm just the problem woman who talks in her sleep.'

'I don't want to fight,' he said wearily. 'Really not. But so you know, I'm staying with them tonight, then going back to Cambridge to see this therapist chap a few more times. Is that OK?'

'Fine by me.'

'What are you going to do? Marrie, I do worry about you too, you know.' His voice softened a little, and like a song remembered from far away and long ago, affection stirred in me. But some small devil told me that it would mean danger, compromise, the snapping of the thin gold thread that bound me to Allie and the child. I kept my voice flat and pretended to be sleepy.

'I'm fine.' Yawn. 'Just let me get some sleep.'

'The girl Jackie is going away for Christmas in a few days,' he said, tentatively. 'To her people in America or somewhere.'

'Why do you say that?'

'Just – you know. Things getting back to normal.' That therapist's tone in his voice again. I kept quiet. Normal! Normal, meaning no more 'crazy dykes' and 'manufactured children'. I could read him like a book. No, a pamphlet. After a pause he went on:

'Carla's invited us both over for Christmas Day but we don't have to decide anything yet. Couple of weeks to go.'

'Mmmh.'

Then he burned his boats.

'It'll be nice to be with family.'

I sat up rigid, suddenly bristling with furious alertness.

'I know why you said that!'

'Why?' His therapized calm made me want to launch myself across the wide bed and hit him.

'Because you don't think Sam's child is family!'

He stood up then, snapped the light on and looked down at me.

'Marion. You have to stop this. Even if you find this – this pair of women, they won't welcome you. You'll get hurt. There may not even be a child. And if there was – face it, it's a chimera, a mirage. We need to grieve and accept our real loss. Not chase after moonbeams.'

'Is that what your therapist said? That your grandchild didn't matter?'

'I haven't raised the subject. It isn't important. Even if it exists it isn't—' He paused and then carried on, in a tone I recognized as almost brave. 'It isn't a grandchild.'

'What – is – it – then?' Between gritted teeth. He was silent for a moment but at last said:

'Marion, all I am saying is that you should mend your fences with Sarah, who is fond of you, and try to get a sense of proportion over this – this masturbatory donor business. Sam's gone. What happened is an aberration. If it existed at all, you couldn't say it was the child of a marriage or even a love affair or a fling. It isn't the child of his love, or even of his carelessness. It's just . . .'

He shrugged, and could not finish. I could.

'It is the child of his kindness,' I said, and lay down again, to roll away with my back to him. 'His last kind deed.'

Sarah was to say, much later when we were speaking again, that she didn't think Tom should have walked out at this point.

But he did, and after weeping for a while in rage and self-pity I fell asleep, still knowing I was right.

On Monday I went in to work, and took solace from Eric's relief and grateful appreciation. There was far too much to do; wage adjustments were behind and employees grumbling. I stayed until six and came home exhausted, promising to be in on Tuesday. As a result my other client firms began to get worried and demanding, and Tuesday afternoon, Wednesday and half of Thursday were taken up in straightening out those things which my supposed illness had left askew.

The steadying effect of work was miraculous. It proved quite possible to let slip, over instant coffee with Eric, the fact that Tom was away in Cambridge 'on a job' and that I was taking the opportunity to have a good spring-clean of the house. These cosy domestic details seemed to reassure him: in the first few hours of my return I had seen poor kind Eric glancing at me in a worried manner I had never seen before.

I did clean the house a bit, in the evenings. Television seemed pointless, books unattractive, and I was still avoiding Sarah. She came round one afternoon while I was at work and left a cheerful note, a poinsettia in a pot and a box of After Eight chocolates. This was behaviour so unlike her that for a moment I thought I was the victim of some strange reverse burglary. Sarah is not the kind of woman who leaves poinsettia and confectionery. She faces things head-on. If she couldn't face my defiance of Tom, I ascribed it to her guilt over having discussed me so legibly with him.

Mainly, though, I leafed through Sam's old baby photos in their white albums, trying to trace the new child's features in his. It was not hard. Not for me, anyhow, flying on wings of wishes. There was a full moon on those nights and it was unusually warm for December; I would lie on the bed, arms and legs outspread, remembering how in legend a woman lying naked beneath a full moon would be made pregnant by its beams. Too late for that, but I sent thoughts, love, strength across the ether to the nameless child. I spoke them to the moon, hoping that its brightness poured down on him through the skylight of the Dalston attic.

'You may have cost me my marriage, babysweet,' I said to the shining disc above, 'but it might have died anyway. Aberration, indeed!' My laugh sounded odd even to me; I shivered, pulled up the duvet and tried to sleep.

* * *

Some days, not many, went by. It was the twentieth, five days before Christmas and not a leaf of holly or pine in the house; but then, why should there be? I came home from Eric's factory at lunchtime, having tied up all the loose ends necessary until New Year, and found the answerphone flashing a '3'. The first message was from Sarah, as was generally the case.

'Marion? How are things? Wondering if you fancied supper? Do give me a buzz.' She had given up on the mints and poinsettias at least. 'Pot luck, I'm on my own tonight.'

The second was Tom, sounding unnaturally normal and ignoring the gulf between us as if he had forgotten it.

'Marion. Just to say I'll be home the day after tomorrow. Carla and Jeremy are expecting us on Christmas Eve through till Boxing Day, shall I do the presents or will you?'

Rather than think about this I pressed the button again for the third message. A shock ran through me as it played, so that I sank against the wall for support. It was a taut, hysterical but familiar voice.

'Marion? Are you there? Pick up. It's Allie. Please. This number, not the office one. Please.'

What number? My hand shaking, I dialled 1471, thanking heaven that she was the last inward call. The pencil by the phone was blunt, but pressing hard I wrote down the long mobile phone number it gave, before pushing '3' to recall it. It rang for too long, and I despaired; then Alexandra's voice cut in.

'Hello? Hello – sorry – the baby—' There was a wail, a sound that cut through me, but moments later it came closer and gentled to a snuffling whimper. A small clatter as she picked up the mobile again with, presumably, her one free hand.

'Marion? Oh, Marion. Thank God. Look, I need help. Julia . . .' My heart hammered.

'Is she there?'

'No. It's complicated. She's off to bloody *Africa*!'

'Why? When?'

'Got a grant. For her bloody refuge. African women outrank *me*. And Con.'

'Con?'

'The baby. Condor. We named him.'

'Isn't that a vulture?' I was so relieved to hear of Julia's impending absence that the irrelevance popped up despite the note of hysteria in Allie's voice.

'It's a wild bird, it soars above canyons. That's the point. But Marion, I can't cope on my own!' She was almost crying, and the baby's whimpers rose alongside. 'She says millions of single mothers do, she says I'm being pathetic, she's being vile. But it isn't her who doesn't get the *sleep*! I can't shop and cook proper stuff to eat, and cope with Condy as well – he cries and cries – and the bloody stairs – Julia just won't accept that it's difficult—'

'Allie, when does she go? I'm coming.'

'She goes tomorrow. She's out getting her fucking malaria tablets and seeing the Trust woman. Might be a month she's away, more even. I could kill her – oh darling, don't cry, Condy, *please*!'

'I'm coming. Tomorrow.' A great joy rose in me, the joy of the needed.

'No,' said Allie's voice, half drowned by a rising mew of baby rage. 'Please, can't I come to your house? I hate it up here, the stairs, the fumes off the lorries, it's so horrible, I never saw how horrible it was here until I had the baby. He's so little and fresh, and everything bloody smells round here, and I daren't leave him and the stairs—'

'Yes. Shall I come and get you?'

'Oh please! I don't have anyone else – I can't go to my dad's—'

'When does Julia leave?'

'Nineish. I could kill her. I *will* kill her.'

'See you at half past. Feed that baby!'

The sun was slanting in, motes of dust dancing with crazy vitality. I put down the phone and felt a great smile spreading through my whole body.

A clear afternoon to prepare. I went up to the spare room and looked around; it faced north, clean and chilly and with its own tiny bathroom, but barely room for a cot alongside the bed. Across the landing, with sun streaming through the dusty panes, was Sam's room. I had not been mawkish or superstitious back in that dark spring: I did not leave his room just as he had left it, as some mourners do. I had cleared and boxed his things, put them in the attic, and given the least iconic of his clothes to the charity shop. However, the bed had never been made up since, and its duvet and coverlet lay folded with heartbreaking, sterile neatness. The room smelt unused; his books still lined one wall, and the pictures were those he chose, or had borrowed on bandit raids from the walls downstairs. There were vivid colours, cloudy abstracts, a watercolour of the Cornish beach where he learnt to surf, a small, striking sketch of a bird with ragged wings against a copper evening sky. Maybe it was a condor. Anyway, a baby would like to look at such things.

It was a big room, light and happy. I set to work to prepare it.

22

'Why do you call him after a South American vulture?'
I asked, to distract her from her fretfulness.

'Condors are beautiful. They soar for miles over the Andes.
I saw one once, on a trip I did when I was performing. It's
the most graceful thing in the world. And lots of people are
called Con. So he won't get teased, people will think he's
Irish.'

We were on the train, a crowded Christmas-holiday carriage
overstuffed with luggage and shopping-bags; the baby's bag
of clothes and equipment had to balance on my knee, and
our feet were jammed next to Allie's scruffy suitcase.

'I looked it up in the encyclopaedia,' I said, 'and apparently condors sometimes don't eat for days, then eat so much
they can't even get off the ground.'

'That's another reason, then,' said Allie, shifting her limbs
with cautious discomfort lest she wake the child curled in a
cloth papoose on her chest. 'He has no pattern whatsoever.
Sleeps five hours then feeds for three, then sleeps forty
minutes and hungry again.'

'That's babies. They don't grow a routine for a while. He
isn't a month old yet. Think of new babies as a bit like weather
– just because it rained at ten yesterday doesn't mean it has
to rain at ten today.'

'I can't keep up.' She yawned. 'Oh God, I might be dropping off right now—'

'Do. I'll keep an eye. Sleep.' She folded her arms around

the form of the baby on her chest, and closed her eyes like a child herself.

I had found her at half-past nine in the morning, ragged in a nightshirt, surrounded by unwashed mugs and plates and a background reek of disposable nappies in an untied bin-bag. She was tearfully apologetic. 'I'm sorry, you see how I can't cope, I'm useless, I shouldn't have done this, I'm not fit to *have* a baby, I never knew . . .'

I bustled. So benevolent did I feel, so powerful and delighted by this unasked-for gift of my grandchild Condor's company, that I washed up the dishes and took the bin-bag downstairs, properly sealed up, and threw it in a skip so that Julia, if she got there first, didn't come home to filth and chaos.

'Though she bloody deserves to, bloody, bloody Julia,' said Allie vindictively, stuffing baby clothes into a canvas bag. 'Leaving me, and sneering at me for panicking—'

'Just before Christmas, too, it's a bit hard,' I said, but in a lightning shift of mood Allie said repressively:

'We don't do Christmas. It's a meaningless commercial rip-off. Julia says if all the money we spent on rubbish every December was put to use in the Third World it would save millions of lives.' It was as if her momentary anger and disloyalty had to be atoned for by this echoing of Julia's stern views. In my new benignity I found it touching and was glad that in the rush I had not had time to get a Christmas tree and decorate it for the baby's wondering eyes. I stayed quiet, and when Allie was ready rang a cab and bore her off to Liverpool Street. Only there did she ask: 'Where is it you actually live?'

Now, on the train, she drowsed and woke, looking wonderingly out at fields and estuaries flashing by, drinking in the quietness of the small stations and, as dusk fell, the brave little Christmas houses with their shining lights and luminous

Santas. Her childlike pleasure in these confirmed my suspicion that the anti-Christmas feeling did not run very deep. We ate a cheese pastie off the trolley service, changed to a less crowded train on the branch line, and she slept again. Inevitably the baby woke and screamed just as we pulled into the station. Allie panicked – I was coming to recognize that weary panic and learning to forestall it.

'Shit! What do I do? Should I feed him right here, it's so cold – how far do we have to go?'

'Short walk. Give me the papoose.' I strapped it on, baby and all, and wrapped my coat around him. 'If I keep moving he won't scream, and if he isn't smelling your milk he won't be so furious at not getting it straight away.'

'Clever,' said Allie. She picked up her own bag and winced a little. 'Jesus, muscles still hurt—' I took it from her, motioned to her to carry the baby's little canvas sack of clothes, and trudged off down the road with her a step or two behind. Her panic rose again.

'Where's he going to sleep?' There had been a folding cot in the loft, but it was a heavy, old-fashioned one from a charity shop which we could not easily carry. I reassured her, still walking as fast as I could, the baby squirming live and indignant against my chest, the fairy-lights brightening in the village windows.

'He's small enough for a Moses basket. I had an old one in the attic, I ran the steam-cleaner over it yesterday afternoon to kill off any bugs, and it's dry. I've washed a blanket that we can fold as a mattress with a clean sheet on it, till we're properly sorted in a day or two. Improvise! That's the family motto.'

'You are so kind,' said Allie faintly. Then, panting a little at the pace I was setting, 'Is it far?'

'Here.' We were turning into my gate, we three. We were home. 'Welcome.'

I had left the heating on all day, and a breath of warm air embraced us as we came in. 'Oh!' said Allie. 'I didn't know how lovely—'

She began to cry. I led her to the sofa, unzipped the papoose and put the cross, damp child on her lap. Obediently she fumbled with the front of her dress to feed him, tears of unfocused emotion still dripping down her face.

'I'll make some tea. Green, do you like? Or fruit stuff?'

'Is there some real tea, with milk?'

When I came back with the tea the baby, noticeably smelly by now, was feeding blissfully and although the tears had made grimy streaks down her face, Allie's eyes were half closed in the hormonal contentment I remembered too well. I delved into Condor's bag of possessions and found a nappy; I had bought wipes and cream yesterday at the station chemist's, in case, and improvised a changing mat from half Sam's old Scout camp mattress, covered in a pillowslip. It all lay ready on the kitchen table, and when the baby fell dozing from his mother's breast, the thin milk dribbling from the corner of his mouth, I carried him through and changed him, frowning at a patch of nappy-rash and anointing it with the cream I had bought. When I took him back to Allie she was hard asleep, head thrown back on the sofa, legs askew. I put the equally sleepy baby down on a chair and carefully laid her out lengthwise – she grunted but hardly woke – eased a cushion under her head and covered her with a rug. Her golden hair spread like a Christmas starburst and Condor and I settled quietly in the armchair opposite, feet up, clean and safe, warm and fed.

When the phone rang and Tom's voice on the speaker filled the hallway it was not hard to ignore it. Weary from my night of preparations and the long day on the train, I closed my eyes too, and the three of us slept for a while.

23

I had forgotten the turbulent nights of early motherhood. Waking from our afternoon snooze Allie took her bag upstairs and then she and I ate supper together, without much conversation. Halfway through peeling a mandarin orange she abruptly yawned, laid it down and said, 'Do you mind if I go to bed?' The baby had fed again at seven, and I offered to keep his basket in my room until he woke; she yawned more widely and said:

'That'd be cool. Do you mind? In the flat Jules was kipping out on the cushions because she says she can't sleep with the snuffling and crying.'

'I like the snuffling. When he cries I'll bring him to you for a feed, the way the nurses used to do in hospital, back in my day. And you might get a deeper sleep.'

'Cool. You won't let him cry long?'

'Course not.'

I went to bed at ten; Con woke at eleven-fifteen and I took him to her, lit a nightlight and sat watching him feed by its flickering light. Then, without either of us discussing it, I brought the basket back to my own bedside. Allie looked so thin, so pale and confused by the sudden waking that it seemed kinder. The same thing happened at three and again just after five, except that on the second waking he fed only briefly and decided he was no longer sleepy. I took him back again as Allie slumped into unconsciousness and he stayed awake beside my bed, staring and kicking and attempting near-smiles until – on the far side of a brief doze – he abruptly began to cry for another feed.

So by eight o'clock all three of us were asleep again, down deep, when the phone rang. I ignored it, glanced at the sleeping infant with incredulous, reminiscent joy, and dived back into shallower mists. On the way I remembered my own mother twenty years back, intoning the hospital nurse's post-natal mantra: 'You sleep when the baby sleeps. That's the rule.' I wondered what she would think of her great-grandchild's conception; then as I melted back into sleep, the regretful thought came to me that her early death – and Dad's – were perhaps, in that respect, a mercy. If Tom, in my generation, couldn't take it, how would my utterly conventional parents have managed?

Or would they, perhaps, have surprised me? They were, after all, survivors of wartime, unlike me and Tom. My father fought at Monte Cassino, my mother was an air-raid warden. Maybe memories of pointless death make people glad of any new life. Maybe it is us, the squeamish me-generation, who find it hard to accept oddity.

It was only when the door-knocker sent peremptory crashes echoing through the house that I woke properly – around nine-thirty – to find Carla on the doorstep.

'Surprise!' she cried cheerfully. 'Jeremy and I thought we'd come and fetch you. He's picking up my secret Christmas present from the new plant nursery, I happen to know. He pretended he was just dropping me off to see how you were. But I had a brill idea, why don't you come with us now? Jay-Jay will only be half an hour, and we've managed to dump Harry on my sweet sweet neighbour. Hoorah! Pack a bag and come and start Christmas today!'

I stared, dishevelled on the doorstep in my long cotton nightie.

'Carla – the thing is – I don't think I can come for Christmas—'

'But Tom said it was *fine*! And Harry Samuel would miss you!'

'Carla, he's four months old, they don't miss people at that age. They don't even know it's Christmas. Honestly, it's sweet of you, but I can't – I've got a guest . . .'

'Oh.' Carla's lovely countenance, always easy to read, showed quite clearly that she knew Tom and I had had a disagreement, and that there was only one sort of 'guest' who, in her world, was likely to turn up in an estranged woman's house. 'Is he here—?'

'Not he. She. A friend who needs help with her baby.'

'Oh!' Relief flooded her face. 'You are a friend to the lame ducks, Auntie darling, always were. Well, the more the merrier, we can pop friend and baby in Jeremy's study – there's a sofabed, terribly comfy, and Harry Samuel can lend his travel cot for the sprog.'

'No. Sorry. Really, Carla, I can't come for Christmas. It's not something we really feel like celebrating this year. You'll understand why.' Her face fell, and I felt bad for using poor Sam as an excuse, when in truth my grief had been driven into abeyance so wonderfully by his child. 'Tom can do as he likes. He might come.'

'Doesn't he know your – guest?'

'No. It's a girl thing. Carla, really – it's sweet of you, but with this baby in the house I'm too tired even to make you a cup of tea. We've hardly slept, we're frazzled, you must remember what it's like?' But her bright face showed little understanding, and I remembered that Harry Samuel had been, in his early weeks, a 'clockwork baby' who kept a tidy schedule which even allowed for Carla's appointments with her personal trainer to be scheduled between feeds.

'We'll meet up after Christmas, OK?'

Finally she left, but as she wandered down the drive to meet Jeremy on his way from buying her some exotic shrub, I saw her take her mobile out and knew perfectly well that she was going to ring Sarah. Or Tom. Or both of them. Cursing inwardly, I made tea for me and for Allie and wished we were on an island, just the three of us. A warm island somewhere, in a sea sparkling with golden fish, with fruit trees and . . . I was sleepy again.

Allie, on the other hand, appeared a few minutes later and was wide awake. I admired her youthful powers of recovery, but the first symptom was that she seemed suddenly to feel the strangeness of her position as a guest. Over cereal at the kitchen table she said:

'You didn't have to do this for me, but I am so grateful. I was doing my nut, even with Jules to get the food in and tidy up a bit. Christ knows what I'd have done on my own.'

'I did have to do it,' I said slowly. 'For you and for Con. We can't pretend he's nothing to do with me, now can we?' She glanced up sharply, and I added, '—Though obviously, I've no *rights* over him.'

'I'm sorry,' said Allie unexpectedly. 'How did you know what I was thinking?'

'Not rocket science.'

She poked at her cereal with the spoon, submerging the flakes with exaggerated care. After a moment she asked:

'But your husband. What's he going to think?'

I settled on honesty.

'Tom would be horrified. He doesn't approve of me getting involved, and he doesn't think of the baby as a member of the family. Actually, he's quite angry with me already. We quarrelled about it, and he flounced off to his friend Malcolm and his therapist in Cambridge.'

'Gosh,' said Allie, reaching for more milk. 'So we're in the same boat, aren't we? Partners on the run. Heavy disapproval pouring on our heads. Who'd have thought one little baby would freak out so many people? And at Christmas, too. Herod rules.'

'Well, Julia's coming back, isn't she?'

I made myself say it in a hopeful, cheerful tone. The selfish demon in me wanted the crazy woman to stay in Africa indefinitely and leave me with my little miracle and my new young friend. Allie made a face, indicating to me that Julia would, indeed, come back, with all the temperamental problems inseparable from her presence. She didn't answer the question aloud, though. She merely said:

'Isn't Tom? Coming back, I mean?'

'Dunno.' I was a little shocked at the blitheness of my own tone. Deserted middle-aged wives were meant to have at least a tremor in their voice, surely.

'I don't truly know either,' said Allie more soberly. 'About Jules. Though I think she will. Nobody's said she won't. We didn't have a row, as such. But the thing is, she wasn't exactly bonding with Condy. He's got one body part too many for her liking.'

'But she loves you.' I did not know why I said it, but her face showed me that it was, by chance, the right thing to say.

'We-ell . . . yes.' She ate more cereal, finishing the milk, and we sat in a reasonably companionable silence until it was broken by the baby's imperious wail from his basket in the sitting-room.

It was later in the day that Allie returned to the subject, when we had both dozed again, tended Con, admired his pearly little toes and given him a bath in the kitchen sink. It began with one of her sudden upsets. She was changing a nappy upstairs while I cleaned the bathroom, and she accidentally laid the dirty one down on the clean white towel I had laid on the other half of the camping-mat. In our spirit of Blitz improvisation we had set up a secondary mat for the upstairs nappy changes. She gave a little scream.

'Oh shit! I mean, literally shit—!' I ran through, alarmed. 'I am so sorry – the clean towel – I am so hopeless at this – now I daren't put him down, oh God, I am no good—' She was clutching the smeary bare-bottomed baby, who squirmed in unease, and looking helplessly at the minor mess she had made.

'Don't worry – for heaven's sake – there are plenty of clean towels, look, the airing-cupboard's full of them. Here—' I threw the dirty one in the bathroom basket and laid out a fresh one. Allie burst into tears and I took the baby off her, looking with renewed affection on her thin, drawn, beautiful face; the thought flashed through my mind that I would have liked a daughter.

'Don't cry – it's OK – you're doing beautifully, look how contented he is – you're a good mother, Alexandra, don't let little things get you down.'

She went on crying as I wiped Con and dressed him; it seemed not to be stopping so I wrapped her child in an old red shawl and said, to distract her from her formless grief, 'Come on – let's take him for a walk round the garden. He can't have seen many trees yet.'

There was a light frost outside, and the air was coldly clean with a tang of the sea; as I had hoped, it revived her spirits. She brushed her sleeve across her face within a few moments and gave a watery smile. The baby was clearly interested in the patterns of light and branches, and flapped his arms towards them; she watched, fascinated.

'He does see stuff,' she said. 'It's amazing – the way he stares at you. Will he smile, soon?'

'Pretty soon. Four weeks, maybe . . . sometimes sooner. People always say it's just wind. But when it's real, you know. It's always a response to something.'

'Gosh, you do know a lot about babies.'

'I've seen a good few. You do, when you've got one of your own. It becomes a sort of club.'

'Not where I live.' Her face was shuttered again.

'There must be plenty of young mothers, in the city!'

'Yeah, but . . .'

'Julia?'

She turned away, and we walked in silence round the little orchard, then back across the frosty lawn, making a new set of wet footprints on the white grass. Warm in the house I brewed tea, and we sat at the table, Con on her lap nuzzling half-heartedly towards his next feed.

'I need to tell you about Julia,' she said abruptly. 'I don't think you understand how it is.'

Do I need to? I wondered. She ploughed on.

'Jules and I are completely different. Do you mind me talking about us being gay?'

'Course not.'

'Well, you have to understand how it's not straightforward. I'm *gay* gay. Never fancied men, ever. I like them, they're mates, they're a good laugh, sometimes they're actually a bit of a relief when women get too intense. I suppose that's how men feel about going to the pub with other men. Getting away from the navel-gazing touchy-feely girl thing. But when I fall in love it's always been women. I only want to hold women. I only want to go to bed with women. It's who I am. Hundred and fifty per cent woman, so gay gay gay. Ever since I was ten, I reckon it's been hard-wired.'

'You really don't dislike men?' I felt I was being a little slow. I know nothing of her world.

'Nah! My dad's great, in his way, though I don't see him because of the wicked stepmother, and when I was working I was friends with heaps of men on the circuit – you know I did cabaret, and stuff?'

'I vaguely heard. From Jackie.'

'Well, I had mates. Still have. Gay men, straight men, all ages, no problem. One of my best friends used to be my agent, who's fifty-plus with a huge red nose. Gave me bear-hugs. Like a big teddy. But I couldn't marry one. I did try straight sex, but, ugh.'

To my shame, I found myself glancing nervously at the baby, in case his tiny ears picked up unsuitable conversation; the absurdity made me blush and feel older than my years. Allie, with the same air of explaining to a slightly retarded student, carried on:

'Julia, on the other hand, is a different shade of gay. She's very 1970s, very Marilyn French. She wants a woman's world. A woman's realm.' She paused flicking the tablecloth, and irrelevantly muttered: 'Isn't there a magazine called *Woman's Realm*?'

I stayed quiet, and eventually she carried on. 'Jules thinks men are dangerous, and aggressive, and selfish, and altogether the worst half of the human race. She's got reasons for that. She's got history. I told you about her ghastly judge dad, and the AIDS thing. But it's become a sort of universal philosophy and a permanent mood. She can twist everything round to prove the rubbishness of men: every news item, every statistic. But if it wasn't for hating blokes, I'm not sure she'd be gay at all.'

'Really?' I was jolted, confused. Allie smiled.

'She's not that into sex, really. She's sort of austere. It's all principle with her. She isn't even like Jackie – Jackie goes both ways, and she had a horrible dad so she played at gay for a time. But Jacks doesn't really hate men. I think that's why she couldn't cope with Julia for very long.'

'She's dating one now. Sarah said.'

'Good for her. Very mainstream at heart, is our Jacks. Again, that's one of the reasons we had to split up. That, and all the agonizing about whether or not to spell her name with a sodding D. Which is ridiculous. But Julia, you see . . . with Julia, it's all in the mind and the will.'

'But isn't that awful for you?' I surprised myself by bursting out with this, but was overcome by a great sense of waste. Who – straight or gay – could fail to want this golden beauty with her Sam smile and her shining skin and easy sensual grace? 'I mean, if Julia's not really interested . . .'

'Yeah,' said Allie. 'Sometimes it is awful. It was a bit awful when I was working, she didn't like some of the acts I did. Not lapdancey stuff but quite risqué, quite sexy and ironic, I'll tell you about it some time. Only she thought it was just silly and undignified. She used to go spare about my red frilly corset, couldn't get the joke at all. Then with the baby it's been pretty grim, and I know that's about sex, too. The more I got plump and round and earth-mothery, the less interested she was. I thought being pregnant would be fantastic, and it was in a way, but she hated it.'

'So why stay?'

Allie sighed, shifting the baby who had begun to feed with avid determination.

'I love her,' she said simply. 'I understand her. She tries to make people's lives better, even if she does it in weird ways. She's not an ogre, though I can see she freaked you out, and your husband.' She gave me a direct, challenging glance. 'She wouldn't ever hurt Con, you know. Wouldn't hurt a fly. Very high principled.'

'But she won't *love* him.' It came out before I could think. 'Babies need *parents*. Two people who think they're wonderful. Unconditional love. From both directions.'

'Yeah. That is a bummer. But if I love her enough and I love Condy, and it all goes round in a sort of triangle . . .' She tossed her head, and her hair fell gold about her. 'If anything can make it work, Marion, it's love. Going round and round, filling the room, bouncing off the walls till it covers everything and makes everything all right. I woke up last night after the first proper sleep in ages, and I saw that. Like a sort of vision. We'll be OK because there's love and love, and two loves make three. I wouldn't have understood that before he was born, but they don't half teach you stuff quickly. Babies.'

Astonished respect and treacherous regret combined to silence me. Then:

'You're a bit of a heroine, you know, if you really think you can do that. Hold it together.'

'Yeah. Mother Heroine of the Glorious Soviet Republic. Not to mention world's fastest labour. Gimme a medal. But –' she grinned again now, and addressed the sucking baby – 'I do ser-lightly wish, dear Condy, that you'd had the common prudence to be born a girl.'

The baby fed on; we talked desultorily of other things. Watching her with the child was a curious amalgam of pain and pleasure. He looked just like my memory of baby Sam – or else my real memory was fading, replaced by this vigorous scrap of new life. My own breasts ached with longing to be his refuge and his nourishment. But then I glanced down at my fifty-year-old hands on the table between us, the rising sea of wrinkles foreshadowing the storms of old age; and I looked beyond them to where Allie's smooth young skin lay against his. At that moment, combined with the pain came gratitude that he had this strong young protectress, a guard from the right generation, and one who moreover was growing every minute in wisdom about life and love.

Then sorrow came back in a crashing wave, and it was not even sorrow for my lost Sam, but for myself: my youth, the clear-skinned past which would never come back. *Never glad confident morning again.* Who said that? Browning? Yes, *The Lost Leader.* He said it when Wordsworth accepted the

Laureateship. Perhaps people should never idealize other people. Or, indeed, idealize idealism itself. Julia did that, and she must be taught by this golden tigress that love outranks theory every time.

I was sleepy again, my thoughts woozy and confused as I watched the baby, who was now looking out over Allie's shoulder at the frosty garden where birds pecked at the garden feeder.

'Do you mind if I have a nap?'

'Of course not. I'm fine. Thanks again.' But as I stood up, she said hesitantly:

'Can I ask you something? After all the stuff I just said?'

'Mm. Sure.'

'I know you're not a bit like us. Me, and Jules, and Jackie, and most of the people I know. That's why I was so off with you before he was born, in the flat that day. You're almost a different kind of animal. Married, and straight, and all that.'

'I suppose so. What did you want to ask?'

She looked at me, clear eyes over the baby's woolly back.

'Do you think we're a mess? Our lives, I mean?'

'I'm not homophobic—'

'I didn't mean that. But do you? Do you think we're a bit of a mess?'

The polite negative died on my lips; I saw by her face that the question held seriousness. Weeks ago, if I had read about the pair in a magazine, I would probably have taken Tom's perspective and readily dismissed them as a self-indulgent bohemian mess – serial partnerships, odd ways of getting pregnant, disposable fathers, dusty lofts, edgy cabaret turns, stupid theories— Even after my first meeting with Julia, and Jackie's stumbling account of the pregnancy, I might honestly have said, 'Yes, you're a mess.' If the answer now was different, it also had to be honest. I took a moment, then said carefully:

'Actually, yes, I did. Until the last few days. Now, I don't think I can carry on thinking that. You have to judge by results, don't you?'

'Results?' She pulled down her sweater.

'A life,' I said. 'A life. Him. Where there's life there's hope.'

It was all too much and I was tired. A choking sensation rose in my throat. I did not want her to see me crying and turned my back to fiddle with something on the dresser. From behind me her voice, oddly gentle, said:

'I wouldn't have liked your world much, either, a couple of weeks ago. I'd have said it was stuffy bourgeois crap. But I'm starting to see the advantages of a proper airing-cupboard.'

24

'It's Christmas *Eve*!' Carla was on the phone, disbelieving and almost shrill. 'Tom's here, I thought you were coming for Christmas Day at least!'

'Carla – calm down – I told you. I'm here with a friend and her baby.'

'No, but it's Christmas! Bring them! Harry Samuel is making really sweet noises, I think he might say Mama – only they say Dada first, don't they, something to do with tongues developing? And he loves the tree lights – oh, Auntie Marion, do come over! Jeremy will fetch you all – poor Tom—'

I had forgotten it was Christmas Eve, and the first effect of this morning phone call was, even as Carla remonstrated, to make me start scribbling a shopping list. We had run out of some basic things, nursing mothers need good food, and our village shop believes in three-day Christmas breaks. The previous shopping trips had raised Mrs Feaveryear's eyebrows, but she solved the problem of the nappies in my bag all by herself, concluding, 'Ah, you've got your pretty niece visiting with her little one, thass lovely!' On my second trip to the shop I met Sarah and took care to be bright and insouciant and to say nothing. But I heard the proprietress delivering the same news to her as I left. 'Marion's got her little great-nephew staying; lovely to have a baby at Christmas.' I did not wait to hear Sarah's response. She must know perfectly well that Carla was in her own Poggenpohl kitchen making mince-pies and fussing over a goose, and that Tom was not far away. And now Sarah might have guessed which baby I had in the house, and which mother. I had muttered 'Damn' as I left, and again as I hauled the bag home. Damn, damn, damn. And now I must go shopping again.

When I got rid of Carla, I looked out and saw that Allie was in the garden showing Con the frosty bushes and looking for the robin. To my astonishment she informed me that she had never seen a robin: a South London childhood seemed never to have yielded such a sight. Our domestic routine had settled nicely in the past few days, undisturbed by anything but a couple of phone calls from Sarah. The second time she rang, before our cool encounter in the shop, Allie asked baldly:

'This friend who rings – why're you so cross with her?'

'She thinks I'm crazy. She's on Tom's side.'

'How d'you know? Do you mean she's against Con?'

'I think she's worked out that he's here. And you. I wish –' I added savagely – 'that I could hack into her emails again and see what sort of patronizing line she's spinning to bloody Tom.'

'Again?'

'I read them. While I was in London she was soothing him and agreeing that I'm a loony.'

Allie was silent. She pursed her lips, her face taking on a new expression. I was not quite prepared for the question she asked, and it flustered me badly.

'Do you love Tom?'

'Yes – of course – no – I don't know. I did. But when you're my age—'

'What's that got to do with it?'

'We've been married a long time. We've been through a lot. It's not like these great declarations of love that your generation thinks about. It's a mixture of habit and – well, habit.'

'Ever been with anyone else? Since, I mean?'

'No!'

'Obviously you do love him, then. Perhaps,' she added, 'Con and I should go away. Then he'd come back, wouldn't he, and you could sort yourselves out. I don't want to break you up by staying here. That'd be awful. I'll be OK now. I've got the knack.'

'Do you want to go?'

She dropped her eyes, then: 'Course not. Julia's away for weeks, I've had exactly one text which was all about the project. OK, I'll go a bit nuts in the flat. But I didn't come to break up the happy home. I can find somewhere else.'

'It wasn't a happy home you broke up. Not for months.'

'Marion,' she said more gently, with the new, softer wisdom I had seen in her before. 'Your son died. Of course you weren't happy. I get all that mother stuff now.' She looked at her baby, currently asleep in an old dresser-drawer on the kitchen table with a pink pashmina wrapped around him. 'God, if he died . . . ! You couldn't expect to be happy. Nobody could.'

But she stayed, and the comfortable connection between us grew, and the baby's every hour brought new and interesting joys. Carla's call on that Christmas Eve morning made me fleetingly guilty and shocked at my behaviour, avoiding my husband and relatives at Christmas; but the very concepts of 'husband' and 'Christmas' seemed vague and far away compared with the solid, gentle comfort of our lives. Carla rang again at lunchtime, when we were eating an onion soup made, with surprising brio, by Allie, and the domestic warmth of the moment made me use language which I later had good reason to regret.

'Auntie, are you totally sure Jeremy can't pick you up? I know you're just trying not to be a bother. We could make room for your friend and her baby, I'm sure.'

'No,' I said. 'We're happy here, just the three of us. Say Happy Christmas to Jeremy and Harry Sam for me. And Tom. But Allie and I are fine, just the two of us and the baby.' The words were to ring in my head, later.

After lunch we dozed, and then, as Allie and the baby slept on I made mince-pies, because it was, after all, Christmas, and our dinner the next day would be no more than a roast chicken and fruit salad. Seduced by the warm fruit smell I went to the cupboard under the stairs and looked at the decorations; many dated from Sam's childhood, and it had seemed to me that they would never go up again, not in this life. Most of them I could not look at without tears, but I pulled out a string of fairy lights and put them round the fireplace, then fetched ivy off the wall by the front door and twined it round the flex.

It looked so good that I took out the glass angels and added them, trembling on their paperclip hangers. When Allie came down in the early dusk the fire was lit, the lights on, and ivy shadows dancing on the walls. We propped Con's basket at an angle so he could see it all, and reflected in his wondering eyes we watched the flames and sparkles and points of coloured fire. His bare legs bicycled in furious appreciation.

'Christmas Eve!' said Allie. 'I remember . . .' And there in the firelight with the baby, sitting on the floor with her arms round her knees in the graceful comfort of youth, she told me a little about her childhood: her wayward mother and stolid father and the baby brother whose death broke up the family. 'She blamed Dad, I never knew why. It was some sort of quick fever, but apparently my mother said he would have had a car if he wasn't such a failure, and then he could have got the baby to the hospital instead of having to wait for the ambulance. I was five. She left after that.'

'So strange,' I said, staring into the fire, forgetting to be careful. 'To leave a child when you'd lost another one.'

'Well, she took my big brother.' Allie's lips thinned. 'Peter. He was ten. My dad wrote him letters and stuff, it broke him up a bit, but there weren't visits or anything. I never saw him again till I was twenty and he tracked me down at college to say hello. It was really awkward. Nothing in common, basically. He'd gone into the Army. No idea where he is. Or Mum. Though Dad once said he'd heard she died.'

Her bravely casual narration wrenched my sentimental heart.

'Why didn't your mum take both of you?'

'Didn't like girls, Dad used to say. Polar opposite of Julia, I suppose. He once told me that she used to get jealous when he said I was beautiful. Even when I was four.'

'So you stayed on with your dad?'

'Yep. Dad's great. He put food on the table, more or less, till I learnt how to, and from when I was fourteen he paid for my fencing lessons, God knows how.'

'Fencing?' This one was out of the blue.

'Oh God, yes. I was bloody good. It came in handy when I started the turn – you know, the sword act I do. Used to do.'

'A sword act?'

I must have looked comically astonished. Allie glanced across at me and laughed, and it was not the defensive satirical humour I saw so often in her but an open, happy sound. Turning back to the leaping flames she explained. 'Yep. I come on fully dressed, like one of the Three Musketeers and my assistant or one of the ASMs chucks fruit up – I can cut an apple in half and then quarters with two slashes before it hits the ground. Broadsword, obviously, not rapier. And peel a strip off an orange in mid-air. But with my other hand, and the blessing of Velcro—' she was laughing at me now '—I strip. Down to a thong and pasties – tassels, you know. It's a club act. Modern burlesque. I was *good*.'

'So you had to stop when you were pregnant?'

'Luckily for Julia. She can't stand that stuff. I thought she might be my fruit-thrower, but no. Says it's pretending to be ironic but really it's titillating the male punters. Which I deny. Blokes don't fancy a woman with a sharp sword and mask, even if she is in a sparkly corset. But yeah, I did stop when I got pregnant. After the third month it got tricky with the corset. Velcro can't hold everything.'

'Is it a good living?'

'Not bad. You know, that's exactly what my dad asked when I started doing it. Not "How much do you take off?" but, "What do you earn?"'

'I'm starting to like your dad.'

She grinned. 'Dad is great. Probably his fault I got hooked on glitz and showbiz. Once when I was fifteen he asked what I wanted for Christmas – we were always broke – and I said I just wanted something glamorous and sexy to put in the bath. And there on my bed in the morning was a parcel with a plastic duck, and he'd stuck sequins and knock-off Swarowski-type crystal bits on it. And then he came in and saw my face, and winked and handed over a bottle of Jo Malone. It was the latest thing, all us girls worshipped it, God knows how he knew. But I had the duck for years. And I spun out the Jo Malone a fair while, too.'

'Still see a lot of him?'

'He remarried seven years ago. Born-again Christian cow, Christine. Moved to Essex.'

'Ah. Difficult?'

'Every couple of months I talk to him on the phone when she's out. But she thinks I'm a sin machine, basically, so I don't rock the boat.' A brief bleakness came over her face. 'He's happy.' She sighed. 'And I know he doesn't think badly of me. When I came out as gay I was seventeen, and he just said, "Honeybun, you do what you need to do." So now he can do what he's got to do – which is Christine. Fair do's all round. Hey . . .'

'Mm? D'you want a mince-pie?'

'No thanks. Wanted to ask you, what was Sam like when he was a kid?'

I slid from the sofa to sit on the floor like her, using the couch as a backrest. It must have been a decade since I sat like this, sprawled student-style on the floor with nowhere further to fall. The years fell away, and I told her about Sam's first steps, first word ('Ducky! And it wasn't even a sequinned one like yours'). I told her about his enthusiasms and small terrors, his flaring tantrums and instant forgiveness, and the way he would bring back new best friends from school with delighted pride, and give away his best possessions in fits of sudden love.

'Like he did for us,' she said thoughtfully. 'I think he was fond of Jacks, you know. Funny spiky creature she is, but I got the impression he understood her. Better than I did. She said he was really kind, and totally cool about her conditions about the baby. He knew that her own dad was crap, so he understood that she was nervy about fathers. Though actually . . .'

'You mean you reckoned he'd stay in touch, when it came to the point? Know the child?'

She looked at me, mildly surprised at my intensity.

'Yep. I was going to say that. A couple of things he said, that she quoted to me – she obviously didn't realize what it meant, but I did. I didn't want him to have to *pay*, that would be so gross – but, I dunno. I had a good dad, I did look forward to it a bit. Once things had settled down. I quite like blokes, you know.' Suddenly, almost shockingly, her eyes filled with tears and she pulled her sleeve across her face. 'With all the drama, I haven't really taken in that the poor guy's dead.'

More than anything, I wanted to talk about Sam. But there would be other times, and I did not want her upset by the thought of the happy, if unconventional, relationship that might have been. Casting around for a subject while we were so confidential, I said:

'Jackie. How did you get together with her?'

'Oh, she knew my ex. Sonia was one of her tutors. And Sonia was dead against me having a baby, and Jackie was OK about it, so—' She grimaced.

'But then after a bit you left Jackie?'

'Yeah, I was horrible. I see that now. We were only together for less than a year. I shouldn't have fallen for Jules, but I did. It was a double hit for Jackie, since she'd had her own thing with Jules and it was her who introduced us . . . Jeez, I was vile to do that.'

There was real trouble in her face again now, and she glanced at the baby, who was starting to fall asleep, his eyes glazing and blinking. 'Con, your mother is a slut!'

I wanted to reassure her, in the warmth of that Christmas Eve, to soothe her conscience with partisan platitudes. But suddenly I felt that sense of danger. There was peril in this quick confidentiality. Too much warmth flaring too fast might cool into ashy dislike. If this friendship stampeded and declined because we had told too much, I could lose both her and the child. I heaved myself up off the floor, my creaking awkwardness a salutary reminder that we were not of the same generation, and said in a suitably mumsy tone:

'I'm going to make a Spanish omelette. I got eggs from the chicken place up the lane. That suit you?'

'Thanks.' She was a guest again, the danger past.

25

In the depths of that night, after one of the baby's erratic feeds, I went back to the stair-cupboard and pulled out another box. Rummaging in stealthy silence so as not to alert Allie, I pulled out one of the relics of Sam's babyhood: a mobile of mother-of-pearl, bought in Indonesia during our last childfree holiday and far too pretty to be thrown out with the plastic tat of modern infancy. The discs, pale as leaves of Honesty, were beautifully iridescent still beneath the dust; the dim, dead light from the horrid low-energy bulb Tom favoured in the hall was transformed and enlivened. I washed it and spent some time untangling the strings, then wrapped it in a red silk scarf to prevent more tangles, and eased it into an old hiking-sock of Tom's, to lay it across the end of the Moses basket.

'Your first stocking,' I whispered sentimentally to the sleeping baby, then crept back to bed to spend a troubled half-hour reviewing how slim was the possibility of his getting many future stockings. How could it be, how could these simple family celebrations happen in a household headed by the disapproving, the anti-materialist, atheist-feminist Julia Penderby who 'didn't do' Christmas? I consoled myself with the hope that my example, together with the memory of her father's sparkly duck, would help Allie to defy Julia's austerities.

But I could not be sure. I could not be sure of anything. Despite the surge of affectionate empathy I felt for the girl

– I still found it hard to believe she was in her mid-twenties – I knew little of her real life: her life as what Tom called a Crazy Dyke. Perhaps this companionable interlude of normality with me was just a lull, a false dawn. Airing-cupboard love. Perhaps I, and all that I longed to offer the child, were a brief Boden dream of Middle-England security. Allie's real world was one which for so many comfortable years had been invisible to me – a hip, cool, angry, edgy street-urban world, a right-on loft in Dalston where lorries hammered by belching harsh fumes. A world where a strip-burlesque fencing performer lived a vivid life (a screaming, scolding, slapping life) with a sour-faced hater of the male sex who cared more for unknown Africans than for the human beings closest to her. The baby lay in his basket beside my bed: fresh, unmarked, an angelic envoy from a simpler universe. At last I fell asleep, tears damp on the pillow.

Christmas Day dawned grey and damp, as it so often does. The magic frost was all gone, the robin silent. And the stove had bloody well gone out: the faithful Aga, symbol of our provincial Middle-England comfort, had temperamentally rejected its oil feed. I fiddled with the controls in the chilly kitchen and ruefully remembered my own mother stoking a coal stove and, with conscious irony, reciting Yeats's *Song of the Old Mother*:

> *I rise in the dawn and I kneel and blow*
> *Till the seed of the fire flicker and glow*
> *And then I must scrub, and bake, and sweep,*
> *Till stars are beginning to blink and peep;*
> *And the young lie long and dream in their bed*
> *Of the matching of ribbons for bosom and head,*
> *And their day goes over in idleness,*
> *And they sigh if the wind but lift a tress.*

While I must work, because I am old
And the seed of the fire grows feeble and cold.

But like my own mother I did not mind my role. As the warmth returned under my hands, and the kettle sang and the baby clothes dried on the rail, I felt a small treacherous happiness rising again. They were, at least, still with me. My world was not exciting but they were finding it comfortable, and in the long run humans will always edge towards comfort provided it does not hold too obvious a set of disadvantages. Making breakfast, crisp bacon and waffles with syrup, I felt a sudden unexpected wish that I was making it for Julia Penderby, too. Perhaps I could lure her closer to my way of thinking, like a wild bird tempted with crumbs. Perhaps even Tom could be lured, if the bacon was crisp enough. I laughed at the thought, aloud and alone in the kitchen, but the sense of optimism remained.

Allie woke for the final time at ten, glad of breakfast. Con's feeds, I noticed, were starting to form a pattern – an asymmetric pattern, but discernible. We had at least an hour's grace for her to eat, and shower, and dress; but when I went back for the tray I found her in her tattered T-shirt, going through her canvas bag and shuddering at the contents. There was little in it to feed any woman's vanity, certainly no Yeatsian ribbons to match. Remembering the anxious state I had found her in, that day in London, I was hardly surprised at her exiguous packing.

'Oh Jesus,' she said, without any rag of Christmas meaning. 'I have no bloody thing clean to wear!'

'I'm not your size by a long chalk,' I said, picking up her tray. 'But I can lend you some floppy stuff. You look good in most things.'

'And who cares anyway?' she said. 'Anything. Just a

borrow.' I kitted her out in a spare pair of knickers – she rejected a bra as if she had never seen one in her life, or at least not one with proper comfy straps – and a long wraparound black jersey skirt embroidered with red flowers which I sometimes wore in the evening ('Very Julia, very hippie,' she said drily, twirling it round her neat waist). Above it she put on my best red cashmere sweater and a long black cardigan, previously banished to the back of the wardrobe for making me look a frump. On her it could have gone straight to the Oscars, at least in the period of *Annie Hall*.

'Handy,' she said. 'I can pull the jumper up and feed, and hide him inside the cardigan if the vicar comes to call.'

'You might want a belt then, to put over the cardigan?' I rummaged in the wardrobe and found one of Tom's. Allie was in good spirits; so was Con, who showed his approval of the flapping fabric and bright colours with much kicking and staring and almost, we thought, a smile.

'We ought to go to *church*,' said Allie suddenly, after the mid-morning feed.

I was startled. 'Why?'

'It's Christmas Day! It's a village! Like in Miss Marple and stuff. There's a vicar, yeah? And I can see the church from here.' She craned out of the kitchen window. 'Bells. Heard them. Seems like a cool trad thing to do.'

She was full of surprises, I thought. Beguiling in her childlike tendency to seize the moment without consulting either the past or the future. I demurred. I am older. I am cautious.

'People will stare. You don't know what villages are like – everyone knows your business, and it'll already be all over the place that Tom isn't home.'

'So? If they know everything already, why not go sing a

carol? My dad used to take me. Not to a miserable sin-bashing church like Christine's, but we'd go up to Southwark Cathedral. And it was lovely, all Christmas stuff – oh, come on, Marion! There'll be candles, all twinkly! Con will love it—!'

I glanced at the neglected kitchen noticeboard, and there, sure enough, was the parish magazine. '11.30, family service,' I read. 'Oh God. I suppose if you insist – but they'll stare.'

'So we should care?' She danced a few steps round the kitchen, making imaginary sword-feints with a wooden spoon. 'You know, Marion, I feel normal for the first time in months. Yay!'

I saw why Julia Penderby would find her irresistible, for all her multiple disapprovals of pregnancy, boy-babies and swordplay in corsets. I remembered the tears and murmuring reassurances between the two of them up in the loft, and probably blushed. Allie Morris could make people do things, no question about it, and all without ever seeming to use any overt force. I remembered something Sarah said once about a rather sour and severe mutual acquaintance and her problem teenager: 'Never underestimate the power of plain old-fashioned charm in dealing with boys, even if you're their mother.' Con would have a charming mother, at least. And she might charm Julia into being no worse than any detached but benign Victorian father-figure. In my mind's eye I saw Julia with big curling moustaches, and only with difficulty refrained from sharing the image with Allie. Caution, caution.

So we went to church. Walking through the village with Con strapped on her chest in his papoose, Allie looked around, taking deep breaths and commenting, as visitors must, on the thinly invigorating quality of Norfolk air. 'Makes you realize that we basically breathe in chemical soup, where I live,' she said cheerfully. 'I wanted to move to Greenwich, top of the hill, but Julia won't hear of it. Is that the school?'

'Yes – Sam was there.'

'Sweet! Oh, it's so little – I love the climbing frame, is it an elephant?'

'Yes – they put it up in his last year there, and we were worried it wouldn't last, being wood – but they've kept repairing and oiling the teak and it's still in use. Look how polished the slide is.'

'It's wood – doesn't it splinter their poor little arses?'

'No – smooth as anything.'

She stood looking into the empty playground for a moment, then turned to me and said:

'So – it would be polished partly by Sam going down it? When he was little?'

'When he was nine or ten. Yes.'

'You've got history, here, haven't you? It must be funny . . . I mean, not funny, but—'

'Yes. It's OK. I don't mind, I like people talking about him. About all his life.'

She turned towards the schoolyard again, laid her hand on Con's sleeping head beneath its white woolly hat, and said to him:

'That's your daddy's old school, that is.' I marvelled at her ease. We walked on and came level with the village hall; my heart beat faster as it always does. Allie, oblivious, stopped again.

'I love the little hall! Does everything happen there? I mean, meetings and parties and stuff? Is there a stage? I once did a gig in a little hall like that, a local arts group. Some village in Suffolk, I dunno, Grumplingham St Bastard or something. Someone had moved down from London and booked the group I work with. I have to say they were very polite, but I doubt that Grumplingham has had any burlesque artists since. But this is where your village stuff happens, yeah?'

'Yes.' I thought I must tell her or violate the honesty which had grown between us. 'The playgroup was there. The school concerts used to be in there, and the Nativity plays. And Sam died there. An accident. The night before his 21st. We had his funeral tea there.'

She walked on, her silhouette with the papoose almost pregnant again, her hand on the sleeping baby's back. Then she said carefully:

'Have you been in there since?'

'How did you guess that I haven't?'

'Just did. You'll have to, though, won't you? If you go on living here?'

'Suppose so. If I do.'

'Well, it's your home. And it's lovely.'

'Home,' I said. 'Mm.'

We were at the church; people were trooping up the mossy path from the lych-gate, flocking in, saying 'Happy Christmas!' at the gate, glancing curiously at Allie and the baby, trying to place her. We have a fair few holiday cottagers in the village, but they are generally well known by sight. Still, she could have been someone's new daughter-in-law.

We found a pew near the back and I sat, a little nervous of the scrutiny, while Allie looked around quite unself-consciously, enjoying the candles and green branches. Our church does look very like a movie set, probably a movie with a script by Richard Curtis. The vicar emerged, beaming, and the service began with *O Come All Ye Faithful*. As the congregation stood and the flapping coats and shawls in front rearranged themselves, I saw that Sarah was two rows in front of us, protectively assisting her husband Edward to his feet. Every year, I reflected, the age gap between them seemed greater: Sarah's spare, energetic frame never changed but he became an old man by rapid stages. The sight of her gave me a pang; walking past the school had reminded me of how level, how humorous a friend she was during Sam's childhood, and how I never gave enough thought to what this sympathy must cost a woman whose only son died before he had any life at all. I remembered her at the hall, too, in the minutes after the accident, speaking calmly to the paramedics, helping me into the ambulance, quietly making the funeral arrangements work.

During the second carol Con woke abruptly and uttered a mew of protest at his imprisonment; I leaned across and unzipped the papoose for Allie, freeing his legs and lifting him out. She wriggled her shoulders and signalled, still singing Glorias, that I should keep him. He quietened, looking at the candles, his small body vibrating with the deeper organ notes, appearing to enjoy it all. The mew, however, had made Sarah turn briefly; she saw me and gave a guarded smile. Then her eye travelled to Allie, and with a sickening moment of premonition I saw her taking in the skirt and sweater which she had seen me – rather wider in silhouette – wearing a dozen times. She gave a curious, conciliatory half-smile, turned back towards the altar again and sang on. I bit my lip.

I would have to explain. That was obvious. Her nervous smile settled it, and melted my heart. It was the only brave and sensible thing to do: to lay all my cards on the table, get reconciled with my best and sanest friend, clear up all misunderstandings. If I told her quite calmly that I had accepted this child and this odd family and planned to keep it, whatever Tom said, she would have to see my point of view. My forgiving her for the emails would make us even, if I kept just calm about it. I would go up at the end of the service and wish her a happy Christmas, and make a date for a quiet talk.

All through the service I rehearsed inwardly what I might

say; but we were not two verses into *See Amid the Winter's Snow* when Condor was overwhelmed with hunger and original sin, and let out a bawl so piercing, so repetitively ferocious, that Allie and I looked at one another in dismay and of one accord, tiptoed out and dashed home up the dank lane to feed him.

So I never reconciled myself with Sarah that day. Which, as it happened, complicated matters more than it had any right to.

26

It was Boxing Day, and it was Carla on the phone. Again. 'Auntie, darling! Might you come over to lunch? Bring your friend? We're not having our big Boxing Day drinkies this year, it's too much with Harry teething. God, he shrieks! But Tom's here, and your nice friends Sarah and Edward are going to come for a drink on their way to another lunch—?'

'Oh, Carla, I can't – really, I'm just not up to driving over, getting the car out.'

'Jeremy will fetch you! And bring you back! He's started his Teetotal January early because he wants to start boozing again when we go ski-ing on the 26th – he and Tom were up till two o'clock this morning finishing off the Laphroaig to celebrate, but he's awake now and can't touch a drop even at lunch, so of course he'll drive you! So that's settled!'

'No. Carla, no. Really, Alexandra – my house-guest – is very tired, and her baby's very small. It wouldn't be fair.'

'Well, you come!'

'I have to stay with her.'

There was a silence, uncharacteristic of my ebullient niece. Then, in a more careful voice, she said:

'Right. Well, sorry to have butted in.'

There was something odd in her voice, almost a note of satisfaction, as if she had been running one final test and proved a thesis. I spotted danger just too late. She had hung up. But with my new-found skill at pushing away unpleasant thoughts and facts, I went back into the kitchen and showed Allie my favourite quick paprika-chicken recipe, and then we took our naps, all three of us. Then we went for a walk round the garden and down the bumpy field behind, to turn up the narrow lane behind Sarah's house and look back with a luxurious shiver at the welcoming glow of the house. Allie was transported.

'It's like living in a Christmas card!' Suddenly she hugged me, sideways-on so as not to disturb the sleeping bump in the papoose. 'Isn't it lovely?' I hugged her back.

We ate soup at six, then sat by the fire watching an old Bette Davis film about love, renunciation and beautifully tailored 1930's jackets. Allie, it turned out, shared my enthusiasm for high-toned vintage schlock with clear goodies and baddies, and admitted that of all the disadvantages of living with Julia, one of the worst was her partner's distaste for the movies. 'Though she puts up with stuff like *Lady Sings the Blues*. As long as the women are strong and gifted and hideously oppressed.'

'Not keen on the Queens of Country, then?' I said lazily. 'Not Tammy Wynette standing by her man, obviously, but I'd have thought she'd like tough types like Loretta Lynn—?'

'Puh-lease! The woman got married at 14! And put up with him flirting around! She's Hetero Central and proud of it!'

Allie stretched her long, pale, beautiful legs luxuriously to the fire, the skirt rucked up, its red-and-yellow flowers scattered around her. After a moment she said:

'I'm loving my little holiday, I really am. Thank you.'

I was startled by how sharply I was cut by the word 'holiday'. I knew, of course I knew in my reasonable mind, that she would go back when Julia returned from Africa. From our scraps of conversation I had understood a little of what lay between them, and my rational self accepted that it was real. Equally rationally I feared it, for the baby's sake and for mine, too. But I knew that Allie was not on the run from her partner. *Or not yet*, said a treacherous inner voice. All the same I had never thought of this time of ours in Norfolk as a holiday. It was more than that, surely, this almost sacred Christmas time of watching over the baby in the quiet winter house. I wanted to feel that it was a building-block, a beginning. Not a holiday. Holidays are temporary and not part of normal life. Holidays may not necessarily be repeated on the same terms and in the same place. I said carefully:

'Allie, I don't want you to think of it as a holiday.'

She started. 'I'm sorry, I haven't been much help with the meals and stuff—'

'I didn't mean that. I suppose I wanted you to think of this as . . . one of your homes. Yours and his.'

She was silent, biting her lip, staring at the flames.

'You know that could be difficult.'

'I do. Difficult isn't impossible, though, is it?'

'Sometimes.' The warmth of the evening had dissipated; soon she yawned.

'I'd better get some kip. Shall I have Condy's basket by me, tonight?'

Sorrowfully I accepted the offer. The beginning of the end.

It is strange how easy it is to be unaware of other people's mounting rage. You would think that if the person is close to you, even at a distance you would feel some sort of psychic storm brewing, some meteorological-emotional alteration in pressure gradients. A vast thunderstorm of fury should not be able to build undetected and break on you out of a sky you thought was blue. As it was, the only warning I got was a call from Sarah, a couple of days later.

'Marion. Don't hang up. Listen. Tom's on his way over. He's in an awful state, I wanted to warn you.'

'What's the matter?' I was relaxed, unaware. 'I know we took a bit of time out, and he's been upset about this tax business as well, but he's been seeing this therapist and I thought . . .'

I stopped, confused, because the fact is that I had not really thought about him at all for days. I had almost forgotten the grim, nocturnal conversation in my room. The new life, Con's life, had wiped away such darknesses. I suppose I just assumed that when Allie left, Tom would return and we would both begin to reorganize our attitudes. Sensibly, like adults of mature years.

'Oh, Marion!' Sarah's voice rose above its normal quiet contralto pitch. 'He's in a state, I've never seen anything like it. I tried to calm him down but I may have made things worse. Look, shall I come round—'

'No. Yes. I don't know.' I was getting frightened now. It was unlike Sarah to have her voice running up the octave and cracking in panic. The idea that Tom could harbour rage against anything more immediate than the Inland Revenue was almost ludicrous. 'I'll have a word with him. It's probably nothing—'

He was on the doorstep, banging and shouting.

'Marion! Let me in!'

'It isn't *locked*,' I said, banging the phone down and running to open the door. 'For heaven's sake, Tom, what is it?'

'What – how can you ask? You humiliate me, you spring this – this *lifestyle* of yours on everybody, you scandalize the village – you embrace your *woman* in full view – Sarah says I have to understand that people change – but common courtesy! Even Carla knows – she said I was like Ross in *Friends*, she said she understood how I felt—'

He was inside the hall now, taller than I remembered – I suppose I was used to Allie's delicate presence and the softness of the child. His face was flushed, almost purple. Even in the shock of the moment I found myself thinking that the old clichés were true: 'purple with rage'. It really happens. I put my hands up in front of me – another cliché, hands thrown up in defensive amazement. I said:

'Tom, what is your problem? I know we had a disagreement but—'

'You – you!' he stuttered. Tom is articulate, he is a lecturer and a television scientist, he never stutters. 'In my house, in our home, you publicly shack up with this dyke stripper woman half your age, and you ask what *my* problem is?'

'What?' I was thunderstruck, glad Allie was in the bathroom running taps and Con hard asleep in his basket in her room. 'I do *what*?'

'Don't you dare,' he hissed, his puffed fury filling the narrow hallway. 'I've had Boxing Day with Carla and Jeremy sympathizing, though I have to tell you Carla is actually pretty shocked. And Sarah and Edward were being all politically correct, telling me I have to understand people's –' he slipped into a sneering parody tone "– multiple sexualities" and comparing you to that dozy little researcher of hers who's suddenly given up dykeing and run off with a bloke—'

'But I'm not!' It burst out. 'Tom, we are not . . .'

Allie appeared at the top of the stairs naked, clutching a towel in front of her, a pink Venus risen from the foam, eyes wide.

'Are my jeans dry – ooh – sorry – I thought it was just the post—'

Tom stared at her retreating form for a moment, at the flash of her matchless buttock as she turned. Then he took a step back closer to the front door as if to look at me, saggy old me, in wondering comparison. He spoke more quietly.

'Lying makes it worse. Embracing in the lane. And everyone saw you two giggling and whispering in church. She was wearing your clothes. Don't deny it!'

'And did they see the baby?' Temper was coming to my aid now, not before time. 'She's not a lover, she's a friend. I'm helping her because she's got a new baby. As a matter of fact, you smug, stupid tit, it's our grandson. Sam's son. Get used to it.'

He could not speak. I feared for a moment that he would collapse and die in front of me and I actually moved forward, reaching out a hand to support him. The front door was still wide open behind him, and his silhouette against the brightness suddenly changed; too late, I saw that he was raising his fist to me. In slow motion I saw it advancing, then in a brief salutary moment saw him open his hand, so that what landed on the side of my face was a slap rather than a punch. I staggered and – oh, the cartoon quality of these moments! – yelped, 'Help!'

I had not seen the other man coming up the path. When I raised my face from its defensive aversion there he was, quick and fit and young, grappling a surprised Tom from behind, holding him off me.

I could see, even in that moment, that he need not have bothered. Your middle-aged academic is rarely more than a one-slap chap, and my husband's vigorous anger had deflated in shame. Certainly the young man need not have bothered wrestling Tom to the ground. I stood above them and said so.

'It's OK. For heaven's sake. Let him go.'

'You sure, madam?' The young man cautiously released Tom's arm and stood up, brushing down his cheap suit, looking back at the path for the case he had dropped. Tom rolled over and sat up, shaken. He glanced at me and then followed my gaze towards the man and the case. It bore a small but unmistakeable gold logo: the circled crown of Her Majesty's Revenue and Customs. I knew it well from the pile of unopened letters which Allie and I, in our days of maternal peacefulness, had allowed to pile up on the kitchen dresser.

27

There are advantages to having been raised by inhibited, war-hardened parents whose favourite films starred Celia Johnson. I was a teenager in the Sixties, certainly, I wore floppy Indian dresses and paid lip-service to the belief that the thing to do was to 'let it all hang out'. But childhood influences are stronger than cement, and deep down I always knew that in a moment of crisis I was more likely to tuck it all back in. Tidily. I pulled Tom to his feet, smoothed my hair and with difficulty fought back an impulse to smooth his, which was standing on end, badger-striped and crazy. I said to the young man:

'Do come in. I'm sorry about that, it was nothing, but your instincts were very gentlemanly.'

He blushed, poor youth, to the roots of his hair.

'I was in the Army for a bit,' he said apologetically. 'It comes natural.' Blushing more he corrected himself. 'Natural*ly*.'

Tom was still speechless, and when I gestured towards the living-room door he went in without a backward glance and sat heavily on the sofa, staring at the blank television screen as if it might hold an answer.

'Oh,' I said brightly to the taxman. 'The Army. Of course. Why did you leave?' Good God. I was making small-talk.

He tapped his knee. 'Injured, ma'am. Ramadi. Iraq war. From here down is mainly carbon fibre.'

'Goodness, though, you're quick on your feet!'

'One can stay pretty fit.' His accent was a curious mixture of Estuary and officer-speak; I guessed that he had risen quickly and competently in the Army and found himself changing class.

'Well, I daresay you came here on a mission,' I said. 'I think I can guess. Perhaps we should give my husband a moment or two then go and have a chat about it. Tea, or coffee?'

But the lad was staring past me, at the staircase.

'Allie?' he said, and his officer voice had vanished again. 'It never is!'

The laws of coincidence – 'elfin coincidence' Chesterton called it – have been argued and debunked down all the centuries. Novelists and playwrights eschew it for fear of being mocked by critics, yet when you think about stories of reunited twins, unlikely meetings, or long-lost engagement rings cut from the belly of fishes forty years later, you find that these marvels occur just as often in sober newspaper reports as in fiction. Some time after the dramatic events in my hallway I read Milan Kundera and copied out the lines:

> Without realizing it, the individual composes his life according to the laws of beauty even in times of greatest distress.

Kindly Kundera concludes from this that it is wrong to chide novelists for mysterious coincidences, and equally wrong to be blind to them when they happen, lest you deprive your life of 'a dimension of beauty'. I have thought of this often, remembering the odd phenomena – a vivid anniversary sunrise, a flower blooming out of season – which I connect to my lost Sam. Accept the dimension of beauty, accept the coincidence because it is beautiful.

Such sweet philosophy was far from my mind in those

confused moments when it became clear that some gently mocking fate had enlisted the help of a misguided war, a shelling outside Ramadi, and Her Majesty's Revenue and Customs service. And that it had done these things simply in order to bring Alexandra's brother Peter to the bottom of the stairs where she stood, wearing a borrowed skirt and holding a new baby.

'Peter?' she said, incredulous, and I found myself darting forward in case she dropped Con in her shock. 'How the fuck did you find me here?'

'I didn't,' said the tax collector helplessly. 'I was sent to see Mr Faulkner. The office sent me. Are you – I mean, do you live here?' He remembered himself and said to me: 'Mrs Faulkner, I am so terribly sorry, this is – this is – it's just that my sister . . . I haven't seen her for a bit.'

Allie descended the last few steps and handed the baby to me. She put her hands on her brother's slack arms, said, 'It's actually rather cool to see you,' and (not having been raised in quite such a stiff-lipped generation as me) burst into tears. Peter, startled but game, his reserve perhaps eroded by war and hospital and disappointment, folded her in a ready hug and said, 'There, pet, it's OK. It's good to see you. Why are you here? Is Dad OK?'

'Dunno. Months since I spoke to him. I live with this woman—'

'Not Mrs Faulkner?'

'No! Not *this* one. A woman called Julia. So seeing Dad wasn't really easy—'

'Ah. Yeah. He visited me a couple of times when I was in hospital with the leg. He said she was sort of anti-family.' He let her go and turned to me. 'We'll catch up later, perhaps. Mrs Faulkner, I really am sorry. It's just my sister, we haven't seen each other, it's complicated.'

'Yes. I know all about it. Don't worry. Was it tea or coffee?'

The offer popped out without thought for the problems involved in making either. I was still holding the baby, and Allie did not look fit to take him, as she was leaning against the wall, her head thrown back, eyes closed, hair loose as a Maenad's, saying, 'God . . . so strange . . . I don't get it!' and other unhelpful exclamations. I went through to the sitting-room, glanced at the staring figure of my husband, his hair still standing up in grey-black tufts, and pulled a couple of cushions off the armchair to lay Con down on the floor. The baby was awake and seemed temporarily quite content, his big eyes fixing with interest on whatever came into view. I was just about to put him on the cushions when Tom's voice behind me said:

'No, give him to me. Be safer. He might roll off.'

'He can't roll yet. And are you – are you fit?'

'I'm not crazy,' he said quietly. 'I was, but I'm not. I'm sorry. I can't believe I hit you.'

'Slapped,' I said. 'Not hit.'

'Same thing. Look, I could hold the baby while you give this man his tea.'

I still could not give up the child to him. I glanced out into the hall, where Allie and Peter were talking quietly, his hand on her shoulder, she still sniffing between words. At least she was close, in case anything happened. All the same, fear prickled in me.

'Tom,' I said suddenly. 'You do know what baby this is, don't you?'

'Yes. I guessed. Look, I won't hurt him.'

'He's called Condor.'

Amazingly, like a shaft of sunlight after a storm, Tom's face lit up in a smile and he said drily:

'Even that won't provoke me. I've shot my bolt. Come on, Condor.'

I walked back to the kitchen, barely able to feel the floor

beneath my feet, shaking with emotions I could not name. I burned my hand, not badly, on steam from the kettle but eventually managed four cups of instant coffee and took them through. Peter was standing, still awkward, near the window with his briefcase at his feet. Allie was sitting on the cushions, regarding Tom, who was watching the baby watching him. She looked up at me, accepting the coffee, and said:

'I don't think I've ever seen a grandfather. Not in the act of grandfathering, as it were. Pete and I never had one.'

'We did,' said Peter unexpectedly. 'Mum's dad. We used to see him after we left. He and Mum made up, we lived there for a bit. He'd refused to see her after she took up with Dad, because he'd been in jail.'

'He *what?*'

'Only for a bit. Robbery. When he was nineteen or something.'

'Bloody hell!' said Allie. 'Family skeletons bursting out of every wardrobe today. Oh Pete! Do you know you're an uncle?'

'Bloody hell!' echoed the young man, apparently relaxing into the occasion and forgetting his tax-gatherer status. 'That's yours, then? I thought you might be nannying it or something. Cute baby.'

'Yep. And this is his Grandma Marion, and that is his grandad you just knocked over.'

'I don't mind,' said Tom quite meekly. 'I asked for it. No, not there, it might spill on the baby.' I put his mug further away and took a long, too-hot draught of my own.

We all paused and drank in a kind of amazed contentment. I found myself gazing at Allie's brother: he was darker than her, but hardly looked his five years older, though in repose his mouth showed lines of past pain. His eyes were good though: clear and honest, and when they rested on his sister they held a surprised fondness I found almost too touching to observe. Family, I thought; and felt a familiar pang of sorrow that I had never given my own son a sibling. Still, he or she would have been a sad sibling now, so perhaps it was best. And it was not as if my own brother and I ever give one another such fond looks. One must not be sentimental.

A silence had fallen on the five of us, and it was Con who broke it first with a whimper, a wriggle and an imperious, hungry cry. Allie jumped up and went to get him.

Peter, as if woken from a dream, remembered his own needs and struggled back to formality. Tom's newly baby-free status perhaps made him a more legitimate target for taxation's arrows, even though his hair was still standing on end and his expression dazed.

'Mr Faulkner. My name is Peter Morris, of the Norwich office of Her Majesty's Revenue and Customs and I have to ask you for payment of monies due to the Inland Revenue, referring to our letters of—'

'Isn't it odd how they say "monies"?' said Allie, hitching up her sweater to put the baby to her breast. 'Monies. Who else says that?'

'There's a story told about Frank Muir and Denis Norden,' said Tom, still rather vague in his manner. 'I think it was them. It's a BBC apocryphal tale. That they got overpaid by the Corporation years ago and when they were asked for it back they just wrote a letter saying, "We regret we have no mechanism for the returning of monies". And that was the end of it. Mechanisms and monies trumped everything.'

'I have to ask,' said Peter rather desperately, 'that these monies due be remitted to me as of this date—'

'I'm sorry,' said Tom, getting up. 'I'll write a cheque. I think I have been a little off my head lately.'

'There's a penalty included,' said Peter, sounding relieved

and human once more. 'Sorry about that. You can appeal against the penalty if you've been ill.'

'No, no. I deserve it. How much?'

Peter named the sum – twenty-five thousand pounds and some random pence – and Tom winced only slightly as he crossed to the desk, wrote the cheque on our offset mortgage account and said to me:

'Sorry, Marion. I'll put it back out of my investments, but this is the only cheque book that'll work straight away.' And to Peter, conversationally: 'What do you do, anyway, if the cheque bounces?'

'Bailiffs,' said Peter with a grin. 'And court. The full Monty. It all seemed cleaner, somehow, in the old days when I just used to shoot at people from a tank.'

'You are *rich*,' said Allie to Tom, a little flirtatiously. 'Just writing a cheque like that! Julia would spit. Capitalist!'

'Surely writing a cheque like that just means I *was* rich. A minute ago.'

He smiled. He was flirting too. I suddenly found the whole situation so unreal that I had to go alone to the kitchen, to shake my head and stamp my feet as if they were numb. Or perhaps what unnerved me was the casual mention of Julia. From where I stood, leaning on the worktop, I could hear shared laughter rising from the three of them with a sense of tension released, like a chorus of reconciliation in the final act of an opera.

But it was not a final act, not by a long way. The gathering had, for a moment, felt so like happy family heaven that the thought of Julia and her inevitable return struck me like a blow. A boy baby, an uncle, a grandfather, a comfortable and undisguisably middle-class sitting-room . . . the scene would appal her. The very uttering of her name in this setting seemed to create a black, swoopy shadow over it, a furious avenging vulture. Suddenly I saw it all through Julia's hard, uncompromising eyes: the almost casual writing of an eye-wateringly large tax cheque, the flowered wallpaper, the pot-pourri, the watercolours and, God help us, even a small hunting scene in oils on the wall. It had belonged to Tom's father and was kept for sentimental reasons, and I am sure no foxes were harmed in the painting of this picture. But all the same. What would Julia say, to see her lover so much at home in this bourgeois cartoon?

Allie and Con would have to go home to her, because in the end it is the primary intimacy that counts. And I would have to mend my fences with Tom for the same reason. This lovely scene, this happy ending, was a mirage.

28

The mirage, the phoney war, lasted two weeks longer. They were good weeks. Peter Morris, reverting to his dutiful Revenue persona, insisted on leaving promptly for his HQ in Norwich with Tom's cheque, saying that he would just have time to call on a farmer outside Dereham 'who'll probably get the shotgun out like he did last time'. The idea seemed to cheer him up; I suppose once a soldier, always a soldier. Allie, equally insistent and with only a cursory glance at me for consent, asked him to come back at the weekend and catch up. 'Such a good chance, with Jules out of the way,' she said, and again I squirmed inwardly at the mention of Julia and the acknowledgement that her absence could not stretch forever.

Tom and I opted to use the last of the day in a walk down to the seashore. 'We need to talk, if it's OK with you.' The beach was his idea; I would not, remembering our last beach walk, have chosen that route. As we reached the door I stopped dead and said: 'Oh God. Sarah. I ought to ring her, she was worried about you coming.'

Tom nodded, and I stepped back inside and rang. There was no answer, so I left a brief reassuring message – 'Don't worry, all sorted' – and we walked on down the path in a silence that was only slightly constrained. I kept glancing sideways at my husband, shocked by his very normality. It had been, I saw now, many months since I saw him like this. We had got to the edge of the shingle before he said formally:

'I have to apologize. I think I went nuts.'

'I haven't been completely normal myself. Not at first, anyway.'

'My therapist chap doesn't like me saying the word nuts, but I tell him I'm a scientist so I like accuracy. Nuts. I was. That business about the tax . . . I was overreacting. For months. It seemed to represent everything, as if it was even to blame for Sam falling off the ladder. Nuts.'

'Would the therapist prefer you to call it post-traumatic shock?'

'Yes, I suppose so. Shellshock. That's what we've had. But are *you* OK, sweetheart?' He turned to me with real concern, and I realized that this too had been missing. On both sides.

'Yes. I think so. But I'm frightened.'

'Of what?'

'Julia Penderby coming back. She was your gipsy-type woman, remember, when it all started, and she's unequivocal about the baby, and us, and, oh dear!'

'Oh,' said Tom heavily. 'I know all about Julia now. And her views. And Alexandra. And that bloody little flake researcher girl Jacqueline. She and Sarah have more or less filled me in.' His lightness of mood had vanished, but after a moment he said: 'I have to admit that to my surprise I rather liked Alexandra when I met her just now. That might just have been the bang on the head, though.'

'No, she's lovely. I've grown terribly fond of her. But I don't know why on earth you got it into your head that we were . . . mm . . . involved.' I felt myself growing pink.

'Oh God,' said Tom. He stopped, stooped and picked up a handful of pebbles. Throwing them one by one into the grey, quiet sea for emphasis he said: 'One – Sarah told me what you'd gone looking for. I was horrified. Embarrassed and horrified and generally off my head.'

'Yes. I saw your emails to Sarah.'

'Oh God . . . how? Well, never mind. Two, I heard you were back, with a blonde woman and a baby in tow.' The pebble splashed. 'Three –' another, more viciously hurled, pebble hit the water – 'Jacqueline told us Julia was against the baby, and would probably throw Alexandra out in the end because she never sticks with the same woman for long. And she said a lot about Alexandra. Made her out to be pretty ruthless, a vamp, told us about her making her living lapdancing with swords.'

'It wasn't lapdancing! It's performance art.'

'As you wish. Anyway, *four* –' he threw the biggest stone, hard – 'Sarah then sees you giggling in church, wearing each other's clothes and dashing off together without speaking to anyone, and then apparently hugging in the lane—?'

'It was a quick, friendly hug. Look, I've hugged lots of women in my time – maybe not Sarah because you know she's not huggy . . .'

He grimaced and raised a hand to stop me. 'I know. I know. But she thought what she thought. And in a caring, Sarah, way she starts to prepare me for the possibility that you might be Finding Your True Self. And how I mustn't take it personally. And how lots of people have dual sexual identities.' He dropped the rest of the pebbles and fell silent. I walked on a few paces and then, without pebbles, I said:

'Well. *One*, I was only ever concerned about the baby. Which, by the way, I delivered. It was an emergency, and providential that I was there. *Two*, Allie only came here because her rather tough partner has gone to Africa for some charity, and left her all alone in this awful attic flat, and she needed help with Con. *Three*, there has never been the slightest thing between us and never would be, I am not remotely lesbian, Allie loves Julia, and Sarah is a dirty-minded cow.'

'She was trying to help. Being liberal and modern, all that.'

'Liberals ought to bloody well wait until they're sure there's something to tolerate, before they start chucking dirty great lumps of toleration at people who don't need it.'

'She meant well.'

'Yes, but how would she like it if I suddenly started being all understanding about her having a drug habit she hadn't got, or shoplifting she wasn't doing?'

'True.' We walked on, and soon of one accord turned back. Dusk was falling and a hazy half-moon brightening. I took his hand and it seemed natural to be holding it, dry and warm and familiar these twenty-five years.

'Will you stay?'

'If I may.'

'It was wonderful seeing you with Con, earlier.'

His hand in mine changed, almost imperceptibly: a tightening of muscles, a loss of ease.

'Marion . . .'

'Yes?' My breathing changed, and our pace of walking slowed. We were back on the lane now, between high hedges, and our footsteps echoed in the emptiness.

'I don't want you to get the wrong idea. I held the baby and I was glad to. Just to help out. As if it was any baby. I hate to see them on floor cushions, all vulnerable. And I won't be rude about him any more because of the way he was conceived. I see now that I was being hateful. But it isn't because I think of him as Sam's child.'

'As what, then?'

'Just as a baby. Someone else's baby. One gives all babies a sort of – a sort of honour. That's all it is. Once they're here, you have to respect them. I didn't want some tax inspector to go tripping over him on the cushions.'

'But he *is* Sam's child! Our grandchild. I feel it, I see it, it's real.'

Tom did not answer.

'He may be. OK, he is. Biologically.'

'You're a biologist. You should respect DNA, heredity—'

'DNA isn't everything.'

We had reached the house. Inside, Allie was chopping vegetables for a stir-fry.

'We're three for supper, right?'

'Right,' said Tom, and smiled at her, an open, easy smile. He had got over our conversation faster than I ever could.

Peter came back, as promised, and Allie – her energy returning with Con's more decorous night routines – made up the spare room for him, and for three nights over the New Year we were four at table, laughing and exchanging life stories like any family of friends. Peter was good value, relating without a trace of self-pity his wandering life with an unsettled mother and his sequence of homes: a grandfather's flat over a video shop in Milton Keynes ('I could borrow anything, my entire sex education has been in the hands of Sharon Stone'), a council flat where his mother traded cannabis, and a brief spell in Morocco ('Unspeakable. Mum had this boyfriend who worked as a nurse orderly in a sex-change clinic and frightened me with pervy stories about it').

When she died he was seventeen and without a second thought left school and joined the Army – 'looking for a family, I guess'. He rapidly gained a commission. He was an infantry lieutenant serving a second tour in Iraq when a roadside bomb sent a chunk of flying metal through his leg.

Invalided home, without family, he managed to make contact with his father, who saw him through hospital – 'though his new wife didn't seem keen for me to come to the house. She's a pacifist, apparently. But I wanted to see you, too, Al.'

'That's so sweet,' she said, fond eyes on her brother.

'I just remembered this chirpy little sister and thought you'd be someone to know. Specially when Dad told me that you'd taken up fencing, because weirdly I did that in the Army. I was good.'

'Oh, wow!'

'Knowing you did it too made me feel I actually had a sister. It was so awkward, that time we met before, when you were at college. But Dad said it was best not to bother you, you live with this troublesome broad who hates guys.'

'She does,' said Allie. 'But who knows, you might have cured her?' She grimaced. 'Now, why did I say something that stupid? But you could have come to see me anyway. She does go *out*.'

'Anyway. I reckoned I'd find you, but I had to find a job first. And the Army were pretty keen not to have me propping up a headquarters desk, and they seemed to have this resettlement deal with HM Rev and Customs. So I took the job. Had it nearly two years. Being out on the road is the best bit, but I'd rather find something else. You don't get many hot dates once girls find out you're a taxman.'

Tom, who had been listening to the young man with approving interest, made a few suggestions which seemed to enthuse him, mostly about the possibility of doing a degree and changing direction.

'I did quite fancy teaching,' said Peter. 'Dunno why, but in the Army I loved the training jobs. But I only got one A-level, maths, and that was only 'cos I took it a year early.'

Tom came up with constructive suggestions, citing fast-track foundation courses at his university and expounding on the intricacy of mature student grants. Allie listened, I dished up food and enjoyed the harmony, and the baby was handed from lap to lap. I watched Tom when it was his turn, but he was impassive, gentle, impersonal. Nothing changed.

When at last the New Year party broke up, Tom said that he ought to go back to the long-suffering Malcolm's flat in Cambridge to collect his things 'and sign off the therapist'.

'You sure about that?' I asked, when we were alone that afternoon in the garden. 'Is everything OK with you, now?'

'Well, what do you think? Looks like it.'

'Yeah, but—' I wanted to talk about Con again, but thought better of it. Instead I came at the subject obliquely.

'Allie had a text yesterday,' I said. 'Julia's got a date to come back. I think it's quite soon.'

'Well, I'm sure you'll miss her. And I do like the brother. I asked him back next weekend, I hope that's OK? I was going to talk to UEA about what sort of support he could expect. I reckon I could get a bit out of the Army, too. And I've been asked to propose a new series, and I'd happily give him some part-time research.'

'That's good,' I said absently. 'But yes, I'll miss Allie. And the baby. We'll all miss Con.' The child had begun to smile, rarely but beautifully.

'I'm sure you will,' said Tom, always careful about pronouns. 'I want to have a look at that loose pane on the cold-frame.' We walked our separate ways in silence.

Allie was in the kitchen. She looked different these last days: pink-cheeked, rested and properly fed, her beauty had become less ethereal and lost its edge of orphan vulnerability. Not for the first time I wished she was my daughter, or daughter-in-law. From time to time I had seen Tom looking at her and been almost certain that he too saw the odd resemblance to Sam: the resemblance which perhaps led Jackie to her fateful choice of our son as a donor. Knowing Allie now, it seemed even more incredible that she had so meekly given in to the erratic Jacqueline over this. Impulsively, I asked her:

'Allie – what was it like with Jackie? I mean, you and her? About the baby.'

She looked at me, amused.

'Why? You're always asking about Jacks.'

'Because it was you two who first decided to have Condor.'
This was not quite true. It was because I needed to get her
talking about Julia, unguarded. I needed to quiet my own
terrors.

'Oh, I get it. Yes, I can see that now. You'd want to know
a bit about that. Well, Jackie . . . !' She paused, an egg-beater
in her hand dripping unheeded onto the worktop. 'You probably think she's a bit of a flake.'

'Well, rather young, certainly. Compared to you.'

'It wasn't like that, back then. There's only two years in it,
and I was much flakier – I was doing my act, waitressing a
bit, and going to gay pub sessions. Jacks was your serious
clever postgrad student, full of causes and all that. And she
was a bit famous because she was political and she'd lived
with Julia and changed her name to spell it with a D. And
she'd apparently dumped Jules, not the other way round . . .'
She looked at me and sighed. 'You won't get it, but I was a
bit in awe of her. It was a funny bubble we lived in, just our
little East London gay lefty gang against the world of homophobic capitalist bastards. And Jackie was struck on me, and
I thought she was sweet, and cool. And we moved in together
and it lasted a while till I behaved so badly and went off with
Julia. Even though Jacks was keener on my having a baby.'

'You were young to be wanting a baby so much.'

'I pretended it was 'cos the biological clock was ticking.
I think I told her a few lies about how old I was, actually.'
She shrugged, embarrassed. 'Really, I think I just wanted
family. And I kept having dreams about my little brother
dying, and Mum screaming at Dad and going. Perhaps I
thought I could make everything better by keeping one alive.'
She began beating the eggs again. 'I didn't know that then,
though, obviously. It's only since Condy's been born that I've

worked it all out. Anyway, like I said, I bullied Jacks into backing me up, and then I went and left her. I'm a cow, you know? I don't know why anyone puts up with me.'

'Everyone does one or two stupid things in their twenties.'

'Did you?'

'Mm. Before I met Tom. I said yes to a man who proposed to me, then panicked and left the ring and a note. I still feel lousy about it.'

'Awful, isn't it?'

'We make up for these things as time goes on. One of the ways we make up for it is by putting up with other people doing rotten things to us, and forgiving them.'

'Would you have been angry with Sam about the sperm thing, if he'd lived?'

'For a bit. Yes. Probably. But now . . .'

'I know.' She was still dripping egg mixture on the worktop. 'Anyway, like I told you before, Jacks threw a wobbler and said if I went to a sperm bank it might be some Tory bastard's kid so she couldn't love it. I told her I don't think they have to put their politics down on the form along with colour of eyes and stuff. But she insisted on knowing who it was. But now I know it doesn't actually matter. He's who he is. Though I'm glad he's got a cool Grandma, obviously.' While I digested this lovely compliment she set the bowl aside and looked vaguely around for the frying-pan. 'I thought I'd make an omelette?'

She dribbled oil into the pan and waited for it to heat, then looked around again, having forgotten where she put the beaten eggs. Watching Allie cook was, to my housewifely soul, halfway between amusement and torment.

'So that was it,' she said, when she had found it on the dresser. 'To be honest, I didn't think it would work first go. Then I went off with Julia and dumped Jackie. Oh, I am a cow!' She put the pan on the heat and frowned at it. 'Julia!

I sometimes think life would be easier if she hadn't been invented.'

'Why?' The conversation had come to the point I had wanted.

'Well . . . like I said, we all sort of worshipped the idea of Jules, who'd turned her back on her crap posh family and all their values and all that, and stood up for women. I badgered Jacks to introduce us. Poor girl, I reckon she was a bit proud of being friends with the Queen Bee.' She grimaced. 'I let her down. But actually it's come out OK, since she's now gone straight. It's much easier being straight than gay in this world, you know.'

'I bet. But you were pregnant. Was Julia pleased?' I held my breath; Julia's feelings for the baby were more intensely important to me than I wanted Allie to know.

'Ah. Well. I didn't actually tell her. I was only two months gone. It was Jackie who told her, on a rather wild night when she came round shouting.'

'What did she say?'

'She went very quiet and strict and dignified. You know—'

'I think I've seen her in that state, when I first came to the DAN office.'

'Yep. Well, she said we had to have the sex test. That was the first thing she said.'

'So you did, with your alternative woman . . .'

'Shona. Hebridean witch magic stuff. Hazel twigs. And it was a girl, so Geronimo! All was well.' The omelette, neglected, was hardening fast; she glanced down and hastily scraped the sides inwards and let the liquid flow. 'Jules started to get quite keen on the idea of us raising a daughter, to be a strong, free woman and an example to all. Tamasin. It means something in some old language.'

'It's the female of Thomas! Thomasina, Tamsin, Tamasin—'

'No, it means warrior woman. In Hindi or Turkish or something. She says, anyway. Only now, obviously, he's a boy.' The egg she had spilled on the hotplate was sending up an acrid smell of burning. With difficulty I restrained myself from helping.

'Will it be OK? Julia and Con?' The question hung on the air.

'No idea.' She folded the omelette untidily in the big pan, looked around for the salad she had made earlier and lost, spotted it on the scullery draining-board and called, 'Tom! Supper!' for all the world as if she had lived with us for years.

29

After the New Year holiday I went back to work; things were slack enough at Eric's and my other clients, and I found that I could do mornings from nine till one and keep the afternoons clear. Tom brought back his bags from Cambridge, and sent Malcolm a case of rather good wine and another to Sarah and Edward (this amused Allie no end – 'You lot have a whole language of your own, hey? Wine instead of hugs?').

He had meetings in Norwich about the new university term schedule, so Allie and Con were left alone several mornings. She explored the village with the ever-heavier Con in his sling, and reported that since Tom's return the shop staff and passers-by treated her quite differently, with cheery greetings and words of admiration for the baby. In the busyness of our early days I had only subliminally noticed the odd looks we were getting in the village, but I now admitted to myself that there had been a certain uncomprehending *froideur* during the days before Christmas. Later, I understood that Sarah had a great deal to do with the returning warmth. With brave humility she had set about correcting the impression to which she contributed before; I know what it must have cost her.

Sarah herself came over one afternoon quite unexpectedly, knocking at the door more formally than of yore but seeming entirely composed. Allie was feeding Con on the sofa and trying to read a newspaper, her head cricked over at an awkward angle as it lay on the sofa beside her. Sarah showed signs of staying in the kitchen, but I led her deliberately into the sitting-room and introduced her.

'Allie. This is Sarah, an old friend.'

'Hi. This human sucker-pump is Condy.'

'He's beautiful.' Sarah looked down, half embarrassed, at the child and I said firmly:

'He looks like Sam, don't you think?'

Sarah looked so miserable, so grey and gaunt next to the blooming Alexandra, that I felt sorry for her. 'Let's not distract him from his feed. We'll sit in the kitchen. Allie, want tea?'

'No thanks.' She craned over to finish reading the article, and Sarah and I went and sat, facing one another as if for interview, at the kitchen table.

'I owe you an apology,' said Sarah formally. 'I jumped to a conclusion, and I didn't mean Tom to pick it up, but he did via Edward. And Jackie. And Carla. And then I perhaps made things worse by trying to make them better. I sort of confirmed it.'

'Jackie!' I said. 'She stuck around, then?'

'She's been invaluable. Workwise. But she does have a bee in her bonnet about –' she lowered her voice – 'Alexandra.'

'I can guess. She thought I'd been bewitched and changed tracks.'

Sarah looked so embarrassed that I took pity and added: 'It was probably an easy mistake to make. Honestly. Tom and I have not been behaving normally lately, we see that now.'

'That's just *it*,' she said eagerly. 'Grief and shock and all the wonderful, dignified self-control that we've all admired so much in both of you. I suppose we thought – Edward and I thought – that if this cracked, the strain would – well, that just about anything could happen. When I told Tom about what I thought . . .' She stopped, blushing.

I put a hand on her arm. We'd rarely touched in the past, Sarah and I, despite our closeness as friends, and she looked up, half startled and half relieved. 'It's OK. Forget it. I think perhaps we should revert to our middle-class inhibition about such matters. Tom's back, we're fine, we're even sleeping together, if you're interested—' Something of Allie's mischief had infected me; I made this last observation purely in order to enjoy Sarah's brief discomfiture. 'It's fine. Allie has become a friend, Tom even rather likes her, he's met her brother and he's talking him into doing a degree. And I adore Condor. Happy ending.'

'Is it?' The old, rigorous academic Sarah was back now. 'Marion, is it? A happy ending?'

I sighed. Things were back to normal: Sarah was back to her usual form, and as in previous times she was right. After a long draught of tea, I said:

'Not yet. It might be. There's Julia, Allie's partner, coming back from Africa pretty soon. She doesn't like men. Or even baby boys, it seems.'

'Jacqueline has filled me in nicely about Julia's views. Very 1970s, I thought.'

'Well, I was young in the 1970s and I never met anything like it.'

'I did. In the Civil Service, there were a few.'

'You amaze me. Not just in the feminist counter-culture, then?'

'No. Marilyn French stalked the earth in Whitehall, too.'

'The other thing is that Tom doesn't think of Con the way I do.'

'As a grandchild, you mean?'

'He *is* our grandchild!'

'I know. But you say Tom doesn't accept that?'

'Oh, he *knows*.' I ran my hands through my hair, oddly comforted by being able to talk about it to Sarah. 'He accepts the heredity, he's not holding out for DNA tests or anything stupid like that. I bet he can see the physical resemblance as strongly as I do. But he has no feeling about the baby. None. It's as if he's refusing to, on principle. And I'm afraid he thinks that what Sam did was rather disgusting. And irresponsible.'

'He's a biologist! They do test tubes, they do cloning, they use donated eggs—'

'This is different. He isn't in that area, he's a wildlife man. Always been a great one for respecting nature. He doesn't much take to lesbians, either.'

'Oh God.' She was embarrassed again. 'When I started talking to him about it – Marion, I am so sorry, I came on all PC, trying to explain, and he went—' She blushed. 'Sorry.'

'Enough. Don't worry. The good thing is that lesbian or not, Allie seems to have charmed him beyond reasonable expectation.'

'What do *you* really think?' asked Sarah, composed again. 'About what Sam did, and people making a baby this way?'

I was about to spring into a spirited defence of it all, but paused, realizing how complex, indeed intermittently crazy, my own emotions had been about the business. I glanced at the open kitchen door and the hallway, but there was no sign of Allie being within earshot.

'When Jackie told us,' I said carefully, 'I collapsed. As you know. And part of it, yes, was a kind of horror. The idea that the only bit of him left was something he'd given away in that rather squalid way. Given to weird strangers. Remember, I'd met Julia. I assumed the pregnant woman would be like her.'

'But then . . . ?' Sarah gently broke the long pause.

'I had to know, and I needed to get away from the house. So I went to find them. And when I saw Allie, she looked like Sam.' In answer to her raised eyebrow I added, 'I know she doesn't really, but it was that shining, fair, happy look she has, even when she's in a mood. There is something.'

'A bit. Yes. Maybe.'

'And she was so beautifully pregnant, and there was just something about the way she took on Julia, laughing and mocking and standing up for herself – I kind of fell for her. Literally, actually. I fainted. In their office. Hadn't eaten since God knows when. Thanks, by the way, for trying to feed me that week.'

'A pleasure. But the baby? I don't see how you got so involved so fast.'

'I delivered him. They rather grudgingly put me up for the night after I keeled over, and the next day she had a sudden labour, really frightening. I was the only one there. I went to the hospital. So you see.'

'Yes,' she said, finishing her tea. 'You were in at the birth. That must have meant a lot. But Tom . . . yes, I see that too. Not the happy ending, not yet.'

'And Julia,' I said, glum again. 'Julia. Coming back soon.'

'Yes,' said Sarah. 'We'll have to have a bit of a think about all that.'

I was strangely comforted by her choice of phrase.

30

Our lives went on during those early weeks of January, the four of us living together in apparent contentment with Peter appearing at weekends and frequent visits from Sarah. She took to the baby with enthusiasm as he uncurled into a kicking, lusty child and began to bestow smiles, random and heavenly, upon any new face. Tom remained aloof from him, but politely uncomplaining even when one or two unsettled nights of prolonged wailing heaved me from my bed to help Allie.

'He doesn't seem to understand that night feeds end with more sleep,' she would say crossly. 'How long does it take before they, like, *get* it?' I no longer took the baby into my room, for Tom's sake, but once or twice carried him downstairs, and held him by the living-room window to gaze at the frosty moon. This had always quieted Sam; it calmed Con equally. One dark windy night, though, he would not settle and we sat on the sofa and I sang until he slept in my arms. Tired as I was, it seemed to me that earth had little more joy to offer than this.

Allie seemed content and calm now; her leaving was never mentioned, and it was almost possible to imagine that we might go on like this indefinitely – grandparents and daughter-in-law watching over the child, friends down the lane. The playgroup, the village school. One day in the kitchen, seeing me gazing through the window at Allie pointing out snowdrops to the baby, Sarah said drily:

'You'll have her enrolled in the WI next.'

'In my dreams,' I said sadly, acknowledging her meaning. 'I know I can't hold on to her, and it wouldn't be fair to try. She's so young. Not to mention gay.'

'Happy right now, though,' said Sarah, looking out of the window. 'And gosh, she's so pretty!' Allie was wearing the black skirt with flowers again, and the long cardigan with a red pashmina of mine wound round her neck. Her hair hung loose and golden around her, and her breath rose on the air like incense.

'Yes,' I said. 'She's been contented lately. She does like it here. I think we'll be seeing a bit of them even when . . . even after . . .'

'Them? Her and Con, or the whole family of three?'

'Don't remind me.'

'She must be in touch? With Julia Penderby? And all her other life?'

'There are texts.'

Indeed there were. Allie could be seen several times a day reading the tiny screen of her mobile and thumbing new messages. Once, casually, I said, 'Friends? What do you tell them?' and she answered readily enough: 'I say I'm staying at my dad's, and that the baby's fine.'

'You wouldn't tell them you're here?'

'Too complicated. Don't want to be complicated.' She pouted, then relented and smiled at me. 'Nothing personal, Grandma!'

'And Julia?'

The pout returned.

'She's been travelling where there isn't much of a signal. She warned me about that. She thought she'd be back a week ago but seems there was more to do.' I stopped myself from commenting on a partner who would happily go into the bush and stay out of touch during a first baby's first months.

In the days of Empire, I told myself, men wouldn't have thought twice about it, pushing off to India or Rhodesia while the little woman prepared to give birth then pay, pack and follow. The idea of Julia unwittingly aping a pukka sahib – I mentally drew on that big moustache again, with sideburns – amused me so much that my anxiety temporarily faded.

But as January drew to a close, one particular text made Allie frown and bite her lip. We two were eating supper, Con asleep in his basket and Tom in Norwich for a university dinner. At last, Allie said:

'Julia's coming back. She's got her funding, not for everything she wanted but for a women's refuge.'

'Not for the IVF idea, then?'

Allie laughed. 'I expect that's gone. I think she went nuts, briefly.'

'So many of us do.'

She glanced at me, understanding my meaning immediately. We had talked a little about me and Tom, and our breakout from normality, and Sarah's misunderstanding; I found her youthful insouciance about it refreshing, and told her so. She lightly replied:

'That's the upside of coming from a drug generation, see.'

'Hang on, I'm a child of the Sixties, we did drugs, too.'

'Pah! Your lot just saw pretty colours and lava-lamp visions,' she said scornfully. 'We did the real thing. Half the people I know have gone totally bloody psycho from time to time.'

'Did Sam?' The question came out before I could stop it. But 'No idea,' she said, and shrugged. 'Don't think so. I know Jackie grilled him about smoking and drink, in the month before he did it, because of sperm quality. So she probably did the same about drugs.'

Now, looking down again at Julia's text on her phone, she

said: 'I guess it'll be a good refuge. She says the local women she's fixed up to run it are ace. So she's coming home, back to the fund-raising.'

'When?'

'Wednesday.'

It was Monday. I felt my breathing accelerate, and turned away to disguise a gasp.

'She'll expect me to be home,' said Allie in a flat voice. 'Thinks I've been there all along. God, the flat'll be bloody dusty by now. It comes down out of the rafters.' She glanced at Con, spreadeagled in his basket like a miniature Superman in flight, his lips just parted, his fair hair lying in spikes of light around his peaceful brow. 'Marion, what'll I do?'

The appeal was so direct that I was nonplussed.

'You don't have to go, you know.'

'I've been living off you for – what? Five weeks? Six? It's been a godsend, I'd have messed up big-time if I'd been all alone in the loft. But I have to go home, don't I? And there's Julia?'

She seemed genuinely uncertain. While I puzzled over an answer she went on, 'And I have to work out some way of starting work again – the idea was always that I'd go back to doing gigs, or at least bar work, and Julia would look after our *daughter* in the evenings while she caught up on the paperwork. But now . . .'

'Do you need to work? Financially? Wouldn't benefits help, for a while anyway? Maternity, family credit, all that?' I cursed myself; I had no intention of talking about money, money was the least of it. But she seemed relieved to be asked.

'Yes, I could. It was more about self-respect and independence and all that garbage. But it turns out that I'd rather stick by Condy, for quite a while anyway. And as for money – well, you know about Julia, don't you? I told you? Her family?'

I racked my brains. 'Her father was that judge, yeah?'

'Still is. Hizonner Justice Macallan Strang Penderby, OBE, standing for Old Bastard Extraordinary. Her mother died after all the flap . . . natural causes luckily for him. He married the sixteen-year-old and retired to Belize or somewhere, to spend more time with his lavish pension.'

'What's that got to do with Julia and money?'

'Her mother was an heiress. Changed the will just in time to stop the old bastard inheriting a bean. Julia got it all.'

I stared. 'But you live . . . !'

'I know. It's political. Jules used a lot of the money to start DAN, and gave a good bit away. But she owns the whole building we're in, and half the street actually, and a lot of developers would just love to take it off her. She could buy a house, no trouble. Several, probably.'

I puzzled for a moment, then said: 'So what was all that stuff about getting funding for the refuge from some Trust or other?'

'She wants DAN to have credibility. Proper backing. Not be just some little rich girl's toy. And Portweigh Trust would take it on for ten years, and they've got good pull with the big aid agencies and governments and all that.' She sighed, looking at the baby with curious intensity. 'And she had plans for Tamasin. The phantom daughter. She thought she might found a girls' school, very alternative.'

'Ah.'

After a moment more Allie said with a sad note in her voice:

'You know something? I miss Jules a lot. Mad bitch that she is.'

'Yes. You love her.'

'And I can't live off her, and lumber her with paying for a baby she doesn't want. Can I? It was my idea, and now it's a boy.'

I was silent. She inclined her head, looking hard at the

baby. 'And you know something else? I'm scared to go back. To take Con back to the way we lived. I never saw it before, but when you've got a baby you sort of want an airing-cupboard. And thicker doors. And some daffodils. Jesus, if Julia could hear me now!' A small, choked laugh. In a mock little-girl voice she added: 'Darling Ju-li-ah, would you mind buying me an airing cupboard and some daffodils and a John Lewis cot for my baby?'

The infant slept on, oblivious. All I could say was: 'You've always got a billet here. A respite. Whatever. Believe that.' My voice was shaking; Allie, refreshed by her moment of drollery, looked at me with drily amused affection overlaying the trouble in her face. Then she jumped up and said, 'Wait a minute.'

I heard her on the stairs, and then she came down, light-footed and quick, and laid an envelope in front of me.

'Remember the day I chucked Julia out of the hospital?'

'Yes.'

'Well, the following morning, before you'd arrived, the registrar man came round. They sometimes let you register the birth while you're still in hospital, specially in areas like ours where heaps of people don't speak much English and they're frightened of official buildings.' She pulled out the paper, folded three ways, and I recognized the format of a full birth certificate. My eyes went straight to the name – Condor Alexander Morris-Penderby – and then widened. Father: *Samuel Thomas Faulkner, decd.*

'How did you manage that?' My voice was a squeak.

'There was a letter he wrote. To Jackie. Confirming who he was, his date and place of birth, everything. He had a lawyer draw it up, confirming he was the donor. She thought that if there was a hereditary disease or a bone marrow transplant or we both got killed – oh God, she thinks of every damn thing. She's so anal, I think that's why it didn't work with her and me.'

'But did they admit that as evidence?'

'I started the ball rolling that day in hospital. It took a lot of to-ing and fro-ing over the first couple of weeks. I did it on the phone – the registrar was a sweetie, I reckon he was gay himself – but he looked up Sam's death certificate and everything.'

'It means a lot,' I said, fighting the tears. 'But why?'

'I was furious with Julia, and we aren't civil-partners anyway so she can't be listed as a parent. And she was being so vile about him not being a girl. She even accused me of bribing Shona to lie about the result of her mad alternative sex test, so I didn't have to terminate the baby. She was horrible, that first couple of weeks. So I thought, What the hell? Sam was a nice guy and you were nice to me, and he was dead and nobody could go after him for money or anything any more . . . and it was true, so . . .'

Her voice tailed away as she looked at me in my increasing shock. I could not tear my eyes away from the formal paper and the name of my son, the father.

'Why are you showing me this now? Why now?'

'Because I want you to know that whatever Julia says, whatever she does, you're his grandmother. I won't let him lose you. At first I thought we'd have to scrub round all that, for a quiet life. But I've seen how much it means, and finding Peter's made me think about families and why I'm so hopeless, what with my mum and never knowing I even had a grandad. And I don't think a quiet life is worth it. And I don't think I'm ever likely to have one anyway, not with Julia.'

'That's what I'm scared of,' I said slowly. 'Babies need quiet contentment around them. Not passion and rows. And children need approval and encouragement from both parents. Or parent-figures.'

I was afraid I had gone too far, but Allie only raised her shoulders in a long, eloquent shrug and said:

'I know. But I can't leave her.'

There was nothing to say. On cue, Con woke, snuffled briefly and then uttered his mealtime roar. We said no more about Julia's return that evening, but turned to the anaesthetic of the DVD and watched three episodes of *Dinnerladies* in succession before Tom got home and found us, all three on the sofa, laughing fit to shut out any future.

31

It was the birth certificate that began to change the landscape for Tom. I asked Allie if I could photocopy it by
running it through his fax machine, and left the result on
his desk, without comment, next morning when I went to
the factory. After lunch, he waited until Allie was out round
the village with Con, and then came out to the battered
garden shed where I was tidying up for the coming of spring.
My heart was immeasurably lightened by Allie's statement
of intent; whatever happened, Con would be part of our life
and we, calm, rural grandparents, would be part of his. I still
feared terribly for his life in the vicinity of Julia's cold distaste
or angry screaming, but my faith in his mother grew ever
stronger.

Tom stood in the shed doorway, blocking out the light,
the paper in his hand.

'OK,' he said. 'You win. It's real.'

I looked up. I could not see his expression, only his dark
silhouette.

'Is that ironic?'

'No.' His voice was flat. 'I still don't love him, I still don't
feel the magic you're meant to. I'm sorry. But, yes, he is our
grandchild.'

I stood up and went to him, putting my arms around his
waist, my head on his chest. His arms hung undecided for
a moment, then just one of them came round my shoulders.

'I'm sorry.'

235

'You don't have to feel sorry. You can't turn feelings on just like that. I was there when he was born, it's different for me—'

'It isn't turning feelings on that's the problem. It's turning them off.'

'What do you mean?'

'It feels like cheating,' he said slowly. 'So neat and tidy and clinical. As if we were replacing Sam with a new, instant baby. As if he doesn't matter.'

I pulled away in tears, my hands flying to my face.

'That isn't it! Not at all! Sam is – everywhere, all the time, for me too! You must know that!' I was shaking, and sat down unsteadily on a pile of seed-boxes.

'It's just that you seem so happy,' he said helplessly. 'And I can't be.'

'Is that so bad? Being happy about one thing doesn't mean you aren't grieving about another.' The boxes creaked as if to give way. I pulled myself up again and leaned on the splintery wall.

'Rationally,' he said, 'I know that. But you and Allie and – Condor. I look at you all, a cosy little trio, like when I came home last night, and it's as if Sam was outside the window, shut out, always shut out, helpless—'

I came close again because my husband was crying, and put my arms around him. We had, even in the first days of shock, rarely seen one another crying. 'Oh, Tom!'

He controlled his tears, brutally.

'It's OK. It's only a feeling. It's not rational. I should be glad you're happy.'

'But I cry for Sam! I still do!' I protested, and guiltily wondered how long it had been – days, certainly – since that really happened. The vigour of new life had, I accepted with silent horror, begun to eclipse the memory of the old. Beyond the formal stained-glass of memory the young trees thrashed and waved. Around my dark old shed the crocuses were springing. Life. Nothing could stop it, any of it. Not anger, not denial, not mourning-bands nor Tom's sad dignity. I held him tight for a moment and said hopelessly: 'He was our boy. There won't be another like him.'

That evening at supper Allie said: 'I'd better go to London tomorrow and tidy up the flat. Julia's flight gets in about eight, apparently.'

'Do you want a hand?'

She gave me a look that was untypically shifty.

'Is it that obvious?'

'Well, with Con . . .'

'The thing is,' she said awkwardly, 'I rather hoped I could leave him here. For the day. While I cleaned, and got food in the fridge, and stuff. Con could take a couple of bottles of formula off you.'

She had taken to supplementing her breastfeeds with powdered formula, partly so that I could help in the night but really because all my National Childbirth Trust persuasion had failed to convince her that she could make all the milk he needed, provided she kept suckling. By day, though, she still fed him three or four times.

'But you'd have to be away twelve hours,' I said. 'With the trains and everything. And then you'd miss Julia getting back.'

'I have to switch the heating on, she's been in Africa,' said Allie with a hint of desperation. 'And I have to get the flat right. I could leave a note saying I was back in a few days, or something.'

I disguised my private rejoicing at any delay in the baby's meeting Julia, and only said doubtfully:

'I suppose Con would take milk out of a bottle by day.' But then I could not resist adding: 'Would you take him up with you the day after, then?'

I had never seen her angry. Scornful, frightened, irritable, but never angry. It was a shock when she shouted, 'Don't interrogate me!'

I was so surprised that it was Tom who spoke first, in a tone I daresay he uses on over-emotional female students. 'Alexandra,' he said. 'Calm down. Nobody is doubting your judgement. Marion's question was quite reasonable.'

She deflated instantly, and reached across the table to grab my hands, in one of the impetuous physical gestures of affection I had happily become used to. 'Sorry. I'm a cow. A nervous cow. You know how it is.'

'It's OK. Con can stay here,' I said. 'And if he doesn't like the bottle, he'll take it when he's hungry. He's healthy and got plenty of weight on. It'll do no harm even if he grizzles. And you have to do what you need to do.'

In the morning, though, it was painful to see her go. She gave Con a long, nuzzling feed, kissed him and me, and inclined her head to Tom with a grave respect I had rarely seen. She took a small bag with her, and when I had watched her go down the lane towards the station, Con wriggling in my arms, I put him down in his basket with a mobile to paw at, and ran upstairs to see what she had taken. Her night-shirt, a deckchair-striped thing from the village craft shop, lay crumpled on the bed, but her washing things were gone, and half her clothes. Slowly I went downstairs, thinking hard, made up three bottles and put them in the fridge, and at nine o'clock rang Eric to say I wouldn't be in. And maybe not the next day, either.

It was surprising what hard work the baby was with Allie gone. All the harder because Condor Morris-Penderby (absurdly aristocratic name for a child so louchely born!) had fixed views about bottles, tolerating them only when intensely hungry by night. He arched and screamed and spat out the rubber nipple specially shaped for breastfed babies, and whenever he opened his eyes between bouts of screaming he glared at me as if I were the enemy. More poignantly, he would bring me to tears by rooting and nuzzling against my chest in search of what I could never again give a baby. By early afternoon, though, he quietened down and, still shaking with tiny sobs, took the whole bottle and fell into a heavy, sated, sullen sleep. I was glad Tom was at work and could not see my struggle.

At seven, I thought about the great plane crossing northern Europe, the travel-weary Julia heading for home comforts in Dalston while Alexandra made for the Liverpool Street train. At eight-thirty, making up still more bottles, I glanced out of the window at every footfall in the lane. Allie's supper kept warm in the bottom oven. At half-past nine I accepted that she had missed the first train, fed and changed Con again and threw away the dried-up shepherd's pie, checking that there were eggs for an omelette.

Tom came in and glanced at me as I scrubbed the bottles in the sink after the ten o'clock news headlines.

'She's not back, then?'

'Obviously.'

'Do you think she stayed on to see – the Der-joolya woman?'

'The D is silent.' I said it between gritted teeth.

'As you say.' He wandered back to the television with an air of studied calm. 'No doubt she'll ring.'

It was the phone, not Con, which woke me at 4 a.m. I jumped up, startled both by the sound ringing through the house and by panic at the baby's unwonted six hours of silence. I ran to him in his basket beside the bed in Sam's old room, my heart in a death-panic, but he was breathing evenly, lost in a milky dream. Perhaps Allie was right and he hadn't been getting all the milk he needed from her. The phone rang on as I stumbled downstairs to answer it. A low voice said:

'Marion? I'm so sorry—'

'What happened?'

'She's ill. Really weak. I thought the flight was at eight, but she meant 1800, so she turned up in a cab just as I was leaving. Julia *never* takes cabs! And I found her on the stairs, she couldn't even climb up without sitting down on the office landing.'

'What's wrong with her?'

'Malaria. She thinks. She only got really ill during the flight, but hasn't been so good for a couple of days. And she was too stubborn to say anything to the aeroplane people.'

'But didn't she have malaria tablets?'

'She was taking the tablets at first. But seems she gave hers away about ten days ago to some African woman. She isn't making much sense, and she's so so hot, and shivering and being sick, and says there are ants on her.' Her voice was unsteady. 'She says I'm not to fuss, but Marion, she looks like she's dying – I'm so scared – and Con, did he cry? Did he take the bottle, oh shit—!'

I was wide awake now, and this was a daughter in trouble. 'Allie. It's OK. Con is fine. Sleeping beautifully, taking the bottle. He's safe. You have to ring a doctor right now. She needs to get to hospital. It's serious. People do die. Ignore what Julia says, take command.'

'She doesn't like doctors and hospitals, says they're patriarchal, she'll kill me!'

'If the malaria doesn't kill her first. For God's sake, Allie!'

I heard some sobs, and then a tight voice said: 'Right. You're right. Time I grew up. I'm going to ring 999.' A click, a buzz, and I was left staring silently into the phone. Upstairs, a whimper told me that Con's nocturnal truce was over; I went to the fridge and fetched the bottle to warm it before he woke Tom.

32

I could not get back to sleep; I made a cup of tea and sat in the kitchen, waiting for Con's next morning cry or for the telephone. Both came almost simultaneously; a choking wail had sent me upstairs and I came down to the phone with agonized, cautious haste, baby in my arms and bottle stuffed in my dressing-gown pocket. It was half-past five by the kitchen clock.

'Marion? Marion?'

'Yes. How is it?' I juggled the phone, the baby, the bottle.

'They've taken her. The Hospital for Tropical Diseases. I wanted to go but there was so much sick and chaos here I decided to get her stuff together and follow. The paramedics gave me an address. It's up West.' I could hear that she was close to tears. 'And they were quite angry she didn't take her tablets. She's got a heart thing anyway and – oh shit, Marion. She's so thin, and she was talking nonsense and trying to fight the guys. And my tits hurt so much!'

She was really crying now. I made soothing noises down the phone, which was jammed under my neck as I fed the baby; if he were to cry now her panic could only be compounded. Luckily, he had given up his war against the rubber nipple and was sucking with greedy contentment.

'Allie. She's in the best place, they're experts. And your breasts are bound to ache for a day or so, but it'll go away. It's lucky you'd scaled down the feeding. Just get rid of a bit of the milk – I showed you, remember? And try hot flannels. Or some people put cabbage leaves in their bra.'

At least it made her laugh, briefly and damply through the tears.

'Cabbage?'

'Cabbage. And Allie, do you want to stay in London till the crisis is over?'

'Is that OK? I have to, Marion, I have to. She looked so terrible. They said if I hadn't rung she might have died really quickly . . .' More choking sobs. 'But Condy . . .'

'We can cope. I'm here, he's feeding well and Sarah will help. I could bring him to London, but I don't know?'

'No,' said Allie. 'I couldn't cope with both of them needing me. Oh God, did that sound terrible?'

'Understandable. Look, you clear up, go and see Julia, keep me posted. We're fine.' And as an afterthought, in dread as I looked down at her child on my lap: 'It isn't catching, is it?'

'They said not. Mosquitoes, isn't it? Oh Marion, thanks for everything.'

When Tom woke up I told him what was going on, and he nodded gravely, made only the briefest comment on people who didn't take their malaria tablets, and asked if I needed any shopping getting in. I gave him a list and asked him to call Eric with yet more apologies; the state of the payroll was something I preferred not to think about. Then he said:

'You're going to need Sarah. I'll drop by and tell her.'

'Yes.'

Alone in the kitchen again I looked at Con in his basket, beadily staring and swiping at a string of plastic animals, and tried hard not to let myself think about what might happen if Julia died. Allie would, clearly, be devastated; but she was young and vital and would still have her beloved baby. And no complications. I doubted there were any more gay women

heaf of photographs of Con enjoying the pram and
gging at the bigger Simpson baby, and leaving a trail of
s for the village team.

Allie met me as arranged at the hospital reception and fell
to my arms.

'I can't believe you've come,' she said.

'You sounded so low.'

'I was. I am. I don't understand any of it, the doctors are
really kind but I don't get it. I thought the fever going was
the end of it all but it isn't, it goes on and on, and they're
not being as optimistic as they were at first. The consultant
mutters about watching out for organ failure. And I dream
of Condy every night, always about him being taken away
by social services or something. Sometimes I dream it's him
in hospital, with all the tubes. And then I wake up and
remember, and in the night I think Julia's ill because I was
so selfish, having a boy, and she couldn't stand it, and I've
killed her—'

'That is ridiculous.' I took her by the shoulders and gently
shook her. 'Get a grip. She's ill because she didn't take her
malaria tablets. For whatever reason she did it, it was an
adult decision.'

'Excuse me.' Behind us, unseen, had materialized a short,
tubby woman in wire glasses, with a face of unusual sweet-
ness and a leathery tan beneath a frame of wiry iron-grey
hair. 'Might you be going to see Julia Penderby?'

'Yes?'

'I'm Arlene Marsh from the Portweigh Trust. I was with
her in Mozambique. I've only just heard.' We stared.

'How is she doing?' said the brisk little woman. 'I wanted
to ask, I do feel a little bit responsible.'

'Well you might!' said Allie fiercely. 'She didn't need to
get ill, lots of people go to Africa and don't end up in hospital
nearly dead!'

in her orbit with views quite like Julia's. And she had her
new-found brother, and friends; a set who had, she sometimes hinted, rather stepped back during her life with that
alarming paramour. She would recover and she would want
grandparental support. If Julia died.

I pushed the thought away, and instead made a series of
phone calls to local friends who might know of redundant
baby equipment. Con did not like lying flat for long when
he was awake, and a bouncy chair would save me holding
him for hours. And he was outgrowing his basket, and –
unwilling to make expeditions into town – we had resorted
to cutting the feet off several of his Babygros as his legs
grew, and found him woolly socks and tank-tops at the craft
shop. 'Pikey baby,' Allie would say lovingly as she surveyed
his haphazard wardrobe. 'Scruffball!'

I called in old favours, spoke to people I had hardly seen
since Sam died because I could not bear their talk of living
sons and daughters. Doing this, I acknowledged to myself
that it could be days or even weeks before Allie came back.
Con was my responsibility for the moment.

Sarah appeared mid-morning and said, without preamble:

'Broken night, Tom tells me. Shall I take him for a walk
in the pram while you get some sleep?'

'Oh Sarah, that's such a kind thought. But we don't have
a pram. Allie used the sling all the time.'

'Umm. I know who's got a pram. Hang on,' she said, and
vanished again before I could even make a move towards
the kettle. Twenty minutes later she was back, pushing into
the porch a vast old-fashioned black pram with a canopy
like a witch's hood.

'It's vintage 1950s, but the mattress is new,' she said as
my eyes widened. 'Mrs Arnold got it done up by the black-
smiths' over at Dereham, for when her daughter brings the
baby down for weekends. But the daughter took one look

and bought a trendy all-terrain buggy which folds up in the boot. Says she wasn't going to go around looking like Mary Poppins.'

'How do you know these things? I've never seen this monster.'

'The daughter, or the pram? Well, I know because Maggie Arnold was going on and on about it in the shop, saying that her Davina wasted four hundred quid on the buggy just because some magazine said that Kate Winslet used that kind, and how they need proper prams to rest their little backs. What d'you think, Condor? Fancy a set of vintage wheels?'

Con loved the pram from the start. We got some string and hung plastic corks and twists of silver foil from the canopy, which gave it a bohemian air, and tucked him up in blankets and a woolly Aztec hat Allie had brought from London. Sarah wheeled him off, mobiles dancing in the breeze, while I went back to bed. When I woke two hours later she and Tom were in the kitchen drinking coffee and laughing over something on the table, and the pram was taking up a great deal of space in the corner. She had, I noticed, added a felt reindeer and a string of bells which I recognized from her Christmas decorations.

'Look. Tom took a Polaroid,' said Sarah. It showed the decorated pram and Con lounging in state inside it, framed by dangle-toys. 'I thought you could show it to Allie, so she knows he's OK. I'll print it up.'

I was puzzled. 'But when I see Allie, she'll be here anyway.'
Tom glanced at Sarah.

'Yes. Of course. But if things go on a bit – we just thought she might . . .'

'. . . need you,' said Sarah, smoothing over his hesitation. 'She looks to me like a girl who wants a mum.'

I blinked. I saw that she was right, and the realization both warmed and dismayed me. While I processed the thought,

she went on: 'If that happens, you w
baby up. Plenty of us here. Maggie Ar
And the Simpson girl does childminding
I bet she'd do an afternoon shift for a fe
nurse before her own baby came. She cou

I was taken aback, a little offended at the
their plan.

'He's my responsibility,' I said stiffly.

'Takes a village to raise a child,' said Sara
'You're a heroine, you're the cat's pyjamas as far
is concerned, obviously. I'm just guessing that
need to go to London and calm down your – mm –
in-law.'

It was the first time any of us had used the express
the look on my face Tom smiled, a less strained smil
I had seen for a long time. 'New times need new langt
he said. 'How about daughter-out-law?'

And so we carried on in the first few days. With Sara
rota of motherly assistants I even managed to get in to wo
for a couple of hours each day, including Saturday, and b
home for Allie's fraught calls. They always came around two-
thirty when she had made her first visit of the day to sit –
so she told us – helplessly at Julia's side in a forest of tubes
and drip-stands.

'She's still mainly unconscious. Since yesterday she speaks
a bit, but then drifts off. The fever's been brought down but
they're not happy about her heart.' There would usually be
another call in the evening, from the loft, where she sounded
lonely and afraid. I asked her about friends and she only said
in a flat voice:

'Haven't the energy. I sleep early. Good for nothing.' Sarah
and Tom proved to have been right, and on the Tuesday
morning I sensed from a tearful eight-thirty call that Allie
was near breaking point. I took the train to London bearing

'How is she?' asked Arlene Marsh again, unflustered by this attack.

'Not good so far,' said Allie, recovering herself. 'We're going to see her. Apparently she didn't take her tablets.'

'No. She did while I was with her, but I left her in a settlement near Madelane, since she was working quite well by then with the refuge team. I had to go to the city to sort something out with a bank. And apparently she gave the tablets away. She also gave away her anti-AIDS sterile syringe kit to a woman who was having a blood transfusion in the rather filthy local hospital. And her supply of Dioralyte to a woman with a sick son. And her water filter.'

She sighed, pushing the wire glasses more comfortably up her nose. 'It's not uncommon. Aid workers arrive, and they're so overwhelmed by the poverty that they can't bear to have things the locals don't. But they get ill faster than the locals. And then they just cause them trouble and use up resources. I lecture them all about it, but the women in the village told me she was very stubborn. I shouldn't have left her on her own that week.'

Allie rounded on her with renewed anger. 'You can say that again! She knew nothing about Africa, she was only a fundraiser!'

'I know. But she's a strong character. And she was warned. Anyway, might I come up with you? I've got some good news that might perk her up. The village leaders have agreed to the House of the Women. And to call it by that name.'

The three of us got into the lift, Allie still visibly fuming, arching herself away from the serene little Portweigh woman. In the ward Julia lay shrunken and unrecognizable in a forest of equipment. But she was awake, her eyes open in the lined and waxen face. Arlene Marsh and I hung back while Allie bent over and kissed her tenderly on the forehead.

'Jules. How you feeling?'

A croak said, 'Nottoobad.' Her lips were dry, and Allie looked around for a nurse.

'I think she's thirsty.'

'Do you think you could manage to drink?' asked the nurse, glancing at the various drips. Julia sucked briefly through a straw and the nurse put something on her cracked mouth, then looked round at us with a trace of disapproval.

'Rather a lot of visitors at once, for a sick girl.'

'Sorry,' I said. 'I came to support Alexandra here, really, and this lady was in Africa with Julia.' I saw the nurse's face take on a disapproving cast.

'I hope *you* took your pills and still are?' she said challengingly.

'Of course.'

Julia seemed to notice me for the first time.

'You're Sam thingy's mother,' she said faintly.

'Yes. I've been helping Allie with the baby while you were travelling.'

'Thasskind,' said Julia surprisingly, and closed her eyes again. 'The baby.'

Arlene waited a moment, then said: 'I'd better go. I just wanted to see how things looked. Tell her about the village and the good news. Oh, and tell her that the Dioralyte did the job. But I'll be back.'

I went with her to the corridor and said:

'I suppose she'll be OK?'

'Yes. Looks like it. They do a good job here. I have to warn you though, she'll be extremely weak for months, and she may be depressed. And there'll be relapses, always are. Need a lot of looking after.'

This idea had struck me too, with ramifications I felt unfit to contemplate. Suddenly I said:

'Might you have a quick cup of coffee with me?'

'Yes, let's.' I went back to the bedside where Allie sat

holding Julia's hand, murmured, 'See you downstairs, half an hour?' and headed for the watery sunshine of the Tottenham Court Road. When we had sat down with our coffee I asked Arlene to tell me more about the time in Mozambique.

'Well,' she said, in measured, donnish tones. 'We travelled a lot, looking for the ideal place for this project of Julia's. I was impressed by her in England, I don't mind saying, because I do like energy. And there are aspects of the DAN idea that we liked. But it seemed to me that some time on the ground would do her good. Focus the vision a bit.'

'Ah,' I said. 'You mean about the IVF?'

'Precisely. We deal with a lot of niche idealists, if I may use that phrase. Her concept was obviously not going to work – we are dealing with human beings here, and she has to face the fact that most women actually rather like their menfolk. And in the kind of conditions we see, the very idea of IVF is ridiculous. Let alone sex selection. But we liked the idea of a refuge for women who've lost men or been victims of abuse.'

'So her ideas really would work?'

'Yes. The refuge would include support and training for microcredit businesses, and security if there are issues with the more predatory men. And we have to think about girls needing protection from pressure over genital mutilation. There isn't much in that region, but it is rather horrifyingly starting to spread. And in the small enclave we're looking at, some of the other aid agencies have lost credibility with local women. It's complicated. Local politics. So we wanted a fresh start, and we've committed some money to DAN. On certain conditions.'

'And she's happy with that? With the conditions?'

'Oddly, yes.' Arlene smiled. 'You'd be amazed how the real Africa changes people. We had another niche idealist last year, who had a bee in his bonnet about "cosmic ordering" and wanted to train hypnotherapists in Malawi. He had a theory that famine and disease were caused by people not doing enough of something he called Positive Wanting. We've got him fundraising for WarChild now, helping former child soldiers. That's what Portweigh does.'

'Funds keen people to give up stupid ideas and get useful?'

'More or less. I wouldn't want it publicized quite that way, though.' She smiled, and I could see how even Julia had met her match.

I took a draught of my coffee and glanced at my watch. 'Can I ask you something else? About Julia? Since you've spent so much time with her lately?'

'Certainly.'

'What I am,' I said carefully, 'is the mother of the boy who was the sperm donor for her gay partner Alexandra. I am therefore the grandmother. You may have heard that my son died.'

'Yes. We talked a lot about her situation, when we were together. And of course, as a grandmother you wonder what sort of life the baby will have with Julia Penderby? I am one myself. I can imagine.'

'You've got it. The baby is a boy.'

'I heard,' she said. 'That's very good. That'll help her.'

'Her? I'm thinking of *him*!'

'Yes. I'm sorry. But I was a psychotherapist before I did this, and I see Julia as someone undergoing a healing change in her view of the male sex. It's already begun. Nurturing a male baby can only be helpful.'

I had never thought of it this way, and wondered whether I ever would.

33

Allie was at the hospital reception when Arlene and I got back. She looked terrible, red-eyed and pallid, and I said instinctively, 'Come on. You need something to eat.'

'I need to talk to – *her*,' she said aggressively, pointing her finger at Arlene. 'Why this happened.'

'Sure,' said Arlene soothingly. 'But I think you'll understand why. Julia talked a lot about you, and it seemed to me that you two know each other very well.'

'You mean it was her fault?' Allie bristled.

'Yes. Of course it was. It was a kind and honourable sort of fault, but stupid all the same. Nobody can be of any use to other people if they don't look after their main tool, which is their own body. In our world it's the first rule.'

'You're very hard,' said Allie, but the anger had gone out of her voice. Once or twice, over the past weeks, fleeting remarks over meals had indicated that she did not think Julia looked after herself. 'Too austere, runs on empty half the time,' she would say, helping herself to more food. 'And the puritan vegan thing doesn't help too much either. I'd be dead without cheese.'

'I'm not hard, I'm just realistic,' said Arlene Marsh. 'I wish she'd kept on with the malaria tablets, that was stupid. But what I wanted to tell her, and perhaps you will, is that the child she saved did live. Little Alberto. The boy who had dysentery. It was his mother she gave the Dioralyte to. She was very involved with that family. Mixed up the salts, sat

251

with the mother during the worst of it, gave the child sips of water all through the night. We had to leave when it was still touch and go – he was so malnourished to start with. But I've heard from the workers, and the little boy is fine. She saved his life. I thought knowing that might give her some support.'

Allie and I glanced at one another with the same thought. Julia had saved a male life. It was some measure of the force of Julia's personality and beliefs that both of us found this so astonishing; a life, after all, is a life. Medical staff save the most reprehensible criminals, prison officers anxiously resuscitate suicidal serial killers. But the fact is that the idea of Julia putting herself out to extend a masculine lifespan astonished us both. Clearly the heat, strangeness, poverty and hope of that alien place had wrought some change in her.

There was to me something embarrassing about our surprise, and it was Allie who broke the awkward silence with 'But she hates boys!'

'Nobody hates half the human race,' said Arlene equably. 'Nobody sane.'

'Julia does,' said Allie, with an edge of hysteria. 'She even hates my baby. That's why I'm giving him up. I realized that in the hospital just now. I can't put Jules through more misery, not after this. It'll kill her. I was going to ask Marion, today. If she'll keep him. For good.'

I could not speak. Arlene, still unruffled, said:

'I really think you two should go and get some food. Alexandra, you will find life much more – nuanced – than you perhaps think right now. If you want any more support, here's my number. Portweigh is now committed to Julia's work, and you can assure her that everything will move ahead and we will look forward to her input when she is better. That might help, too.'

Gnomelike, the little figure gave a ceremonious nod and vanished through the swing doors as discreetly as she had come. We both stared after her for a moment in silence, then I took Allie's limp arm and said, 'She's right. Food.'

I led the way with my mind in turmoil, struggling to suppress a dozen inadmissible visions: Con with his own bright bedroom off the landing, toys in the kitchen; Con learning to walk, chasing butterflies in the garden, starting at playgroup in the church hall, enrolled in the village school. Con happy and secure in clean country air, being taken in to Norwich or Cambridge for the excitement of a little city, Con playing at science experiments with Tom and having bedtime stories from me from Sam's old books. A blond, confident Con in his first lifejacket, preparing his kayak on the beach. As he grew up we might have a dog again, and a donkey – Sam always begged for a donkey, but money and time were tighter when he was small . . .

It was the donkey, I think, that tipped the whole rapid dream into Boden-catalogue absurdity and returned me to the home planet, just as we were reaching an alley off the Tottenham Court Road where a small Italian restaurant was opening its doors.

'OK for you?' I asked the silent, still trembling Allie.

'Yes. No. I don't know.' She followed me in meekly, and stared helplessly at the menu. After a few moments I took it off her and ordered for us both. She slumped forward, head in hands, and said:

'I don't know what's going on any more.'

'Me neither,' I said, as cheerfully as I could. 'But I would like you to know that I am very flattered by your mad idea of giving Con to me to bring up. Flattered, honoured, and aware that it can't happen.'

'Why not?' I was pleased to see a little of her old spirit returning. 'You love him, you're his grandma, you took a lot of trouble to find us, you want him – anyone can see that—'

'I'm fifty,' I said, spreading my hands on the table for her to see. 'I know it's not old, these days, and Tom and I are fit enough, we might have thirty years yet. And if it was a real emergency and he had no mother, of course we'd take him on. You can always be sure of that, as a backstop.'

'Then why not?' Behind the weak belligerence I detected relief.

'I'm old-fashioned. A baby needs a young, strong mother. His real mother.'

Fleetingly, I wondered if this was indeed so, thinking of the resentful, lounging teenagers with buggies and the incidence of women in their late forties, even fifties, now with blithe selfishness creating babies by innovative means. I thought, too, about the baby and child in that dusty loft, the echoing stairway, the rumble of traffic on Dalston High Street, the reeking kebab shops and the impossibility of kayaks, donkeys, even butterflies in his daily world. With a superhuman effort I reinforced my argument.

'You're good at it. You're a good mother, you love him. If I can do one more thing for my son's son, it's to make sure he has a proper mother. Besides, he's your child. You'd suffer terribly.'

'I'm not that good at it,' she said sadly. 'If it hadn't been for you, God knows what I'd have done in the first few weeks.'

'You're fine. You're no more bewildered than any new mum.'

'But I can't do it to Jules,' she said, her voice rising an octave to a wail as she returned to the situation in hand. 'I see that now. I've made her so ill . . . I'm sure her heart got worse because of me and the baby being such a strain, and I know she gave her medicine away because of how awful it all was, with us and Con. I drove her to it. She didn't have anything to live for.'

'Life,' I said, glad of the waiter's arrival with prawns and a theatrical flourish, 'is messy. But people adapt, and move on, and get over stuff. And it helps if you don't talk nonsense and beat yourself up. Trust me. I know. And remember one other thing. Julia just saved a little boy's life. She sat up all night giving him sips of Dioralyte. She'll have held him in her arms, Allie. Doesn't that tell you anything? Doesn't that give you any hope?'

She picked up a prawn, shelled it with absent-minded skill, and ate it. The taste seemed to shock her like a message from another world; with increasing speed and ravenous attention she finished the rest and reached for the bread. I watched her, then pushed the rest of my pâté and toast over towards her, and she ate that too. Colour returned to her cheeks as finally she said:

'I didn't eat, hardly. Since I left Norfolk. I was too scared.'

'I can see that.'

'It felt terrible, the idea of pigging myself while Julia was lying there with nothing, all shrunken and dying.'

'Julia,' I said impatiently, 'is on a drip. She's getting every single bloody nutrient she needs. She's in a top hospital with nurses taking her temperature every twenty minutes and consultants bringing students to study her. You have to look after yourself. It's just like that strange little woman said about the aid workers. You've got a baby, and a partner. It's ir-responsible to fall to pieces and cry and have stupid ideas about giving your baby away.'

'Nobody has said that word to me,' said Allie wonder-ingly, looking round for more bread, 'since my dad. He said "irresponsible" quite a lot.'

'Good for Dad.' I was being so bracing I felt like my old

headmistress. 'Now, what do you most need, and how shall we plan the next few days and weeks? Sarah's doing a good job with Con and the village ladies helping, they all adore him. But I ought to get back.'

'I can't leave Julia,' said Allie, tearful again. 'I don't know what to do.'

'If you're alone in the flat, will you eat properly?'

'Y–yes.'

I did not believe her, or trust her state of mind. The main course came within a few minutes and with it a buzz from her mobile. She took it out and squinted at it, impatient to get back to the food.

'Text.' She pushed the button and her eyes widened. 'Shit!'

'What?'

'Peter. Brother Peter the taxman. Left his job. Ends today. Wants to hook up and talk. Your husband's persuaded him to go and get educated.'

'Wow.' An idea crept into my mind, and I waited while she stared at the phone, then put it down without replying.

'Tell you what. He'll be at a loose end for a few days, won't he? Why don't you have him to stay at the flat? Kip on the cushions, take you to the pub, keep you cheerful?'

She frowned, then her expression eased and she said: 'Yes. I'm hopeless on my own, always was. I'd like to spend some time with him. Julia won't be coming home for quite a while.' More sniffles. 'And it'd be better than . . .'

A look came over her face I did not like; it was my turn to frown.

'Better than what?'

Eyes averted, she mumbled: 'Well, Jackie also offered. To move in. But I thought it might get complicated. Then I did hook up with her the other day, when I was upset. She came up on the train and hung out in the hospital a bit.'

'*I* thought she had got a boyfriend.'

'She broke up with him.'

There was a silence, then I said:

'Allie, I don't belong in your world, and it does sometimes confuse me. But it seems to me that exactly the same principles apply. It's about relationships, and loyalties, and not messing people about, not just giving in to the moment and blowing all over the place like a plastic bag in the wind. You've got a son now. Your private life has to be a bit more thought-about.'

'We didn't do anything.' I had wondered whether I went too far, but there was no resentment in her tone, only a hint of pride. As if, in the days before Con, she knew perfectly well that she might have done a little more than nothing. Especially after weeks of earnest celibacy and a serious shock. I believed her; but in that moment I had seen a glimpse of an earlier Allie, unlike the newly wise one I had come to know in Norfolk. Growing up, I thought, was often a matter of two steps forward, one step back.

'Good.' We ate on in silence for a while. 'So,' I said eventually, 'will you ask Peter to stay?'

'Yeah.' She picked up the phone and thumbed out a message, then squinted at it when it buzzed. 'He says, U READ MY MIND, C U TONITE. ADDRESS?' She picked at the keyboard, and slid the phone shut. 'But Marion . . . ?'

'Mm?'

'Might you bring Condy up to see me? Not for the night, maybe, but I dunno . . . I do miss him so much. And if he forgets me, I won't be able to take him back, will I? He'll scream at the sight of me.'

I nodded. 'Sure. But he won't, you know. He'll be pleased to see you, whenever. He's your baby. He knows that as well as you do. It'll be OK.'

She looked almost happy now, fed and hopeful, the colour

back in her cheeks. Even her hair seemed to spring more vital from her head. I, on the other hand, felt a wave of exhaustion and depression. It is not easy to step with grace into the back seat of life. It takes its toll.

34

Julia collapsed the following night, when I was back in Norfolk giving Con his bath. Allie got the call just as Peter arrived back at the flat with an armful of fish-and-chip packets and a six-pack of lager.

'He took control,' she said to me later. 'I was running down the stairs crying and he just sat me down on the landing, locked up, dumped everything except a bag of chips and a can, and got a minicab in five minutes flat. Which is a record. I think it was the Army voice that did it.' During their journey across London Julia was resuscitated twice, heroically by all accounts, while Allie wept and Peter held her strongly in the back seat of the grimy car, eating chips with his free hand. The doctor explained – 'too much, too technical, but it was basically her heart, the fever just about did for it'. Brother and sister waited together for long frightened hours – 'And he never let my hand go, except to go for a pee. He's such a star, my brother, he reminds me of how Dad used to be when I was little. We do need men, see. Even those of us who don't need men, if you see what I mean.'

It was Peter, too, who rang me at dawn to let me know what was happening. 'I would have,' said Allie, 'but I kept crying, and I thought you had enough on your plate with Con. Julia wasn't your problem, not really.'

She is now. They all are. As I write, this Easter Sunday, the house is full of people, just as it always used to be at the great Christmas and Easter and Whitsun holidays, the turning-points of the year. Allie and Con are back in Sam's old bedroom, Peter in the lumber-room on a camp bed ('Ah, memories of Basra Palace!') surrounded by textbooks from his new degree course at Norwich.

And the emaciated, exhausted, pallid but living Julia is recovering slowly in the guest room. She sleeps separate from Allie not for reasons of propriety, though Tom does roll his eyes a little when his male friends ask about his household. She stays there because she must sleep a great deal, and not be disturbed, and have an en-suite bathroom and shower for Allie or the nurse to help her in and out of with private decency. The nurse is not living here: she comes in at eight-fifteen every morning and six in the evening, to check what she calls the 'Obs'. I am not sure that we are really entitled to this level of service on the NHS, but by great good fortune one of the practice nurses in the surgery not only drives to work right past our house, but is Mozambican.

For which reason she regards Julia as a priority, far more important than the irritating local invalids who turn up at the surgery. As soon as Tom told her the story of how Julia became ill, Marielena took it upon herself to call in night and morning and tend 'this great lady'. She seems in no great hurry to get to work, anyway, and inclines to join us for a cup of tea in the kitchen at eight-thirty. So does Sarah, some mornings.

It won't be long before Julia is up for breakfast, too, though even sitting up in bed for an hour still tires her out. When she does come down we shall need to bring in a garden chair and all squeeze closer together round the kitchen table. Especially as Con makes such thumping physical advances day after day that it can't be long before he stiffens his back and needs to join us in a highchair, rather than be passed from knee to knee, grinning and taking random swipes at anything within reach.

There is a threat of Arlene Marsh from Portweigh Trust coming down to confer with Julia, too. But I have limits. She will just have to stay at the pub or with Sarah. Their spare room is clear now, anyway; the research is finished and Jackie is permanently back in Cambridge. According to Allie she has picked up the threads with her male paramour. That child is flaky. I can't be bothered to keep track of her doings, as long as she stays clear of my daughter-out-law and of the baby. Even though she caused him to be born. Sam presumably had patience with her. That is no reason I should do the same.

I suppose that Julia's resurrection, now confidently expected, will bring problems of its own. Allie says she has agreed to buy a little house in Greenwich, handy for driving out East at weekends and equipped with her longed-for airing cupboard. But one cannot expect a complete personality change, not in a woman turned forty and accustomed to ruling her own man-free roost with a rod of iron.

I pop in and out with food and drink, and occasionally with messages from Chioma at the office. Sometimes Julia talks a little. I get the curious impression that Julia is glad of her interlude of physical weakness, as it gives her a chance to revise her inward life slowly and thoughtfully without committing too much to words. She smiles at me from time to time, a smile which answers the question I have long secretly harboured, as to why anyone would love her. And when Tom put his head cautiously round the door to ask if I needed any shopping in town, Julia raised her head and said: 'Mr Faulkner. It's good of you to have all of us here.'

Quite the civilized house-guest. I said this to Tom and he laughed; it is hard to remember, now, the day when she came to the door and he reported her as a ranting hippie monster.

He is more at ease about Con, too; we two have learnt to talk frankly about Sam and about our uncertain feelings, and about the guilt that comes with any kind of happiness. We have worked through it together, understanding the clear and obvious difference between the wrongness of trying to replace a lost child and the rightness of welcoming a new grandchild.

'Allie makes it easier, you know,' he said in bed last night, laying down his book. 'She's such a sweet little ditz, and a really kind heart. She makes me feel about a hundred and three, but I quite take to the indulgent, patriarch role. And having Peter here in the vacations doing my research will bring the pair of them down here more often. Maybe even all three of them, God help us.' He laughed.

'She's terribly grateful to you for sorting out the money for Peter's degree.'

'Strangely easy. Between us all we're getting rather good at extracting money from Trusts. The peg-leg helped more than a bit. Disabled ex-soldier.'

'Ex-tax collector.'

'Perhaps there's another special Trust somewhere for the rehabilitation of Revenue Rats. If I have done one good thing in my life,' he said sententiously, 'it is to help turn a tax collector into a science teacher. The Recording Angel ought to tick me a lot of boxes for that.' He threw his glasses and book aside. 'Time to sleep.'

Across the corridor, imperious in his late-night hunger, our grandson thought differently. Life, I thought, listening to the sound of Allie creaking resignedly out of bed to soothe and feed him. A raw new life, breaking silence.